Systems Failing

ALLAN McCREEDY

SAPHRIM

SAPHRIM

ISBN: 978-1533673329

For Pamela.

None of this would be possible without the help and support of those around me. You know who you are.

CHAPTER 1

It was the night before the meeting, a damp Friday night and Clark Radcliffe was out with his oldest friend Jackson. Rob and Ed, two computer specialists from back in the day had managed to extricate themselves from their families to join the revelry.

"Ten o'clock. That's me guys, big day tomorrow."

"What?" said Jackson, "Already? Not even one for the road?"

Clark shook his head and peeled his heavy tweed overcoat from the back of the chair. "Not tonight."

Jackson stared at him. "Okay, whatever. Good luck tomorrow, whatever it is you're up to."

Rob and Ed waved as Clark left the Fountain Bar and walked towards the bus terminals at Belfast's City Hall, stopping as he reached the Scottish Provident building and looking over the green copper dome of the City Hall. Tomorrow was playing hard on his mind. He thought back to what he had found five years before, and how he had found it. He thought back to Milton White, the powerful man that he was and how he had fallen. He thought back to Declan Somerville, and the guilt he still felt.

He was brought back to the present by the echo of clinking glass and lively voices as the doors to the Apartment Bar were pulled open by burly door staff seeing off a herd of merry patrons. A smile came to his face. He decided then that he did want one for the road after all.

Clark sat his tall muscular frame on an empty stool beside two bedraggled young men engaged in deep conversation about student debt and the virtues of assignment deadlines. He smiled again recalling the many years he too had spent as a student in this very city, many study sessions spent in its many bars.

"Help you mate?" said the barman.

"Corona," said Clark and slid a note across the bar, waiting for the imported bottled lager he preferred over local draught beers. He nodded as the barman dropped the bottle heavily on a beer mat and after a long pull from the ice cold bottle he spun in his stool to survey the surroundings, to assess the clientele, to look for familiar faces. Not that he wanted to see any. He wanted to be alone. He wanted to think, to reflect. The raucous concoction of men and women laughing however negated any opportunity.

He allowed himself to absorb the warm atmosphere and was reminded of the night Jackson met Tracey. That was a Saturday night in a bar not unlike the one he was in. It was supposed to have been a boy's only night, a night when Clark was consoling Jackson. And then Tracey accidently bumped into him and engaged in conversation, in lengthy conversation. Jackson and Tracey immediately hit it off. Tracey moved in after only a few weeks and now waited expectantly for Jackson to return from his nights out. Clark shook his head at the thought.

He felt a tap on his shoulder.

"Hi. It's Clark isn't it?"

He turned and his eyes were instantly drawn to a short tight fitting dress elegantly displaying a wealth of golden skin. He lifted his eyes quickly and smiled. She moved her head to the side and tossed long dark brown hair away from her shoulders. She too smiled, a perfect smile with full red lips glistening in the light.

"Yes. How are you?" he said although had no idea who she was, nonetheless pleased that she had approached him in full view of the many male eyes glancing her way.

"It's Siobhan. Siobhan Doherty. We used to work together, like a lifetime ago?"

Then he remembered. Siobhan Doherty. It must have been five years since he had seen her. He recalled an ambitious graduate joining his team in the Government's Department of Industry and Trade Development, full of enthusiasm, good ideas and well motivated. He did not however remember such beauty. Perhaps people made more effort outside of work. Perhaps he had been too engrossed in the daily slog at the time to notice. Perhaps she had changed.

"Hi Siobhan, what have you been up to?"

"Still working in computers," she said leaning closer. "A couple of years of public service were enough though. I'm subcontracting now with Peterson's Global. I'm just back actually from six months in Qatar."

"Hence the tan?" said Clark raising his eyebrows and then cringing.

She smiled again showing the perfect white teeth and shook her head gently. "Not all genuine. Much too busy to take in the rays when you are on someone else's clock. What about you? You left the department before me, didn't you? What have you been up to?"

Clark glanced away. She had worked with him five years ago and had gone off the radar. Now she was asking questions about what he had been doing for five years.

And the next day was the meeting.

He returned his attention to her. "What have I been up to?" he said, "Doing a bit of freelance work myself, mostly as an associate with Chesterton and Williamson."

She nodded. "Do you find it better than the old days?" She moved closer, her leg brushing his.

Clark didn't move. "It works for me. It's definitely better than slaving to the taxpayer for little appreciation."

With some difficulty he forced a glimpse away from her chest.

"I couldn't agree more," she said resting her hand on his arm.

A warm glow shot through him.

"We have a lot in common Clark, like two peas in a pod."

"Oh, I don't know about that," his eyes dropping to the floor as a crimson blanket ascended his face.

"Listen, I'm out with the girls tonight." She turned and waved at a corner table in the distance where Clark could just about make out the outline of three or four girls through the haze. A couple of hands were lifted in reply. Another hand beckoned her to return. Clark offered a weak wave although he was not sure why.

Siobhan turned back, leaned towards him and whispered, "I think you and I might have a bit of catching up to do. Why don't you give me your number and I'll give you a call. Maybe we can meet up in the next few days, just the two of us?"

As she pulled away Clark savoured the lingering fragrance, sweet and expensive. She smiled and lowered her head, fixing her eyes on his.

Clark shrugged. They swapped numbers each taking care to enter the digits correctly into their phones, her with an up to date all singing all dancing Smartphone, him with an entry level pay-as-you-go Nokia.

Clark watched transfixed as she walked back towards her friends, the dress pulled tight across her thighs. He gave up the battle and allowed his gaze to fall to her taut tan calves. And a pair of high heeled red soled Christian Louboutins. He shook his head and smiled before quickly finishing his Corona and gathering his overcoat.

Outside the Apartment Bar he walked briskly across the front of the City Hall, just about making the last bus home where he sat at the front behind the driver and thought about meeting Siobhan. He thought about how from time to time he would meet someone or hear something that would transport him back five years. Yes, he could have moved away. But this was his home. This was where his friends were. This was where his family was. And this was where Ellie was.

The bus shuddered to a stop on the Lisburn Road and Clark stepped off, shivering as the cold air hit him and walked the remaining three hundred yards to the front gate of his compact mid-terrace house on Ethel Street. As he fumbled for the door key in his coat's deep pockets he heard a sharp sound from behind. He jumped, turning instinctively just as a shadow fell swiftly behind a silver Peugeot car across the street. He drew and held a long deep breath.

"Who's there?"

A large figure arose, a chilling silhouette in the dim street light. Clark winced and focused his eyes on the figure of a man, a tall broad shouldered man discernible within a full length coat, a man who stood statue still with a stare fixed firmly on Clark, a man with a shaved head and an absurd smile.

"Can I help you?" said Clark slowly and deliberately. The man did not move. He did not speak. Slowly he took his right hand from his coat pocket. He raised his forefinger and pointed at Clark.

Then he turned and walked towards Northbrook Street.

Clark let the trapped breath escape as he watched the man round the corner, a car engine starting and accelerating into the night. He stood shaking and wondered what had just happened. Nothing for five years, and then a phone call. A meeting agreed for the next day and now this. He shuddered.

Inside he hung his coat behind the heavy door before stepping into the lounge and throwing himself onto the brown leather well worn sofa wedged neatly into the bay window. He looked the length of the room, past the granite fireplace and over mirror, past the small pinewood kitchen table to the rear window beyond. He stared through the window, seeing nothing only blackness. The house behind was in darkness, the elderly couple safely tucked up for the night.

Clark had never discussed the happenings of five years ago with anybody. Not even with Jackson or Ellie. Why would he have involved Ellie whom he had not met until afterwards? Jackson had been his closest friend since University, a friend close enough that perhaps he should have shared his burden. But it had never felt like the right time. He decided then that it was time.

He picked up the phone, his landline phone that he intuitively used ahead of his mobile phone. He checked the time and sighed. He dialled Jackson's number.

"Hello?" said Tracey, quietly.

"Tracey, Clark. Is Jackson there?" he said trying hard to disguise his apprehension.

"Hi, Clark, it's great to hear from you. Is everything okay? I take it you are working as hard as ever? You guys have a good night? Jackson said you slipped away early?"

It was in Tracey's nature to talk a lot. One question at a time was never enough.

"Oh, here's Jackson now," she said much to Clark's relief.

"Is everything all right Clark, it's not like you to call and check if I got home in one piece?" said Jackson.

Clark paused and filled his lungs. "There's something I need to talk to you about."

Jackson sighed. "Can't it wait 'til tomorrow?"

"No," said Clark slowly, "I need to talk tonight. Something has happened. Something I think might be to do with tomorrow."

"What do you mean? What exactly is going on tomorrow?"

"Can you come over now?"

Jackson fell silent. "Sure," he finally said. "I'll call a cab."

Clark sat on the sofa in a trance, the thirty minutes until he heard the drone of a car seeming like hours. He moved slowly towards the door and welcomed Jackson with a nod.

Jackson stood with his back to the fireplace and faced Clark, hands in the pockets of jeans that hung loose on his gangly frame. "What's going on?"

Clark said nothing. He walked to the kitchen and returned with two bottles of Corona. He handed one to Jackson and took a long pull himself from the other. "There's something I wanted to bring up with you before but just never could."

Jackson dropped onto the sofa as Clark moved towards the burgundy club seat, the only other chair in the room. He said quietly, "Do you remember five years ago, that thing with work?"

Jackson stared at his friend, nodding gently. "You mean that senior bloke who stole the grant money? He was sacked, wasn't he?"

"Yes. Milton White. He was Director General at the department." Clark paused and took another pull from his bottle. He set the bottle on the floor. "There was a guy who worked in the same team as me in the department, Declan Somerville." He paused again and looked to the ground. He picked up the bottle and began turning it in his hands. "Around the same time as the Milton thing he died in work, collapsed at the rear stairs. Some sort of coronary. He was in his early forties, left a wife and teenage daughter."

"Whoa," said Jackson softly, "Were you there when it happened?"

"No, that's the thing," said Clark and lifted his head to look at Jackson. "He was working late one night on his own. He was found dead by the night watchman during a routine security sweep. I didn't find out until the next morning."

Jackson shook his head.

Clark said faltering, "I don't think Declan had a heart attack. I don't think it was an accident. I don't know what exactly but there was something not right about it." He ran a hand gingerly across his face. "And I think it may be connected with Milton White."

Jackson set his bottle on the floor. "But, what..."

Clark's looked way. He hadn't finished. "It was me who found the coding that exposed Milton White." He looked back to Jackson.

"And that's not all. He's asked to meet me tomorrow."

"What do you mean...Who...What for...?"

"I don't know. I've been playing it over in my mind now for days. I haven't seen or heard of Milton White in five years. And now he wants to meet."

Jackson shook his head again. He stood and paced the room before dropping back into sofa. "Are you bringing him here?"

Clark took another drink, "No, we're meeting tomorrow morning at the Palm House in Botanic Gardens. Some husky voiced girl called, said she was his personal assistant. It was all a bit odd."

He swallowed. "There's more, Jackson," he said, "When I got home tonight someone was here."

Jackson plunged forward. "What, in here, in the house?"

"No. There was a guy standing across the street. He just stared and pointed."

Jackson jumped up just missing the bottle on the floor. "What? Pointed? Who was it, what'd he look like?"

It was Clark's turn to shake his head. "No idea Jackson. I've never seen him before. It was a big guy with his head shaved. He wore a long dark coat, one of those Crombies I think."

"And he didn't say anything?"

Clark stared ahead. "A meeting arranged with Milton White tomorrow and now this. It must be connected."

Jackson let out a long sigh. "What are you going to do?"

Clark looked to the ground. "I need to go and see Milton. I need to meet him tomorrow," he said quietly.

CHAPTER 2

Clark watched as the cab pulled out of sight. Jackson had asked many questions, none of which could be answered. He was concerned and had offered to stay to offer some form of numerical advantage should the man return. Clark had given the offer some thought but had satisfied himself that if the intention had been to inflict physical damage then the opportunity had passed. He was satisfied the altercation was to intimate, although why exactly he had no idea.

Jackson had made sure the curtains were closed and the windows and doors locked and with some reluctance agreed to leave for home, where Tracey would be waiting, waiting with a barrage of questions of her own.

Clark sat on the sofa with head in hands. His mind drifted back to his time in the department.

He'd had many roles back then, one of which was painstakingly checking and verifying computer data and code. This was his area of speciality, something he was good at and enjoyed. He could immerse himself for days interrogating systems and avoid meaningless office chatter. Clark could see no point in engaging in the daily ritual of mind numbing pointless conversation with people with whom the only common denominator was the fact they worked in the same office. One thing that frustrated Clark above all was small talk. Incessant conversations kicking off with some comment on the weather, conversations developing further into speculation about what the weather might be like the next day and even, ludicrously, forecasts on the weather system that might influence the summer months. Clark too paid no attention to television or radio weather forecasts, preferring to look at the sky and if it looked cold or wet, he put on his overcoat. If it looked like being dry or mild he took off his overcoat.

He thought back to his first day in the department, inducted alongside two other young computer graduates, Rob and Ed. Over the years they had become friends of sorts in that they were the only two colleagues he met with outside of the Friday night soirees, and had actually met their partners as oppose to listening to beer fuelled tales of anonymous relationships, not many of which were complementary.

Rob and Ed were both married, two weddings that Clark and Jackson had attended. While Jackson had never worked with Clark, Rob or Ed he did frequently attend the Friday nights. It was there that he grew to regard Rob and Ed as friends also. The feeling was mutual, hence the invitation to their weddings.

Clark had focused on software development and data investigations while Rob became a computer security specialist and Ed project managed large system infrastructure development. In practice therefore their work rarely brought them in direct contact with each other. Hence their friendship was a social one. Indeed rarely did they discuss work when they were out.

Clark's reflections turned to his final investigation in the department, his uncovering of Milton White. He shook his head and sighed, checking his watch. It was already well into tomorrow. He climbed the stairs wondering if sleep would come.

With the bedside clock illuminating eight he awoke from a fragile and interrupted slumber and groped his way down the stairs to the kitchen. It was Saturday, a mild fuzz in his head from the bottles of beer but no more or less than expected or used to.

At the small kitchen table he stared at the cafetiere brewing industrial strength Columbian coffee, his mind full of questions, questions he hoped he could at least find some answers to at his meeting later that morning. A shrill ring roused him. He jumped and reached for the phone, the landline phone that sat on the small table beside the burgundy club chair. He lifted the handset from its cradle.

"Hello?"

"Good morning and how are you?" said Ellie.

He screwed his eyes tight as he remembered. Ellie was due home later. She had gone to spend a couple of days with her mother who was recovering from another session of chemotherapy.

"How's your mum?" he said half-heartedly.

"As well as can be expected, thanks. Are you all right, you sound a bit distant?"

"No. I'm fine. It's just the usual morning after the night before."

"Where'd you go?"

"Just a couple of beers in the Fountain. I left early," he said failing to add that he had in fact strayed into the Apartment Bar before catching the bus.

"That's not like you. Are you sure everything's okay?"

"Yes, fine. What time are you coming home?"

"It'll not be until later. My cousin's calling round after work. Is that all right with you?"

"Sure. Take care. See you later." Clark rang off relieved that Ellie would be out of the picture for the rest of the day.

Home for Ellie was not in fact Ethel Street. Ellie lived in a third floor one bedroom apartment within Victoria Square. She had just recently moved there from a two bedroom apartment overlooking the River Lagan beside Belfast's Central Train Station, an apartment that was among the first apartment developments to emerge in the city. It had however become dated in comparison to the modern developments such as the Obel Tower with its imposing walls of glass, the Boat building with its sail shaped structure replicating the shipbuilding heritage of the City, and the Victoria Square complex.

Ellie was a busy lawyer specialising in conveyance. Her apartment was somewhere she could call home, to be alone when she wanted. She spent a lot of time with Clark of course, many nights staying over at his house. This suited them both, together when they wanted, and space apart when they wanted. Clark had never stayed over at hers however. There was no particular reason. It was just that he liked being in his own home. Ellie didn't mind. She liked the house in Ethel Street, she liked the sense of community, the many and varied neighbours all living so close by, separated by thin walls and narrow streets, but with lives so different. She equally liked maintaining her own little personal space, a space never compromised with overnight guests. Clark had been at the apartment many times however, meeting after work for dinner, sharing a bottle of wine before heading out to a restaurant, or as a meeting point before catching a movie at the cinema within Victoria Square. He had played his role in baptising the bed and in checking that that the large shower was indeed suitable for two. He had just never stayed over.

Clark checked the clock on the fireplace. It was not yet eight thirty. He was not due to meet with Milton White until ten thirty. He climbed the narrow stairs to the small bathroom and stood for what seemed like an eternity in the hot steaming shower over the bath before changing into fresh chinos, shirt, sweater and brown leather brogues and heading back down the stairs, lifting his overcoat from the hook behind the door.

Nine thirty, sufficient time for him to walk to Botanic Gardens. Turning right at his gate he started the walk up the hill towards the Lisburn Road, crossing to the other side of the street when it was safe to do so between the steady line of cars and vans. At the end of the street he turned left on to the Lisburn Road itself. He could sense the bustle of the road already, shoppers, commuters, deliveries all fighting for space on the roads and pavements. He walked past the shops, the cafés and the restaurants along the road, crossing when he reached the City Hospital and headed along Elmwood Avenue towards Queens University. It was a place he knew well given the years he had studied there, its iconic Lanyon Building of soft red brick and sandstone dominating the City's University Quarter.

He turned right and headed for the Stranmillis Road where he entered Botanic Gardens through its ornate black metal gates. It was a stunning entrance overlooked by the Ulster Museum, its morning shadow darkening the lawns and shrub beds of the magnificent Victorian municipal park. Straight ahead was the prodigious cast iron glasshouse that was the Palm House conservatory. Opposite the Palm House across an expansive lawn stood a cluster of oak trees offering protection to the lawn and affording visitors a screen from the buildings beyond. One tree at the forefront of the cluster stood taller than its partners.

In front of the Palm House was a line of benches, benches that provided rest and relief to weary mothers pushing buggies, ageing couples on a weekend stroll, students hastily organising paperwork, and lovers with arms around shoulders surveying the parkland for wildlife, whispering sweet nothings. It was here where Clark was to meet Milton White.

He checked his watch. Five minutes before ten thirty. Guardedly he approached the benches, hands in pocket and coat collar raised to protect from the crisp air, or maybe to provide a degree of safety, security, anonymity. The altercation on the street the previous night was still on his mind.

Clark squinted ahead, his eyes resting on a thin yet tall figure who sat alone on the nearest bench staring at the ground through thick framed glasses, a bushy mop of salt and pepper hair on top, shaggy and uneven. He was unshaven and gaunt with hands clasped tightly together on his lap, feet nervously tapping on the ground. He was barely recognisable.

The man looked up nervously as Clark approached the bench. He offered his hand.

"Thank you for coming."

Clark accepted a weak and sweaty handshake.

"Please, sit with me."

Clark looked over each shoulder and sat, keeping as much distance as the bench would allow.

"Closer," said Milton. "My voice is not what it used to be."

Clark could not disagree. The man was clearly failing, both in health and stature. Clark had remembered a confident, intimidating man who was in control of every room. He was no longer that man. Clark had remembered a knowledgeable, powerful man revered within his department, a man who stood ramrod straight and was without exception impeccably dressed. He had been a man in his late fifties that could easily have passed for a decade younger. Now, five years later, the man had withered and aged beyond all comprehension. He had the appearance of a man into his seventies, if not eighties. What a difference five years can make thought Clark, fighting to resist any feeling of pity or sympathy as he remembered the man's misdemeanours.

"Thank you for coming," he said again, "I imagine you are wondering why I asked to see you."

Clark said nothing. He waited.

Milton turned to look at him. "I don't blame you for exposing me," he said, "In fact I should thank you. For five years I have been living with the shame. The scrutiny, the invasion of privacy, it has all had a devastating effect on my life, on my health. However, thank you. What happened was wrong. It could only have gotten worse for the department. Your intervening when you did made sure that was not the case. Thank you."

Clark stared at him. "I don't understand," he finally said, "Why thank me?"

"Money was missing. It was a bad time for the department, but I was glad a stop was put to it, even though the finger of suspicion pointed towards me." His darkened eyes betrayed the bravado, a fear tightening his brow.

Clark thought at once of Declan Somerville. He said nothing.

"I was implicated," Milton continued. "All indications were that the money was transferred to an account in my name, an off-shore account in the Isle of Man."

This at least Clark knew as it was he who had uncovered the data within the grant payment system.

"It wasn't me," Milton said, "I had nothing to do with it. I received no money." He looked at Clark again. "I am innocent, a fall guy."

As far as Clark was concerned it was an open and shut case. Milton White had opened a bank account on the Isle of Man in person, with closed circuit television footage to prove it. Clark himself had found the computer data showing a transfer from the department to that very account.

He shook his head. "The evidence says otherwise Milton, bank accounts and money transfers, all with your name on them."

"Evidence of what? That I opened a bank account, that money was transferred into it? Ask yourself this, where is the money? Why do I not have it?"

"It was your bank account."

"It was an electronic transfer, Clark. You are the expert. The money was transferred into an account in my name. Records show it arriving into my account and then transferring out. I don't know where it went."

"Hold on a minute," said Clark. "There was a police investigation. Are you telling me police detectives and forensic accountants were not able to trace where the money went, never mind the bank's own

17

tracing systems?"

"Yes Clark. You do indeed ask questions that need answers. Ask yourself this, why was there no trial? Why did a police investigation not uncover sufficient evidence that the Prosecution Service felt could take to trial? You yourself have said the evidence pointed in one direction. I say there is more to this. The police seem to agree."

"Why? What have the police done?"

"Nothing. That is the point. The case has lost momentum, and from what I can tell it shows no signs of progressing. It's as if the case is frozen, as if someone or something wants it to go away."

"What about the money?"

"It's currently unaccounted for. Officially the case is still open but as I have said there does not appear to be any progress. I have heard nothing in nearly two years. I don't even know if I am still a suspect. I used to receive regular visits from a Detective McArdle from Financial Crimes, but now nothing. I have over the last couple of months tried to contact him, to seek some form of update or progress. He hasn't returned my calls."

Clark reflected for a moment. "Why now?" he said. "Why are we having this meeting now, after five years?"

Milton looked at him. "I have my reasons," he said. "For now let's go with my curiosity as to why the police investigation has stalled. Why have I heard nothing in two years? Perhaps I feel it is safe now to ask questions, to try in some way to find answers."

"If you were innocent why were you sacked? Why was the outcome of an investigation not waited for?"

"You don't understand, Clark, I am saying I was innocent of any accusation of embezzlement. I was however accounting officer for the department and as such any misappropriation of funds was my responsibility. I was responsible for what happened regardless. The department had to be seen to be taking firm action and while there was a police investigation ongoing, a complex investigation that could run for some time, letting me go was the quick win. I suppose I can't really argue with that."

"Seems a bit harsh," murmured Clark although not convinced.

"I was the most senior official, Clark. It goes with the territory." He paused and moved closer to Clark. "I need your help," he said softly, "I know you can get to the bottom of this."

He then put his hand into his pocket and produced a small package, a light brown bubble wrapped envelope, no more than ten inches by five. He handed it to Clark.

"Take this."

"Wait," said Clark, "I don't know what you are talking about. I don't know how I can possibly help you. And besides, what makes you think I want to help you?"

"Take this. Look at it and then decide."

Clark reached hesitantly for the package. While he felt the story was incredulous he was intrigued. He removed a corner and looked inside to a small portable disk drive, the sort that can be attached to a computer to provide additional storage.

"On this is a copy of all the files from the Dubai Wire and Cable project. Don't ask how I did it or got away with it, but I was able to make a copy before I left the department. On this I am convinced are the answers to what went on. I know you Clark. You have a reputation for being one of the best. You will not want to miss the opportunity to challenge yourself. Have a look. You don't need to commit yet. Just look and see if you can find any answers. You already found data associating my name with the money. Look deeper. See if you can find more."

Clark nodded. Yes, he had found the file with Milton White's details, and that was as part of a routine system audit. If he was now being given access to copies of all the files he could explore further into the system unhindered by departmental access protocols. He would have opportunity to look deeper than he had ever opportunity to do before. If there was anything at all to what Milton was claiming, he was sure he could find it. Yes, Clark was good as what he did.

"Okay, I'll take a look," he said. "No promises. Give me a couple of days. How can I contact you?"

"I have your number. I'll have someone call you."

Clark slipped the package into the deep pocket of his overcoat.

"Be careful with that," Milton said. "It's the only copy. Please be careful."

Clark looked away. "Did the police not have full access to the original system? What makes you think I can find something they did not?"

"I don't know, maybe your reputation?"

Clark turned slowly back towards him. "Last night there was a man outside my house. He just stared and pointed at me. Any idea if that has anything to do with this?"

Milton's gaunt face turned the colour of snow. "I don't know, please be careful," he said again.

Clark nodded. He rose and moved away slowly, leaving Milton gazing at some point on the ground.

Behind the large oak tree across the expansive lawn and with a clear view of the benches in front, Jackson watched.

CHAPTER 3

Clark walked towards home reflecting on his conversation with Milton White, deciding he would at least for the moment give him the benefit of the doubt. Not that he would regard himself as easily influenced or manipulated but there was something about Milton, something about the way he had clearly suffered over the incident, the way he had physically deteriorated, the emotion in delivering his story. A frail aging man had called for his help.

He felt too a degree of relief over the incident the previous night. Concerns about the man being a companion of Milton seemed ill founded. Milton had however warned Clark on two occasions to be careful. Yes, he would be careful. He was excited by the prospect of having unchallenged access to a complete set of files from a government department's software system. What would he find? How was the system structured? Of course he had carried out a range of more complex data analysis and system development work in his current freelance consultancy role, the role he had moved into when he left public service. But he seldom had full unaccountable access. And here was an opportunity to interrogate deep into a system he previously only had limited and restricted access to.

He walked briskly down Ethel Street and turned the key in his door, his excitement growing as he climbed the stairs to his study, the black box package gripped firmly in hand.

The study held a large maple desk with twin storage drawers, a desk Clark had assembled himself from a Swedish instruction leaflet. A small swivel chair on castors gave the freedom to move about whilst remaining seated. Clark sat on the chair and carefully slid the black box from its bubble wrapped parcel, seeing it fully for the first time. In his hands he held what might give him some answers to the questions he had asked himself many times over the last five years. Often he'd thought about Declan Somerville and how his life had ended so unexpectedly, he thought about his wife and daughter, about how they coped with the news, about how they were continuing to cope. Had they moved on with their lives? Could they move on with their lives? Is it possible to move on with your life when you lose a close family member? Clark had often thought too about Milton White, about what he had done, about why he had done it, about what he hoped to achieve. As he turned the black box over in his hands the questions returned.

On top of the maple desk sat Clark's computer, a Dell, a desktop replacement laptop that he favoured. It was a computer that met his needs, adequate storage capacity, uncomplicated operability, and plentiful ports to facilitate external devices.

He powered up the computer and signed in his security password. The screen came to life, running through its start up routine before settling on a picture of fields with water lapping against shoreline rocks in the distance.

He placed the black box beside the computer, connecting it via its port which served also as a power source to the box. The box buzzed as the Dell identified the attached device and registered it on screen. A routine *Explore* procedure called up a large number of folders, the sight of which caused Clark to exhale loudly, both in anticipation and appreciation of the extent of the task ahead of him. This was what he studied for, this was what he had worked hard for, and this was what he lived for, to be alone with a computer and a problem, just him and no one else, no one to disturb him with banal conversation. He was happy. A broad smile spread across his face.

An initial scan of the folders showed the expected list of hardware, software and support folders. Ignoring these Clark found what he was looking for. Opening the *Program Files* and *Program Data* folders he slowly read down the alphabetical list dismissing those with which he was familiar. He would check each of these later for any irregularities.

He recalled carrying out the computer audit back in the department when an examination of what should have been a routine program folder for the QUIROS financial system identified a rogue nine digit code deep within its data. Clark's curiosity was drawn to the code as it sat within a wider set of data, but was different. It was the only numeric data that was not preceded by alpha text. Extracting the code and running a system check raised no error. Clark then wondered why the code was there if it had no function in running the program. He ran the nine digit code through a number of his diagnostic programs but nothing obvious was identified. He re-ran the code back into the QUIROS system. Here it was identified as a staff number, a number attributed to receive departmental payments, usually a refund of travel expenses. A further check identified that this number was attributed to Milton White, the department's Director General. An investigation followed and Milton White was eventually dismissed for embezzlement. Clark was heavily praised for initially identifying the code within the QUIROS program file, a code that many other analysts commented was so deeply embedded that it should have been impossible to find. Yet Clark had found it. Clark's reputation for data investigation quickly spread around the public services, further spreading to private sector companies and consultancy houses. He began to receive offers.

He would examine the QUIROS program file again later, in some detail. If he could find what he found before on a routine audit he was sure he could find anything there was to find on a deeper concentrated investigation. He glanced at each of the program files, looking for something unusual or unexpected. His attention was drawn to one program file towards the end of the alphabetical list, a program file entitled *Wire and Cable*. Wasn't this part of the name of the company whose grant funds Milton had been accused of embezzling? Wasn't Dubai Wire and Cable the company that Milton had mentioned during their meeting that morning? Clark opened the folder.

It was a program to run a database, a database set up to register and store all communications between the department and Dubai Wire and Cable. It held details of contacts, locations, meetings, schedules, and spreadsheets of financial projections. It also held legal Letters of Offer and Acceptance specifying business start up and relocation grant offers and payment arrangements. Clark smiled and rubbed his hands together. He had accessed the documents detailing Dubai Wire and Cable's negotiations with the department to establish their European base in Belfast. He remembered they were a company specialising in all grades of voltage cabling for the construction industry. He remembered also they were a major player in Asia and Africa and were looking to expand into Europe. Financial support was offered by the Department of Industry and Trade Development.

He read carefully through the documents with growing interest and excitement, his foot beginning to tap uncontrollably on the floor.

And then the telephone rang. The landline telephone. He was annoyed at the interruption and briefly considered ignoring it. It might however be relevant. He pushed himself back from the desk and bounded down the stairs.

"Hello?" he said.

"Clark, it's Amy," his sister replied.

He hesitated. "Oh. Hi." he said slowly.

A long pause as each thought of something to say. That was the way it was with Clark and Amy. A brother and sister who had been very close growing up but who had drifted slowly apart as they began to discover their own lives, lives that now had very little if anything in common.

"Long time, no speak," said Clark to break the silence, "Is work okay?"

"Yes" she replied.

"Everything all right with Spencer?" he then asked not really knowing why given he had never met the man. He supposed it was probably the next logical question to ask, although he was struggling for a credible next question. He was saved from this dilemma.

"Spencer's good. Listen Clark, this is as awkward for me as it is for you. I'm just letting you know Dad's collapsed and an ambulance has taken him to hospital."

CHAPTER 4

"What? What do you mean? What happened? When?" was as coherent a response Clark could muster.

"I don't know much. Mum just called and said Dad had collapsed in the garden."

"When did she phone?"

"Just now. She called me as soon as the ambulance left. She didn't even tell me what hospital he was taken to. She sounded terrible. She hung up as soon as she told me."

"Probably the Ulster Hospital," said Clark, "That would be the closest." He could feel the frustration and anger well inside him. "Why call you and not me? For goodness sake, you are in London and I am twenty miles away?"

"I don't know. Maybe if you had shown some interest in them, shown that that you even remotely cared about them, or about anyone else other than yourself for that matter, it might have been different."

"Now's not the time for this. I'll go to the hospital."

"Good. Let me know." She hung up.

Amy was four years younger than Clark. He had adored her as a baby, old enough to help their mother and father to change her nappies, hold her feeding bottles and entertain her by shaking stuffed toys and rattles. Clark loved to sprinkle the warm bath water gently on her stomach to elicit what was the broadest of smiles and most affectionate of laughs. They grew up on the fringe of a rural village close to the shores of the Lough where there were no friends of a similar age living nearby. Playmates had to be invited, collected and returned. This required planning and could not be arranged spontaneously. Clark and Amy were therefore each other's primary playmate, and whilst the difference in age, gender and the fact they were siblings led to the inevitable squabbling, they were the best of playmates. Given the choice of inviting other children to play with them they would often decline, preferring to play together.

The large garden and the fields of the farm beyond were their sanctuary, their world of exploration and discovery. Many long hours were spent tracking, catching and releasing the myriad of insects and bugs to be found in the sheltered fields, with the sounds and smells of the Lough drifting towards them. Sometimes, on particular warm evenings, they were allowed to venture the short distance to the Lough shore. Here they explored the rock pools and sandbanks safe from the low tide rippling far out in the distance.

Towards the end of primary school, as Clark began to spend more time developing his sporting interests and increasingly spending more time with his team mates and class mates, Amy began to spend more time on her own. Although her mother endeavoured to arrange a variety of play days, many weekends were spent helping her mother carry out the chores of the house, the cleaning, the washing, the tidying. If she was really fortunate she might even be offered the opportunity the help her father in pulling weeds from the many flower and herb beds around the garden. This was all while Clark was playing football with his friends. She resented him for this, for leaving her alone with their parents each and every weekend.

Transferring to grammar school Clark had begun to develop an insatiable interest in video gaming and computing, leading to him spending the time he was at home hidden in his bedroom playing on the consoles or exploring the in and out workings of his computers. Amy resented him all the more for this. He was growing, developing, changing, and leaving her behind. He didn't want her to be a part of his life any more. Or at least that was how she saw it.

Clark did not share the view. To him he was just doing what he wanted to do and whilst he held no conscious hostility to his sister he was, on reflection, perhaps guilty of shutting her out too quickly, forgetting that she was younger and required greater understanding and attention.

And so they had grown apart, irreconcilably as it transpired. Amy finished primary school and transferred to grammar school, a different grammar school to the one that Clark attended. She had chosen to attend an all girl school rather than the mixed school that Clark had attended. Perhaps the resentment for her brother had resonated in some form of distrust in all boys.

As they moved through their teens Clark was spending more time devoted to his computers, gradually leaving the gaming behind and focusing on the art of programming. He was oblivious to the many girls' parties and sleepovers that Amy began hosting in their home. They were living separate lives under the same roof.

Clark chose to stay in Belfast during his university studies in Computer Science and as time went on his visits home became fewer, meaning fewer opportunities for contact with his sister. It also began to create friction with his parents. Clark was slowly drifting away from his parents, just as he had drifted away from Amy.

Amy had successfully secured a place at the London School of Economics to study Accountancy and Finance, eventually qualifying as a Chartered Accountant and establishing herself professionally in the City of London. She had set up home in Greenwich and was living with a City Analyst called Spencer Livingstone, a long term relationship that so far had lasted some seven years. Very rarely did Amy come home and when she did it was to visit their parents. It had been many years since Clark had actually seen her.

The black box would have to wait. He would have to go to the hospital. As if he didn't have enough to do today without this distraction he thought. And Ellie was arriving later. The house would need cleaned.

'I'd better go,' he said to himself. 'Get it over with.'

He ran up the stairs and powered down the computer, disconnecting the black box and dropping it into his coat pocket. He grabbed his keys and folded the coat over his arm. He would not need it when driving.

Clark was not one for cars. He was more of a public transport person. He liked the freedom of hopping on and off busses without the need to seek car park spaces in a city that seemed to be either attracting more cars, or reducing the number of parking spaces, or maybe both judging by the length of weekend queues into the city centre shopping car parks. And the cost of parking, never mind the inconvenience, grated him. No, Clark was more suited to the bus. It had of course the added advantage of allowing for spontaneous nights out after work, with Jackson, Rob, Ed, or even with Ellie, without the worry of a car and having to drive home.

Clark however kept a car on the road, making sure all the required tax, insurance and road worthy inspection certificates were maintained. The car was a requirement of his consultancy job, should he be required of travel any distance outside of the City. It allowed him also to drive, on the very odd occasion, to Rob or Ed's houses both of whom lived in Belfast's outlying suburban towns where public transport links were not as frequent or convenient as the City's Metro bus service. His car was not much to look at, an eight year old sandy coloured Toyota Corolla, the shade of which seemed to be permanently fading. The car was seldom used. It was however there when he needed it. Now was one such time.

Clark locked the front door of the house, cautiously checking left and right. All clear. He closed his gate tight, opened the passenger side door of the car and set his coat on the seat before checking left and right again and moving around to unlock the driver's door. There was no central locking on this model.

He checked his mirror and pulled away from the kerb towards Northbrook Street heading up Surrey Street towards the Lisburn Road and the city centre. He passed the many bars and restaurants on the Dublin Road, once hailed as the Golden Mile of Belfast's night life, an accolade no longer applicable as entertainment had since spread across the city. He passed the BBC building on Ormeau Avenue, the home of the Corporation's regional television and radio news, turning onto Cromac Street and eventually East Bridge Street where he passed the recently constructed soaring office buildings that stood proudly over the city. Opposite was the Central Train Station with its direct Enterprise service to Dublin. He crossed the Albert Bridge over the River, the River Lagan with its long history so influential to the growth of the city. The Albertbridge and Newtownards Roads eventually fed Clark on to the Upper Newtownards Road, a long and wide road serving as a main channel for moving commuters and goods in and out of the East of the city. He passed Stormont and its grand parliament building, a building that was as equally impressive as it was iconic. Beyond Stormont's domineering entrance gates and long undeviating Avenue lay the Ulster Hospital. The journey had taken a little than thirty minutes.

Clark circumnavigated the car park, completing two circuits before he found a space. It was always like that for hospital visitors, or so he was told, not being one to make regular spirit raising visits himself. He lifted his coat from the passenger seat and got out of the car, making sure to lock the door. He pulled on his coat and checked the pocket. It was still there. He kept his hand on it, inside the pocket.

He looked instinctively around the car park. Whilst he had

suppressed some of the fear and anxiety, he remained apprehensive. He had to be careful, as he had been advised. Not that he needed to be told.

The hospital was like any other, austere yet functional in appearance. Clark followed the signs to the Accident and Emergency wing where he found a tired looking receptionist encased behind a glass screen. He bent down to speak through the small opening.

"Hello, is there a Malcolm Radcliffe here, I think he was brought in an hour or two ago?"

The girl smiled warmly and asked if Clark was a member of family.

"Yes, a son." Not *the* only son or *his* son.

She checked the computer, excused herself and lifted her phone. Clark couldn't make out what she was saying but was aware of her nodding. He turned to look around the Accident and Emergency waiting room. He saw a room filled with parents holding distressed children, older children cradling distressed elderly parents, makeshift bandages on arms and legs, heads in hands. A discernible murmur could be heard, a combination of wincing from pain and expectant chatter about when it would be their turn to be seen. Hopefully not long Clark thought to himself.

"Hello? Excuse me?" the girl at reception was saying, trying to get Clark's attention.

"Yes, sorry," he said.

"Your father is in surgery. If you follow the arrows though the double doors to the family waiting room someone will let you know what is happening."

She smiled again, a well practiced smile, and pointed to a set of large doors at the far end of the waiting room.

Clark made his way through the doors and found the waiting room. It was a simple room with hard backed chairs along three walls and a small table at its centre, peppered with yellowing, dog eared and well out of date magazines. A wall of half glass faced on to the corridor. The door also had a half glass panel. Inside the room Clark saw a short woman, stocky in build, and well dressed in short winter boots, navy trousers and sweater, with a red and yellow neck scarf adding colour and distinction. Her head was held low. She was motionless.

Clark entered the room. "Hello Mum," he said.

She lifted her head slowly and looked at him. Her eyes were welled with tears, her cheeks and neck crimson with the strain of fighting to keep the tears within. She did not speak.

"How is he Mum?" Clark asked.

She shook her head slightly, and started to say something. She stopped and turned to look again at the floor, to look away from Clark. "Why are you here?" she said.

"Amy. She phoned."

"Did she tell you to come?"

"No. I ...," he hesitated, thinking what it was he was trying to say.

She lifted her head and looked at him. She raised her voice slightly. "You were going to say what? That you wanted to come? You told Amy not to worry, that you would sort it all out? I don't think so."

"Mum. I ... Why did you not call me? Why did you not let me know?"

"Why would I let you know? Why would I even think to let you know? When was the last time you called to ask how we were? When was the last time you came to the house to see how we were?"

"I've been busy," was just about all he could say.

"Don't give me that Clark. You live a half hour away. You work Monday to Friday. When you were with the government working nine to five we still didn't see you. Offices have phones you know. You have a phone at your house. You probably have a mobile one in your pocket now. This has been going on for years Clark. God knows your father and I have tried. We tried inviting you to dinner, to visit, and you still couldn't come. Even when your Uncle Charlie died you couldn't be with your family. But you took your share of his estate all right. We came to visit you, although we needn't have bothered. What is it with you Clark? What have we done to deserve you?"

She was off on one. Clark didn't know what to say, what to do, where to look. She was right, of course. But he couldn't quite understand why it had turned out the way it did. In his mind he had simply moved away and found a new life, his old life no longer relevant. His interests were a million miles away from those of his parents. He had friends who shared his interests. His parents became people with whom he only had a bond of blood. No meaningful conversation or pleasure could be derived from their company. The visits home had become a chore. Visits culminating in nothing but inane small talk and idle gossip about people he didn't know or care about. The visits home and the phone calls became less frequent. Incoming calls and visits from his parents quickly dried up also as he had nothing to say to them, even expressing distain at conversation topics raised by them. Calls became awkward exchanges of words, so they stopped calling.

"I'm sorry Mum," he said, "I don't know what to say."

"Maybe it's too late to say anything. Did you know your father has had a number of turns in the last year? Heart scares? Did you know? No, you did not. And do you know why? Because you don't care. You don't care about anyone only yourself."

She was sobbing, trying in vain to wipe the tears away with the sleeve of her sweater. Clark put his hand into his trouser pocket and produced a handkerchief that he offered to his mother. She looked at him coldly, but accepted.

The truth was Clark did care. He just did not know how to express it. He experienced hurt and upset like anyone else. He was empathetic, albeit inwardly empathetic. He often wanted to reach out to people, to offer reassuring words, to offer some form of physical comfort. He just couldn't do it. He felt awkward, embarrassed. Now he felt ashamed. His own father had been suffering and he hadn't known. What if he had of known? Would he have become a regular visitor bestowing bunches and grapes and gardening magazines? He doubted it, but he couldn't really know. What he did know was that he was hurting inside. He wanted to hold his mother, to cradle her head on his shoulder, to tell her it would be all right, that he was there for her, that he would make everything all right. But he couldn't do it.

"I'm sorry Mum," he said again, "I'm here now."

Clark sat slowly on the seat next to his mother. He raised his hand and let it rest lightly on her knee. She turned to look at him, seeing tears forming in his eyes. She mellowed, slightly.

The door opened and a tall middle aged man in surgery scrubs entered. "Mrs Radcliffe?" he asked.

Clark quickly let his hand fall from his mother's knee.

"Yes. This is my son, Clark Radcliffe," she said

Clark looked to his mum and smiled.

"I'm Keir Earnshaw, one of the surgeons. I have just finished with your husband. He is stable. That was quite a nasty attack. We got to him just in time. Thank goodness you were with him when it happened."

"Thank you Doctor," she said, visibly relieved, "Will he be okay?"

"We'll need to keep him in a while. No reason why he shouldn't make a full recovery. He'll need to take it easy though."

"Thank you Doctor," she repeated, "Can we see him?" We, not I.

"Yes, for a second. He is sedated but you can see him. I suggest you then go home and come back tomorrow. He is in good hands."

He led Clark and his mother to the recovery room. There, enshrined in bed sheets lay his father, pale and drawn, connected to a variety of tubes and machinery. Clark leaned close and with his back to his mother gently placed a kiss on his father's forehead.

"I'm sorry Dad. Get well," he whispered.

He nodded at his mother and turned, moving towards the door, leaving his mother with her husband.

Safe in the knowledge that his father should recover Clark's attention quickly returned to the black box in his pocket. He had to get home. He needed a few hours alone before Ellie arrived. He had places to be, things to do.

His mother joined him in the corridor outside.

"I have to go Mum," he said.

"So that's it?" she said, "Duty done and away you go? No, how are you Mum? How are you coping? Will you get home okay? Do you need me to go with you? Do you want me to stay?"

"Sorry Mum, I didn't think," he said.

"No, you never do," she said and turned and walked towards the exit leaving Clark standing alone in the corridor with his hand on a small black box in his pocket.

As he drove home he tried to focus on the task and challenge ahead. He could however not shake the hurt and anger he had seen in his mother's eyes as she turned and left him. He drifted into memories of growing up in the house set in rural County Down by the shores of Strangford Lough.

He'd had a good childhood he had to admit. With his father a Professor in the Faculty of Business at the University of Ulster and his mother the Headmistress of a local primary school they were a relatively affluent family. Two cars were always in the driveway, at a time when two car families were rare. They owned a small holiday cottage in Donegal, Ireland's rugged north western county. Many holidays were enjoyed at the cottage, long extended holidays made possible as both parents worked in the education sector, with its long holiday breaks between terms. This meant they were always around when he and Amy were not at school. There was no farming out to child carers. They were a happy family, at least until Clark began to grow, and change.

Clark was on the Lisburn Road before he realised. His recollections had consumed the entire journey home. He signalled right and waited for a break in the line of early evening traffic making its way into the city centre. He made the turn into Ethel Street and surveyed both sides of the street in search of a parking space. He was fortunate. Directly outside his house was the space he had vacated earlier.

So engrossed was he in reverse manoeuvring that he failed to notice the two figures sitting on the wall between his house and the house next door.

CHAPTER 5

Clark climbed out of the car, his overcoat securely held over his left arm. It was only when he turned that he saw them, sitting with arms folded, deep in conversation, waiting. Two men, both stocky and muscular with large crew cut topped heads resting on short necks the thickness of tree trunks. Tattoos were visible on exposed arms protruding from tee shirts, tee shirts that were pulled tight across burly beer bellied torsos, tee shirts worn despite the crisp cold air.

Clark's heart skipped, his chest dropping into his stomach. But there was nothing he could do. He held the coat even tighter and stood tall, in deference to his true sense of fear.

Both heads turned to face him.

"All right Clark, how's it going?" the one nearest asked, raising his head in a reverse nod.

"What about you Clark?" the second man added.

Clark sighed, his face breaking into a wide smile. "Hi Vince, Hi Ryan. Are you heading out?"

"We're going down to the social club. Just waiting for the taxi,"

Vince said. Ryan said nothing.

They were two neighbours of Clark, living next door in a house sharing arrangement, each with a bedroom and paying equal share of the rent to the landlord, a landlord that Clark had never met despite having lived next door for over a decade.

Clark nodded and moved towards his gate.

"You look like you seen a ghost," Vince added.

Clark smiled again. "Enjoy your night," he said and opened his front door before stepping into the entrance hall.

He put the black box in the kitchen drawer, the drawer whose contents had no logical structure, its purpose being the drawer that anything went into that did not have a planned or predetermined home. It was his drawer of random things. He quickly tidied the kitchen, putting away dishes and wiping the worktop. A hasty vacuum of the lounge carpet completed the downstairs clean up. He carried the vacuum cleaner up the stairs; stairs that he felt could survive without vacuuming for another week or two, and went into his bedroom. The room contained a large queen sized bed with brown leather headboard. The bed was much too large for the room, leaving just about enough walking space around it to the chest of drawers opposite the foot of the bed, and to the wardrobe that filled the entire wall across from the windows. Not much room indeed, Clark thought, but he liked it. He liked a large bed that he could stretch across. It was only a bedroom after all. And Ellie liked it. A shake of the duvet, a vacuum of the narrow carpeted pathway around the bed and the bedroom was suitably cleaned, or at least in Clark's book it was suitably cleaned. The bathroom was next. He looked inside, not much to see, a white stand alone sink and low flush toilet side by side against the left wall. The opposite wall held the bath with an electric powered shower over, the floor protected by a glass splash screen that covered about one third of the bath's side. The bathroom was clean enough, he thought, it would do. He didn't bother with the study, the only other room in the house. The study was the second bedroom with a single window overlooking the back yard and the house behind. A small compact house it was, but quick and easy to clean.

As he was carrying the vacuum cleaner downstairs he heard the phone ringing. He dropped the cleaner on the lounge floor and reached for the handset.

"Hello?"

"Hello, Clark."

It was Jackson.

"How did it go this morning?" Jackson said.

Clark remembered the night before, his call to Jackson to come round so he could share his story, his burden, with him. He quickly processed in his mind how much he should tell him. On one hand he didn't want to tell him anything, he just wanted to be left alone with the story that Milton had given him, left alone to explore the black box. On the other hand he had asked Jackson to come to him. And Jackson had come when he had asked, when he had needed him. Jackson was always there when he needed him. Jackson was always there when anybody needed him. Jackson would, and always did, go out of his way to do what he could to help anybody.

"It went okay, I suppose," Clark said. "He was there as arranged. I suppose I didn't know what to expect but he is a failed man physically. He is a shadow of the man I remember, has aged almost beyond recognition."

"Yes, and?" said Jackson.

"He said it wasn't him. He said he was set up."

"But did you not find his fingerprints all over the money transfer?"

"Yes, in a manner of speaking. What I found was his bank details buried in a program file, a file that transferred grant funds. But he said he didn't see any of the money."

"Is that possible? Possible that money was transferred to his bank account and he didn't receive it? Do I not remember something about him opening an account on the Isle of Man just to receive the money?"

"I don't know what to think at the minute. On the face of it everything points to him."

"What about the police?"

"Well that's the thing," said Clark, "While I am saying everything points to him, the police seem to have gone cold on the investigation. Milton says they couldn't provide enough evidence to prosecute."

"That seems strange," said Jackson and paused. "But was he not sacked over this?"

"He was sacked, yes, but he is saying he was sacked as he was responsible for the department's governance. The fact that grant money disappeared on his watch, and in such a high profile way, was grounds enough for dismissal."

"So he was never formally found to have embezzled the money?"

"No. Hence there was no trial, or jail time."

There was a long pause as Jackson digested the information, a pause allowing Clark to consider how much more to tell.

"Why now," Jackson finally said, "Why after five years, where has he been, why call you, what does he want?"

A barrage of questions, all valid questions, not all of which Clark could answer. He knew of course why Milton had contacted him, and what he had asked him to do, but he did not know why then, where had Milton been, or what he had been doing for the last five years. These were questions he was asking himself, questions he would have to find answers to.

"I have no idea where he has been," Clark said and paused. "He has asked me to help him." He paused again. "I said I would consider it."

Jackson's throat gurgled. "Help him?" he managed to say. "Help him how? Last night you were in fear of this man and now you want to help him?"

"I don't know, Jackson. Maybe you had to have been there. He is a frail man who has lost much in recent years. He is not a man who looks like he has gained from a secret offshore stash. He is not a man who looks like he was, or ever has been a criminal mastermind. The police have found nothing, yet he is still implicated in the whole thing. I think he just wants to clear his name."

"But what can you do?"

"He claims that as it was me who found the data that implicated him then I will find the data to clear him."

"Find the data to clear him? What are you talking about? How can you find the data to clear him?"

"He gave me a portable hard drive. He says all the files relevant to the embezzlement case are on it. He wants me to take a look before committing to helping him. I agreed I would do that."

"A portable hard drive? And you think you can find what might clear him in that?"

"I don't know. I think so. If there is anything in these files I am sure I can find it," Clark said, well aware of his own capabilities and dogmatic desire not to beaten. "I have already identified a couple of interesting files."

Jackson paused. "Where is this hard drive, Clark?"

"I have it here, in the house."

"Are you going to keep it there?"

"Yeah, I'll find somewhere to hide it."

"Yeah," said Jackson, "you'll need to keep it safe. Clark, did he mention anything about the guy you worked with, Declan wasn't it?"

"No, it wasn't mentioned."

"What about the man outside your house last night?"

"I asked him if he knew anything about it, but he just said he didn't know, and told me to be careful. I'm sure he knows more than he is telling me. It was just a first meeting after all. Time will tell. Like he said, for now I will be careful."

Jackson didn't answer. After a moment he said, "Clark, you need to get out, take your mind off it, relax for a bit. What about tonight?"

Clark sighed. "Not tonight, Ellie's due home." He omitted to say that Ellie would not be home until much later. In truth he didn't want any further distractions. He just wanted to be left alone with his computer.

"Tomorrow night then? What about the four of us heading out for dinner? Zen? We haven't been there for a while. Tell you what, leave it with me, I'll organise a table."

"I don't know Jackson, I have a lot on."

"Never mind you needing to chill, Ellie will want to take her mind off things too."

Clark had to admit it was tempting. An offer of a night out to Zen was always hard to resist.

"Okay then," he said with a further sigh. "Listen Jackson, I have to go. I want to get back into it."

"No problem, good luck. Assume eight o'clock tomorrow night unless you hear from me otherwise. And stay safe," said Jackson as he rung off.

CHAPTER 6

Clark returned to his study and tried to refocus on the Dubai Wire and Cable file. He was hungry, but dinner could wait.

He began reading through the database, taking notes in a small reporters pad. He recorded dates of what looked like key meetings, who was there and where the meetings took place. He wanted to learn more about the background and was sure that if there was anything suspicious about the meetings then the police would have found it during their investigation. He was not an expert in police matters but assumed all names would have been checked and followed up. He was sure also that the police investigation would have included a search of data within the program files. He could not be sure however of the extent or detail to which it would have been carried out, or what data analysis skills or experience lay within the police Financial Crime Unit. He made a mental note to find out.

His summary highlighted six names. These appeared to be the chief negotiators who were present at all meetings. Representing Dubai Wire and Cable were Abdul Alim, Anthony Tobias and Jennifer Maitland. Together with Milton White from the Department

43

of Industry and Trade Development were Delores O'Reilly and Fiona Mitchell. Clark recognised these names, remembering two ambitious, assertive and capable senior officials. He had no idea what had become of them. He would check with Rob and Ed.

He began to plot a timeline. According to dates within the *Schedule of Communications* the earliest meeting was an exploratory meeting when introductions were made and the Dubai Wire and Cable Company's outline plans to expand into Europe were discussed. A series of meetings then followed over a twelve month period when these plans were discussed further and the prospect of establishing a European base in Belfast developed into a serious consideration. Possible incentives were discussed, ranging from providing back office support and a ready skilled workforce to financial incentives for machinery. The financial incentives seemed to Clark to become a main focus of discussion. He thought this interesting.

Clark's timeline had noted eight meetings over the twelve month period. The same six names had been present at the all meetings, all of which took place in Milton White's office. At the last meeting two additional officials from the department were present, Terry Davidson and Charlie Cappelli from the Finance Division, their attendance to present actual grant forecasts and the process for their payment. This was the last meeting that Clark could find reference to. He thought there should have been more.

He knew the Dubai Wire and Cable Company had ultimately agreed to set up its European Assembly and Distribution Centre in Belfast, yet there were no records of meetings giving the detail of the final negotiations and arrangements. All he could find were these preliminary discussions and the final Letters of Offer and Acceptance. Surely there would have been other meetings to discuss the details? He wondered where the records of these meetings were. Milton had told him that he had copied all files relating the Dubai Wire and Cable project onto the hard drive. Was Milton aware that there may be records of final detailed discussions and meetings missing? Did the police investigation have access only to the files that Clark now had, or did they have access to more? Perhaps these records were somewhere else on the hard drive? Clark made a note on his pad.

The sound of a key rasping in a weary lock jolted him.

"Hello, is there anybody here? I'm home," called a tired voice.

It was Ellie. Clark looked at the clock in the bottom corner of his computer. Ten o'clock. He had been engrossed and had lost track of time.

"I'll be right down," he said as he hastily shut down the portable hard drive and the computer, placing the hard drive in the drawer of his desk, hiding it carefully underneath some outdated computer magazines and a pile of blank printer paper.

He blew out a long sigh, frustrated at having his focus and concentration interrupted yet again. He'd had momentum and was gearing up to drill beyond the explicit information in the database into the program and data files. However, as frustrated as he was, Ellie had arrived. He missed Ellie, even if he did not always show it. He liked her company. The portable hard drive could wait.

Clark ran down the stairs two at a time and found Ellie draping her coat and handbag over the back of a kitchen chair. They embraced and kissed.

"How's your mum?" asked Clark.

"No change," she answered.

Clark nodded and moved away from her. He put his hands in pockets.

"Are you all right?"

He dropped his head. "My dad collapsed today."

Ellie looked at him, aware of but not understanding the complexities of his relationship with his family. "Oh no! How did you find out?"

Clark held his eyes on the ground. "Mum called Amy and Amy called me. I went to the hospital."

"What?" said Ellie and stepped forward, "Your mum called your sister in London and not you here in Belfast?"

"I don't want to talk about it."

Ellie stepped back again. He rarely spoke of his parents or of his sister. In the years that they had been together Ellie had never met Amy, and could recall only once meeting his parents, and even then it was by chance. Ellie loved her parents. She visited at some point every week despite them living in another County. She had a brother who she was in regular contact with, by phone, by text, by email, and by social network. Social networking was something she would have to encourage Clark in to. She could never understand why someone so proficient in the ways of new technology did not embrace modern communication. The mobile phone he insisted on using was basic. He rarely texted and when he did he typed full sentences and paragraphs, in defiance of any accepted abbreviated modern alternative. Social networking was a non starter for him.

Ellie had tried to engage Clark in conversation on a number of occasions about his family, each time for him to close up. She stopped asking. He would talk when he was ready she thought. She looked at him, saddened, wishing she could understand how to help. She knew him well enough to know that whatever had happened at the hospital was gnawing at him. She could tell from his stance, his forlorn expression, his head held low. She decided to leave it.

"Have you eaten?" she asked.

"Not since lunch. I kind of got tied up in something when I got back from the hospital."

"What was that then?"

"Oh, eh, nothing. Nothing important," he said quickly.

Ellie knew nothing about five years ago. He did not want to tell her about it, not then, maybe not ever. He and Ellie had met four years ago when Clark was already established as a freelance consultant. As far as he was concerned it had no bearing on their relationship.

Ellie sighed. "Fair enough," she said. "Grab yourself a beer and I'll fix us something to eat. I haven't had anything since this afternoon either."

Clark lifted a Corona from the fridge and poured a Sauvignon for Ellie. She opened the fridge after him to investigate its contents, finding nothing of worth. It was the fridge of a bachelor she had to remember. Pasta and a jar of tomato sauce would have to do. They sat together at the small kitchen table.

"Jackson has suggested we go to Zen tomorrow night," he said.

"You and the boys?"

"No, a foursome. Us, him and Tracey."

Ellie glared across the table. "Oh," she said. Must I?"

Clark smirked. As much as Ellie liked Jackson she had a difficulty with Tracey, a feeling however that was not mutual. Tracey liked everybody. Tracey liked everybody too much. Tracey liked to talk, and talk she did, incessant talking about nothing. While Clark despised small talk this was the partner of his greatest friend. Jackson was devoted to her and Clark would not do or say anything to upset him. Tracey was a hairdresser with a popular city centre salon. She had become a master of salon conversation, specialising in the weather, holidays, television, and the weekend destinations of clients. This was the conversation topics Clark and Ellie could look forward to the following night.

"So I'll assume you're okay with that?" he said, the smirk developing into a broad smile.

"Sure. Why not? It's been a while," said Ellie mirroring Clark's smile.

"Tell you what, for putting me through it you can tidy up. I'm going for a shower."

Ellie had a drawer in Clark's bedroom where she kept clothes and cosmetics sufficient to allow for a spontaneous stay over. She liked to look well and made every effort to do so. She was a couple of years older than Clark, maybe a pound or two heavier and an inch or two shorter than she would have liked, but she looked after herself, attending gym classes when she could and enjoying regular facial and manicure treatments. She had short mousy fair hair, large blue eyes, and long natural lashes. Her nose was a bit on the large side and her lips a bit thin. Some would say plain, curiously attractive she liked to call herself. Designer glasses gave her that librarian look. She loved clothes. She lived for quality clothes. Clark would always comment on what she was wearing. She liked that. On visits to Clark's house she would intuitively open his wardrobe door and survey its contents. Clark too enjoyed his clothes, his wardrobe stocked exclusively with Boss, Lauren, Armani and Hilfiger. He always dressed immaculately. She liked that about him too. Well, apart from the overcoat.

She could however never correlate his approach to personal grooming and presentation with his lack of interest in cars. To her good presentation extended to driving an attractive and desirable car. While, like Clark, she would use public transport around the City she kept an Audi convertible in the garage beneath her apartment. The Audi was now parked in the street outside Clark's house.

Clark was sitting on the sofa finishing a second Corona when Ellie came back into the room. His eyes lit when she entered wearing his blue towelling Hugo Boss gown. He raised his bottle to her to acknowledge his appreciation. She walked casually across the room to the sink and poured a glass of water, leaving an alluring scent of jasmine in her wake. Clark rose from the sofa and walked slowly towards her, sliding both his hands around her waist as she stood with her back to him, drawing her close. She lifted her head as he bent and kissed the side of her neck, her scent arousing him as his mind cleared. She purred and held his hands tightly, one in each of hers. She gently pulled his hands away and turned to face him. The towelling belt came away and the gown opened revealing a full curvaceous and naked body. Clark smiled. He slipped his hands inside the gown, onto the small of her back, pulling her tightly towards him. They kissed long and hard before pausing to look at each other, smiling. She slowly began to undo the buttons of his shirt. Reaching the bottom button she pulled the shirt aside and caressed his chest, a chest taut and muscular from bench pressing. Her fingers slipped gently into the waist of his jeans, his back arching. Slowly she unfastened his belt and led him to the sofa, the well worn leather sofa by the window.

CHAPTER 7

Clark awoke the next morning and reached across the bed, his heart skipping a beat when he felt nothing but empty space. His mind rapidly shifted away from the comfort of his wakening thoughts, the thoughts of the night before, the intimacy, the solace and closeness from lying and falling asleep in Ellie's arms. Where had she gone?

The aroma reached him, the unmistakable smell from a sizzling pan. He smiled as he placed his hands behind his head and stared at the ceiling, reflecting on his good fortune to have a friend such as Ellie. He had never got round to calling her his girlfriend, although everyone else referred to her as such. He had never been one for girlfriends. Yes he'd had relationships, but nothing that had lasted longer than a few months. Miranda was different. They had met just after finishing university, staying together for almost two years. They drifted apart however as Miranda became increasingly uncomfortable with his inability to express emotion or to display affection.

It was different again with Ellie. He loved being with her, he loved many things about her, but did he love her? She meant a lot to him for certain, and he was making every effort. He tried, not always successfully, but try he did. It was four years since he had met Ellie at a work function and he still looked forward to seeing her. He still enjoyed their times together. He was sure that she too shared this feeling. She seemed to accept him for who he was. Maybe it was time for a girlfriend he thought.

Clark and Ellie ate a quiet breakfast together, during which Clark found it increasingly difficult to keep his attention away from his investigation. The portable hard drive was waiting in the study, its contents calling out to him.

Ellie sensed he had his mind on other things, and if she was honest, she did too. She had to get home to her apartment, where she hadn't stayed for a number of nights. She had to check in with her family. Tomorrow was Monday and she had to return to work. She had case files to prepare.

Clark arranged to meet Ellie at her apartment later that night and walk the short distance to Zen. They held each other tight for a long moment before he walked her to her car, watching as she manoeuvred her Audi from its parking space and travelled towards Northbrook Street.

Back inside he tidied the kitchen and was starting for the stairs, his mind planning the next steps in his investigation when a phone rang, a different ring than that he was used to at home. It was his mobile phone, a ring normally associated with business calls. He found the phone resting by its charger on the kitchen counter and lifted it, neglecting to check the caller ID.

"Clark Radcliffe," he said, adopting his professional business voice and approach.

"Milton White would like to speak with you," said the husky voice, the personal assistant.

"Put him on," said Clark.

"Not on the phone. He wants to meet you tomorrow morning, ten thirty, Café Nero, Victoria Square."

"I'll be there," Clark said and rang off.

In his study Clark removed the portable hard drive from the desk drawer and connected it with his computer, reading over the timeline in his notepad as he waited for the computer to power up. He sighed deeply. The absence of information on meetings finalising the Dubai Wire and Cable deal bothered him.

He accessed the Dubai Wire and Cable program file and examined its program scripts. It was a slow process requiring careful concentration, but Clark was determined. He was doing what he did. He followed each coded script looking for irregularities or evidence of tampering. After more than an hour of studying the screen, barely blinking, he stopped abruptly. He'd seen something unusual, a line of script that did not sit with the script before it or after it. He ran a diagnostic test to check if there was any similar script within the program file and its associated data files. However he found nothing. And then a realisation hit him. He was focusing on finding a complex solution when the answer was something much simpler.

He realised he was looking at a text rather than a coding fragment.

Excitement built as he considered the most likely cause, a document moved and a partial trace left behind. He would look for other text fragments. If they were there he would find them.

Perhaps, just perhaps, he had found trace of a missing document. Perhaps the document would relate to a meeting, a meeting finalising the negotiations between Dubai Wire and Cable and the department. He was charged and enthused.

He continued for another two hours finding three more isolated text fragments, four in total. He recorded them in his notepad and was contemplating his next steps when his phone rang, the landline phone. Frustrated yet again at the interruption he ran down the stairs and lifted the hand set.

"Hello?"

"You were supposed to phone me," said Amy, his sister.

He had forgotten. What was it with him, would he never learn. "Amy, sorry …"

"Stop I don't want to hear it," she said cutting him off. "Mum is upset with you, but what's new?"

"Really Amy, I had to be somewhere. I went to see him. He was in recovery and the Doctor said he would be fine. I tried with Mum. I had done all that I could do."

"Is that really what you think? That you did all you could do? What about Mum? How do you think she is? Did you think to ask?"

"I, I don't …"

"Enough. Not that you care but Dad is getting stronger. He's still in recovery but at least he's getting stronger."

She hung up.

He had messed up, again. He would try to see his dad later. But right then he had to get back to the Dubai Wire and Cable files.

A few more hours and he would have to get ready to go with Ellie to meet Jackson and Tracey for dinner. He was hungry, having not eaten since breakfast but his hunger could wait. He rechecked the Dubai program and data files making sure he had not missed any text fragments. For completeness he would eventually have to identify and search other program and storage files on the hard drive. That would take time, but would be time worth spending.

A phone rang. Again. This time his mobile phone that he had brought to the study with him. Yet another interruption. He grabbed the phone again neglecting to check the caller ID.

"Hi, Clark. How are you today?" said a voice he did not recognise.

"Eh, Okay. Who is this?"

"It's Siobhan. Siobhan Doherty from the other night? Remember we met in the Apartment Bar?"

He closed his eyes tight as he remembered. It was the stunning brunette with the tight dress and the Louboutins. A lot had happened that night, and since. It seemed like so long ago. Was it only the night before last?

"Hi Siobhan," was all he could think to say.

"Well, how about us getting together?" she said.

"Eh, I don't know. I'm kind of busy at the moment."

"Busy with work? I hear you have built up bit of reputation as an expert analyst?"

"I'm always busy. Listen, I really need to get going."

"I might need some help to finalise a contract, a bit of follow up from the Qatar thing. Would you be interested? Just a chat, say over a drink?"

Clark hesitated, and immediately felt guilty. He was just for a moment actually considering meeting this girl for a drink. Yes, she had dressed it up as a work meeting, but at that moment all he pictured was the hair, the low cut dress, the tanned legs, and the perfect smile. He recalled the moment when she rested her hand on his arm, and the sensation that had resonated through him. He then remembered the night before with Ellie.

"Really Siobhan, I have to say no."

"Okay. I'm cool with that," she said, "but I must warn you I don't easily take no for an answer." She gave a mischievous laugh and rung off. Clark regretted exchanging phone numbers with her.

He returned to the program files starting again at the top of the alphabetical list and reading down them, more slowly than before. He hadn't got very far when he stopped. A program file entitled *Inspection* had caught his attention. He chewed on his pen as he recalled from his days in the department a process where grant monies were released only after a verification process. Yes, there were upfront grants available to help with business start up, but in the main funds were released only after asset verification. In other words, after an inspection.

He opened the file and found, like before, that it was a program to run a database. He ran the database and was presented with a long list of Company names, including Dubai Wire and Cable. Many of the names he recognised as local established businesses, others he recognised as overseas companies who had invested locally, and some he did not recognise at all. He found that the database contained schedules and records of grant inspections carried out within the department. He quickly established that the local businesses listed had been in some form of grant assisted expansion programme, the overseas companies with a local presence had received financial assistance of some kind, and the others were potential investments into the local economy that did not materialise.

He remembered his computer audit back in the department that identified the grant funds released to an account held by Milton White. He reflected on the effort someone had expended to disguise the details. He thought that if someone was embezzling or siphoning funds and had gone to that effort to hide details, they would not have risked exposure through some routine process irregularity, an irregularity that could have been picked up at any number of levels within the department. He was sure therefore that they would have followed the full grant payment process. An inspection of some kind would have been part of the process.

He accessed the Dubai Wire and Cable inspection schedule and found many dates, all of which were from five or more years ago, dates relating to planned inspections for machinery. There were no details however of the inspections having taken place. Clark was curious. He knew payments had been made, and assumed they were made following inspections. Where therefore were the records of these inspections?

He began to search for fragments, eventually finding three buried within the scripts, text fragments that only the very keenest of eye and the most experienced, capable and conscientious analyst could have found. Of interest was that each fragment contained an identical set of alpha numerical data, *FC1067*. He had no idea what this related to, and took a note within his pad.

He set his computer to run a data search of all program and data files within the portable hard drive for the *FC1067* data set. He knew this would take a few minutes so went to prepare a pot of coffee, his mind digesting the information he had gathered. It wasn't much he accepted, but enough to raise his curiosity, enough for him to consider that there may be something to what Milton was claiming. So far he had missing minutes of meetings and missing inspection details to go with the missing money.

Clark's mind shifted unexpectedly to his father. He wondered if he was well enough to sit in his bed. He wondered if his mum would be by his side. He wondered if he should visit. His mind quickly reverted back to *FC1067*.

He returned to the study with the cafetiere of coffee just as the computer was posting the result of its search. *FC1067* was flagged within a folder named Corporate Assets. He sat hastily, excited and clicked on the folder, a folder that contained an extensive list of similar alpha numerical codes. It didn't take him long to identify that *FC1067* was factory number 1067, an advance factory in an industrial estate at Mallusk on the outskirts of Belfast. He recalled advance factories were built and retained by the department as an incentive to new businesses. *FC1067* was the factory allocated to Dubai Wire and Cable.

He checked the time on the computer's clock. It was five thirty, time to get ready for Zen. He shut down the computer and disconnected the portable hard drive.

CHAPTER 8

Clark took the bus to the City Hall and walked the short distance to Ellie's apartment in Victoria Square, a journey that took him down Chichester Street past small independent retail businesses, street cafes, tall unsightly office buildings and ground level car parks operating from undeveloped land. Victoria Square was to Clark a magnificent and ambitious building in its combination of retail, entertainment and chic urban living. He had watched the development emerge from the ground over a period of years. He liked it. He liked its huge glass dome creating a striking addition to Belfast's skyline, a dome that itself had become a popular attraction offering panoramic views of the City.

Ellie's apartment was a single bedroom duplex, an open staircase leading to a minstrel gallery from an open plan living, kitchen and dining area. The bedroom and bathroom were off the gallery. It was small, but stunning with views over Chichester Street towards the City Hall and the Scottish Provident Building. It was a home to be proud of for sure. Clark was proud of Ellie for owning it. She worked hard for Geddis, Kenny and Marshall and deserved to have what she had.

Ellie buzzed Clark into the building and he took the lift to the third floor. She was waiting for him at her door looking as beautiful as ever, a flowing nude coloured dress to her calves, low cut revealing her curves. Dior thought Clark as he looked to her feet and nodded upon seeing the Valentinos with two inch heels.

Ellie was equally impressed at Clark's attire, his Hugo Boss combo of navy jeans, sky blue button down shirt and brown Derbys, and his overcoat of course. They embraced, kissed tenderly and moved inside. A bottle of Sauvignon was open on the worktop, with two glasses beside it. This was a usual routine for them, sharing a drink before heading out, sometimes a cocktail, sometimes bourbon, and sometimes wine.

"How was your day?" she asked as she poured.

"Busy," he said, not elaborating.

Ellie smiled accepting the terseness, this being his normal response when focused on a work project. She found his work fascinating and enjoyed their conversations about it, when they had them. She equally respected that he would talk about it only when he wanted to.

"How's your mum?" he asked.

"She's just the same. I went to see Aunt Agnes this afternoon. We had a good laugh about the things I used to get up to when I was younger."

Clark had no idea who Aunt Agnes was. He looked away, thinking about his own growing up and the mischief he used to get up to with his sister Amy. He smiled at the thoughts.

"Are you okay?" Ellie asked, "Any more news on your dad?"

"He's still in recovery, but getting stronger. Amy called to tell me." He looked away again. "Are you looking forward to tonight?" he asked quickly changing the subject.

She laughed, and added an exaggerated nod. "Can't wait," she said.

They walked back up Chichester Street the way Clark had come earlier, turning left at the City Hall and making for Adelaide Street and Zen. They walked side by side, close together, but not holding hands.

They crossed May Street and walked down Adelaide Street, one of a number of streets that ran in parallel behind the City Hall towards Ormeau Avenue. They passed Adelaide House where Clark had worked five years ago, where Milton White had been Director General, where Declan Somerville had died. Zen was fifty yards beyond, disguised within a nondescript red bricked building.

Zen specialised in Japanese cooking. It was a popular restaurant often requiring a reservation long in advance. It was not uncommon to dine in Zen alongside famous football players or golf stars with their ex-model or tennis playing partners. The assumption was Jackson had secured a reservation as Clark had not heard otherwise.

Clark gave Jackson's name at the reception podium and they were escorted up the stairs to a circular red velvet booth. Jackson and Tracey were already there, each enjoying a Martini. Welcoming kisses and handshakes were exchanged, Clark receiving an extended hug from Tracey.

"How about a Martini to start?" said Jackson.

"Not for me," said Clark, "I think I'll wait for the wine."

"Me too," said Ellie as she began leafing through the wine list that had been left to the table.

"Well," said Tracey to Ellie, "you look lovely tonight. Is that a Dior dress? I love Dior. I have a client who is a buyer for House of Frazer. She swears by Dior. She says their finish is far better that Stella McCartney. Can you believe that? I must say I prefer Stella …" And so she went on. Clark tapped Ellie playfully on the knee under the table. Ellie said nothing in reply to Tracey but had the grace to smile and nod politely.

They all settled on a set menu of Sushi, duck Samosa, Kimichi chicken, Kakuni, Tobanyaki, Angry Crab and Chilli Squid.

The meal was pleasant, washed down with two bottles of House Sauvignon. Conversation flowed, albeit one way and from one source. She was a harmless girl all the same Clark thought, not forgetting that Jackson was smitten with her. Clark had known him to have had two long term relationships over the years, one lasting almost eight years. He was the type who liked the security of long term relationships and worked hard at maintaining them. Sometimes however it was not meant to be. Beth, after almost eight years, met someone else much to Jackson's regret. Clark had helped him over it with many nights out. Diana was next. She was a relatively young divorcee that Jackson had met through work. They were well suited and were together for four years until she too met someone else. Jackson was distraught again. More nights out ensued with Clark, and with Rob and Ed when they could make it, and then he met Tracey. Tracey Fox.

It was in the Café Vaudeville, a converted bank building in Belfast's Arthur Street, not far from Victoria Square. Café Vaudeville was an opulent bar and restaurant favoured by an older, affluent clientele. It was somewhere you could dress up in your finest and blend in. It was a popular destination, often with a spiralling queue of hopefuls waiting to gain access. Tracey was there with one of her work colleagues, a small round girl who had little to say. Not that she needed to say much. All Tracey needed was a willing ear, a mannequin might have sufficed.

Tracey was glamorous. She was tall and very thin, but shapely. She had short red hair in a spiked style and wore a lot of makeup, expertly applied. She was, by all accounts, very fit and spent a lot of time at spin classes, and at the swimming pool where she would swim one hundred lengths without pausing. She was well into her thirties and worked hard at keeping in shape. She was an excellent cook and enjoyed nothing more than spending her days off sourcing ingredients and preparing lavish meals for Jackson. He adored her. They adored each other. Clark could tell this was different than it had been with Beth or Diana. It was hard to explain why, but they appeared so much at ease with other. Clark was happy for his friend. He liked Tracey for making his friend happy, despite the talking. If he was honest, he really liked Tracey.

When the coffee was served Jackson nodded at Clark and pointed toward the restroom, a signal that he wanted to talk.

They stood in a small cloak area.

"I haven't had much of a chance to talk to you tonight," said Jackson.

Clark laughed. "I know, but sure we're used to it."

Jackson laughed too. He knew what Clark meant but took no offence.

"How's it going with the black box?"

Clark checked over his shoulder and lowered his voice. "I found some stuff, but I need to do some more digging. There might just be something to what Milton has said."

"Really? Tell me more."

"There's not really much more to tell. There are signs of missing documents, documents that may have been deleted. I don't know yet what was on them but I am determined to find out."

"And you think you will get answers from the black box?"

"Yes. I'm pretty sure. If not then the box will give me clues to where I can find them."

"And where is the box?"

"Don't worry, it's safe."

"Yeah, well be careful. What about Milton? Does he know?"

"Not yet," said Clark, "I'm meeting him tomorrow morning for coffee, in Victoria Square."

"What are you going to tell him?"

"I don't know yet. I have a lot of questions for him. But I think I'll accept his challenge. I'm intrigued enough to help him. And I don't know why exactly, but I think I believe him."

Jackson looked away and after a moment looked back at Clark.

"Do you know what you may be getting into?"

"No idea Jackson, but I need to see this through."

"Yeah, well, as I said, be careful."

They returned to their booth just in time to rescue Ellie from an inquisition about her family and their caring responsibilities for their mum.

"One for the road?" asked Jackson, his usual line at the end of a night.

Ellie shook her head subtly at Clark and he declined on their behalf. "No thanks," he said. "I think we'll go."

"Why don't you and Ellie go back to hers for a while, share another bottle of wine?" said Jackson.

"Yeah, we might just do that," said Clark as he rose from the booth and helped Ellie slide out. He folded some notes from the wad in his trouser pocket and left them on the table to cover their share of the bill. Farewell hugs and handshakes ensued and Clark lifted their coats from under the booth and they left Jackson and Tracey to their nightcap.

At the top of the stairs Clark turned to wave. Jackson had his back to Tracey and was talking into his phone.

Clark walked Ellie home, stopping at her apartment only briefly. They both had Monday mornings to prepare for. They kissed gently and he left her resting on the sofa as he let himself out. It was too late for a bus so he made for the front of the City Hall to catch a taxi.

At Ethel Street he paid the taxi driver the amount displayed on the meter. He opened his front door and entered the hall, pulling the door closed behind him. And then he stopped abruptly. Something wasn't right. The door from the hall to the lounge was lying open. He was sure that he had closed it before leaving. He always closed the inside door before leaving.

He stepped into the lounge and froze.

CHAPTER 9

Every drawer and cupboard door was pulled open, contents strewn across the floor and worktops. He ran up the stairs, perhaps foolishly not knowing if someone was still in the house but wine bravado did not allow for such rational thinking. The drawers from the desk in his study were overturned on the floor. He ran to his bedroom. Clothes were scattered across the floor and the bed. He held his head in his hands and dropped on to the bed. What was going on? What had he let himself get into, recalling that exact warning Jackson had given earlier?

"Think," he said aloud. He hadn't seen any damage, any defacing or breakages. It was a search, not random vandalism or a burglary. But a search for what? And then it struck him.

He jumped to his feet.

He ran again to his study and lifted the drawer contents onto the desk. He looked again around the floor and behind the desk. It was not there. His computer was nowhere to be seen.

He put his hand into the deep pocket of his overcoat and felt the black box. It was where he had put it after removing it from Ellie's kitchen drawer when he had taken her home. He breathed a sigh of relief.

Although his computer was missing he was not overly concerned. The computer contained a lot of software but there were no records or findings from any of his freelance investigatory work stored on it. Clark preferred to use CD ROMs for storage. He knew this was outdated with the advent of other external storage devices such as flash drives and of course portable external hard drives, but it worked for him. It allowed him to store all his work in progress for different consultancy projects on different CD ROMs.

The CDs had been strewn across the floor. Clark tidied them to the top of the desk and they all seemed to be there. He checked inside the CD cases just to be sure. All seemed well. Whilst he had used the computer to access the portable hard drive it had served as no more than a portal. There would however be some trace data deposited within its files that would indicate the folders he had accessed from the external device, but there would be no detail, at least not the detail that could not be found by anyone other than an expert. Of course he did not know who he was dealing with but he was reasonably sure that there was nothing to be found on the computer that could compromise what he had been doing, or what he had found.

And then he remembered the notepad.

He searched through the contents of the desk drawers. He could not find it. He righted the overturned computer chair and sat, elbows on the desk and head in hands. His head was spinning, in equal measures from the break-in and its implications and from the wine. He had to think. What had he written in the notepad? Was there anything explicit or had he just noted ideas and thoughts? He recalled recording the timeline of meetings, and the key players at the meetings. He had found text fragments from what he thought were missing documents, but did he write them in the notepad? He could not remember. He had found *FC1067*, the code for the factory. He was fairly sure he had recorded that in the notepad.

He would have to relocate the text fragments on the drive, but he was sure he could find them again quickly as he knew where to look and what to look for.

He went out to his car and lifted a computer case from the floor behind the driver's seat. In this case was his second Dell, a slightly older model but just as capable. This was the computer he took to work meetings. He liked to keep one computer at home and one he could transport. He didn't really know why, it was just the way he had always worked, idiosyncratic some might say.

Clark tidied the downstairs putting everything back where it belonged. He didn't notice anything missing. The guitar was still sitting beside the red burgundy club chair, untouched. He was relieved, further evidence that this was a search for something specific and not some random burglary. He checked the back door and found the source of entry. The key hole to the lock on the back door was scratched, and had dislodged by a fraction. It had been picked and forced. He lifted the key from the windowsill at the side of the door and tested. It still worked, if only just. It would do. He would replace it eventually. He set the security bolts at the top and bottom of the door, extra bolts that he seldom set as he felt the lock and key to be sufficient. He decided then he would keep them closed.

He contemplated calling the police, but quickly dismissed the notion. There was limited damage and it was clear what was taken. He would just be faced with a number of questions he did not want to answer.

He thought about calling Ellie but didn't want to worry her. She knew nothing of what he was doing with Milton White and he did not want to have to explain it, at least not yet.

Perhaps he should call Jackson and tell him. No, that could wait too.

Clark climbed the stairs and tidied the desk. He powered up the replacement Dell, connected the portable hard drive and began to search again for the text fragments. He lifted another notepad from the drawer, a notepad he would keep closely guarded with the hard drive.

The next morning Clark awoke and checked the clock by his bed. He bolted upright and threw his feet to the floor. It was after nine o'clock and he needed to get ready for his meeting with Milton White. He yawned, having spent a late night in his study, a late night that had led to only a few hours sleep.

His mobile phone rang.

"Now what," he said out loud as he looked at the caller ID.

His face drained when saw the name.

"Clark Radcliffe," he said.

"Hold please for Fabian Townsend," said the well spoken voice in reply. It was Charlotte, Fabian's secretary, someone Clark had known for some time. She was however as officious as ever. No niceties, just straight down to business.

"Why are you not here?" barked Fabian, in his thick English home counties brogue.

Clark had forgotten. He had been so focused on the black box and the meeting with Milton White that he had forgotten about his meeting at Chesterton and Williamson, a consultancy house for whom he was an associate, a consultancy house that proffered much business his way. Fabian Townsend was the Managing Partner, a man not known for his social skills. He was aggressive, impatient and condescending.

Clark closed his eyes and grimaced. He should have been in Fabian's office at nine o'clock. "Sorry Fabian, something has come up," he said.

"Not good enough. I have a client meeting at ten. What am I to tell him?"

"That the system interrogation is ongoing?" said Clark, cringing that he had not come up with anything better.

"You said your interrogation was finished. Your report was due with me last Friday. I still don't have it. And you are not here today as arranged to discuss it. Not good enough."

The truth was Clark had not finished the report. While he had completed the security analysis of the bank's customer database, he had not written up his findings. He had been distracted at the end of the week, with his first meeting with Milton White looming. And now he was preparing to meet with Milton again.

"I'll get it to you in a couple of days," said Clark.

"Make sure you do," Fabian shouted into the phone and abruptly hung up.

Clark sighed and looked around the room, nodding his appreciation that it now looked more or less back to normal. He reflected on his inheritance some five years ago, something that he did not tell anyone about. It was around the same time as the Dubai Wire and Cable incident and he did not want to complicate matters by drawing attention to himself. If he was honest, he was embarrassed by the money. It was a modest but not insignificant amount, enough to buy his house outright and leave enough on deposit to draw on when he needed it.

He had been left a one third share of his Uncle Charlie's estate, his mother's only brother who had died relatively young and who had never married. He'd had no other family. Clark, his mother and his sister shared the proceeds from his house together with some investments he had held in bonds. This allowed Clark to leave the relative job security of the public sector and move into freelance self employment, where he could pick and chose the work he wanted. While in theory he could take a few weeks off or work shorter weeks, in practice he worked more than ever, inundated with work from firms to which he had established himself as an associate.

Maybe that was reason he liked his house so much. It was his, no debt, no payments, no landlord. His only extravagance, apart from his clothes, was the Gibson J200 guitar. Clark loved music, Springsteen, Dylan, Joel, Morrison and Cohen frequently playing in the background. The guitar was a present to himself. He had abused an old second hand Yamaha guitar for over ten years, since buying it on impulse from Belfast's Smithfield Market. He had mistakenly thought that someone who enjoyed listening to music could readily make music. He tried. He persevered. He'd tried playing in a day with Bert Weedon. Eventually the chord shapes and progressions fell into place and recognisable tunes could be played. No singing though, at least not in earshot of anyone else. The Gibson was indeed an extravagance, a beautifully crafted instrument of maple and spruce with mother of pearl crown inlays. Clark kept it on a floor stand where he could admire it, beside the burgundy club chair in his lounge.

He pushed Chesterton and Williamson to the back of his mind. He would get round to his report and inevitable confrontation with Fabian Townsend eventually. He had other things on his mind.

He pulled on his overcoat, ensuring the hard drive and notepad were safely in his pocket. He closed the door behind him and headed for the bus stop on the Lisburn Road.

Milton was waiting for him when he arrived at the coffee shop, a mug of coffee waiting at the empty seat opposite. He still looked gaunt but fresher. He had shaved and his hair was tidier. He appeared relived, perhaps satisfied that a burden may just be lifting.

"I took the liberty of ordering for you. Americano. There is milk if you want it," he said.

Clark nodded and sat. He tasted the coffee. It was lukewarm but strong. It would do.

"Well?" said Milton.

CHAPTER 10

"I have taken a look," said Clark checking over each shoulder. "I have many questions needing answers."

Milton nodded.

Clark said, "How many meetings with Dubai Wire and Cable did you have to scope and negotiate their investment?"

"I don't know. Many. A lot. Why?"

"Please Milton, I need to know."

"There were many, as I said. There were many lunches, phone calls, informal meetings in hotels to encourage them to give us serious consideration for their European operation. That was the way it worked. There was a lot of smoothing behind the scenes."

"What about formal meetings, with minutes?"

"There's no way I could remember that. This was over five years ago."

"Try, Milton. This is important."

"The best I can do is think through the process we would have taken." He looked away deep in thought, "There would have been a number of formal meetings to outline a potential incentive package we could offer, meetings to negotiate the package and then meetings to finalise. There would have been meetings with legal teams to ratify Letters of Offer and Acceptance."

"How many Milton?"

"I would say at least six formal meetings to outline and negotiate, and maybe three or four to finalise. Why is this so important?"

"Just stay with me. Who would have been at these meetings?"

"That is something I can remember quite well. It was always the same six people, three from the department and three from Dubai Wire and Cable. Others would have joined us on occasion for specific input but it was by and large the same six people, me, Delores O'Reilly and Fiona Mitchell from the department and Abdul Alim, Anthony Tobias and Jennifer Maitland from Dubai Wire and Cable."

"Where were the minutes of all these meetings kept?"

"There would have been hard copies kept on file somewhere I'm sure, but don't ask me where. It wasn't really in my pay grade to know where paper files were kept. It was however departmental policy to keep all records electronically. That's why I gave you the hard drive. Everything that the department held electronically relating to Dubai Wire and Cable is on the hard drive."

So far what Milton had said was consistent with what Clark had found. He then decided to share some of his findings to gauge Milton's reaction.

"Some of minutes of meetings are not on the hard drive."

"What do you mean? Everything is there."

"No, Milton. Documents are missing. There is some evidence that they may have been removed."

Clark looked at Milton and waited.

"What? How?"

Milton paused and then lifted his head to meet Clark's stare. "Wait, a minute, you think I removed the files in some way to cover something up?"

"The thought had occurred to me, yes."

"But why? Why would I give the hard drive to you, you of all people with your reputation if I had manipulated the electronic files? The reason you have the hard drive is that I trust you Clark. You are dedicated to your craft. You will search and find what needs to be found. You say files have been removed. I ask you to find out by whom? It certainly was not me. I have told you I was the fall guy, and I fell for this, I fell over something that had nothing to do with me."

He sighed. "Clark, look at me," he said, "I am not a well man. This has taken its toll on me. I just want to clear my name once and for all so my family can live beyond me without the shame, without accusing fingers being pointed, without murmurings behind their backs. Clark, I want my family to be proud of me."

Tears welled in his eyes. He sniffled and reached for a handkerchief, wiping his eyes and face.

Clark grimaced. Milton was appealing to him. Clark then nodded. Perhaps he was hearing the reason why Milton had appeared from nowhere after five years and reached out to him. Milton had spent years living in shame. His health had suffered and now it looked like he thought his health would not allow him to go on much longer. He wanted to lift his shame. He wanted to lift the shame from his family. He wanted to leave a positive legacy.

Clark understood. He nodded again, deciding then to do what he could to help Milton.

"Okay, documents are missing. I need to find out more about them," he said and stared at his hands on the table, his fingers clasped together. He checked over each shoulder one more time and lowered his voice. "Who else knows about the hard drive Milton?"

The colour drained from Milton's face. He too lowered his voice and leaned forward. "I don't know. That is the point. I just don't know. I must be honest, I am nervous. I don't know what went on then and I don't know what will happen now. People were involved, Clark, of that there is no doubt. Who these people were, or who these people are I don't know. They may be around, they may not. I trust you Clark, but I will say again, be careful."

Clark stared at Milton and said slowly, "Someone was in my house last night, and ransacked the place."

"Oh no" said Milton raising his hands to his mouth, "Is the hard drive gone?"

"No, it's safe."

"Thank goodness. It's the only one." He looked away into the distance. After a moment he returned to face Clark. "I'm sorry, that was insensitive. I should be concerned about you. It just the hard drive is … it's the only way I have of putting this all behind me."

"I know, I understand. I'm okay. I wasn't there," said Clark. He didn't mention the computer or the notepad.

"Did you contact the police?"

"No. There was no real damage, and besides, what was I going to tell them?"

"Yes, quite. Thank you for that. You know Clark something is not right with the police investigation. I don't know what, but something is not right."

"I will have to speak with them," said Clark, "I need to know what they know. If you say you copied all the Dubai Wire and Cable files from the department's server to the hard drive then I will need to know when you carried out the transfer, when the files were removed and when and how the police carried out an investigation of the electronic files, or indeed if they investigated the paper files. In other words, did they have access to the missing documents or did they even know the documents were missing?"

Clark paused and looked over the other patrons in the coffee shop. "The fragments left behind from the documents were not easy to locate. I would need to know what level of IT expertise the police have, and to what extent an analysis of the electronic files was carried out."

"Yes," said Milton, "I can see where you are coming from. If you found the fragments is it safe to assume they did too?"

"No, that is the point. They were hard to find. I don't know if they found them."

Milton thought for a moment. "Yes," he said again, "It is very curious why the police investigation has stalled. Initially I was a slam dunk suspect. And now I hear nothing. An open case means to many there is still doubt about me. Yes, talk to the police, although I don't know what you can, or should tell them or indeed what they will tell you, if anything."

"I'll figure something out," said Clark, "What was the name of that police Detective?"

"Detective McArdle, Financial Crimes."

Clark wrote the name in his notepad that he had removed from his pocket.

"Milton," he said, "what do you remember of Declan Somerville?"

Milton looked troubled. "I remember Declan Somerville," he said softly, "a terrible business, a young family too. I remember there were rumours at the time that his death was suspicious. I suppose that he was found lying at the head of an isolated set of stairs might have raised some questions. But no, the police and the coroner both concluded it was some form of critical cardiac arrest."

"And did you have any suspicions?" asked Clark.

"So much was going on at the time Clark that really I did not know what to think. But yes if I am honest then yes I thought it suspicious that whilst I was being implicated for something, a junior work colleague working on the case should unexpectedly suffer a seizure and die on the premises. And late at night when no one else was there. Yes suspicious it was. Think about it Clark. You told me the other day about someone confronting you outside your home, and now you are telling me you have had someone break into your home. And all this after I approached you to help me. Something is not right. Something is going on, something potentially dangerous. Maybe there was more to what happened to Declan Somerville five years ago and a can of worms is opening."

Clark could not disagree. He had always maintained there was suspicion around the sudden death of Declan Somerville. Declan had been working alone, late into the night as he was prone to do such was his dedication when a deadline had to be met. Declan was one of Clark's team members, the only one who had been assigned to help Clark on the Dubai Wire and Cable system audit. Declan had been doing some follow up work on the coding that Clark had found implicating Milton White. Clark did not know what exactly he was doing, or what he might have found on the night he died. Yes, it was safe to say Clark was suspicious. He had run it over in his head many times since. Did Declan find anything that might pose a danger to Clark? Would he be next for some mysterious accident? This uncertainty, this fear, this paranoia had sealed Clark's decision to leave the department. He had by then the means and opportunity to try and make it in the private sector.

Clark had to agree with Milton, that there had to be some connection to what may have happened then and what was currently happening. He would indeed need to be careful.

There was silence as Clark and Milton both gathered their thoughts.

"You mentioned missing documents earlier," said Milton, "something about meetings?"

"Yes, the only records of meetings are the initial exploratory meetings. There are no documents relating to the detail of what actually was agreed and how the agreements were reached."

"That is curious. Everything should have been there. You had asked when I carried out the transfer on to the portable drive. I did it just before I left the department, five years ago. It wasn't last week if that was what you were thinking." He paused, "The later meetings were critical," he said, "I recall a lot of debate around figures and the timing of any financial incentive payment. We managed to negotiate a higher level of advance payments, which are upfront payments before any manufacturing took place. The idea was to get the factory ready for production before any recruitment and training took place."

Milton thought for a moment. "Tell me Clark, was the Letter of Offer still on file?"

"Yes, and the Letter of Acceptance. There's not a lot of detail though, just legalistic terminology decorated at the end with Company seals."

"Of course," said Milton, "legal documents in legal language. And this was all the more reason why the final meetings were important in capturing the full detail of negotiations. And you say the records of these meetings are missing."

"All is not yet lost Milton. I have just started looking into this remember?"

Milton appeared reassured. "Of course Clark, forgive me. I have been waiting for such a long time and now I am being impatient." He managed a weak smile, a smile that Clark interpreted as gratitude and encouragement.

"Just a couple more things, Milton," said Clark, "What exactly were the grants paid for?"

"Machinery. It was all machinery. We had provided an advance factory."

"F C one zero six seven, Mallusk?" interrupted Clark.

Milton paused. "Yes, yes, that rings a bell." He thought for a long moment. "A state of the art advance factory it was. Fifty thousand square feet of production space, with offices on a raised floor overlooking the production area. It really proved to be a selling point, just what they were after. We were able to promote the proximity to Belfast and Larne Ports for transporting to their European markets. We even negotiated advance transportation contracts for them. The whole thing was meticulously arranged. All they had to do was employ people and start production."

"What about the machinery?" Clark said, by way of a reminder.

"I have to be honest Clark. I never saw any machinery. After negotiations were complete and the Letter of Offer was accepted it was the end of my involvement. The whole project would have passed to one of the Client Executives to provide any operational assistance and advice."

"I assume if machinery grants were paid then machinery would have had to have been in place and have been inspected?"

"Yes, but as I say we negotiated a higher than normal advance to allow some minor initial machinery to be purchased. The main machinery however would have had to have been installed and inspected before payments were made. To the best of my knowledge all machinery grants offered were paid. So they would have to have been inspected."

"What happened to the Dubai Wire and Cable Company?"

Milton sighed heavily, his face lightening to the colour of snow. "Production never took off," he said, "What with all the furore about payments to offshore accounts, and about me, the whole project crashed."

"With grants paid?"

"Grants were paid but the money remains officially missing. And the factory never opened."

"Despite the media fanfare that it was opening?"

"Yes. Good media management on the part of the department. We managed to build strong positive coverage, and equally managed to bury a lot of the negative. Yes, there were, and still are from time to time, media stories about what went wrong, why the factory didn't open, and why the promised jobs did not materialise, but by and large the negative story remains suppressed."

"Where do you think the money went, Milton?"

"I don't have it if that is what you are still thinking?"

"No," said Clark, "one last thing, whatever happened to your colleagues Delores and Fiona?"

"I've lost touch with the department, Clark, as you can probably imagine. I have been living mostly over the last years in the family cottage in Sligo, trying to get on with my life. The last I heard, and this was some time ago, was that Fiona was still in the department. Delores left shortly after me. I have no idea where she went, or why."

"Who was the Dubai Wire and Cable Client Executive?"

"I can't remember."

He looked directly at Clark. "But I can remember they worked directly to Delores O'Reilly."

CHAPTER 11

Clark shook Milton's hand as he stood. Milton said he would contact Clark again in a couple of days. He did not leave any contact information.

Clark left Café Nero through the rear door of House of Fraser and entered the main shopping concourse of Victoria Square at what was the second floor. He went straight to the railing and leant over surveying the many shoppers scurrying from boutique to boutique on the ground floor. Mostly office workers he imagined from the way they were dressed, men and women in a combination of off the peg and bespoke suits. It was approaching lunch time.

Clark reflected on his conversation with Milton. Much had been discussed, answers had been given. He had of course other questions he needed answered, but he felt he had covered enough ground for one day. He felt Milton had been honest. He had witnessed the emotion in Milton's eyes, he had felt his pain. And he was certain he shared Milton's desire the find the truth.

Something about the factory and the machinery grants still bothered him. He looked at his watch, nearly midday, thinking it was not far to Mallusk. Maybe seeing the factory might give him some comfort, might satisfy his curiosity. He would have to go home and collect his car.

Clark walked down the stairs to the ground floor not able to resist the opportunity for window shopping, especially in the designer stores that had established themselves within Victoria Square. He stopped at Ted Baker and was admiring a deep purple long sleeved shirt with floral design wondering if Ellie would approve, when someone caught his eye at the back of the shop. Clark made his way through the rails of shirts and suits to the shoe display, passing by the sultry shop assistants with skirts that were too short and smiles that were too wide. There crouching down examining a pair of formal oxfords was Jackson.

"I don't think they'd suit you," said Clark.

Jackson turned. He stood, his face a cherry flush that had risen quickly from his neck.

"Oh, Hi, Clark. Didn't see you there," he said, "I'm just browsing. Early lunch. Just finished a meeting. Need to get back I suppose. Eh, what brings you here?"

"I've just met with Milton, remember. I told you last night?"

"Oh, yes, I forgot. How did it go?"

"It went well. Listen, Jackson, now that you are here, do you want to grab a coffee and I can run some things past you?"

"I, eh, need to get back."

"It's nearly lunchtime Jackson. Are you not entitled to a lunch break at the bank?"

"Okay," said Jackson, "you got me. A quick coffee and then I need to go."

Jackson had moved into banking directly from university. He worked in the Ulster Bank's Headquarters at Donegal Square, right beside the City Hall. He had started as a trainee analyst with the Corporate Client Database Team and was now second in command over the same team. Here he provided IT management and support to the bank's many corporate banking systems, including on occasion providing advice and assistance on IT finance matters to the bank's many clients. It was a good job. He was well respected and well paid allowing him the luxury of an attractive three bedroom semi-detached house in South Belfast, just off the Stranmillis Road, easily accessed on the city's metro bus service. The house was always immaculate, never anything out of place. Tracey kept the house spotless.

Clark and Jackson rode the escalator to the second floor food court and ordered coffee and blueberry muffins at Costa Coffee. They sat beside each other on a sofa by the door, a full length window affording a view over the hoards of workers scampering in search of nourishment, many seemingly grabbing to go such was their apparent eagerness to get back to work.

"Someone was in the house, last night," Clark said in a low hushed voice, a voice that Jackson could barely hear.

Jackson's eyes opened wide, "What do you mean? When? What happened? Are you okay?" he said, a tremble in his voice.

"Everything's fine. The house was a bit of a mess but no damage done," said Clark, "I lost my computer though."

"And what about the hard drive?" Jackson said, his voice still quivering.

"It's okay. It's safe. I had left it at Ellie's."

Jackson paused and nodded. "When did this happen?"

"It was sometime last night when we were all out. When I got home I found the house in a mess, drawers lying open, everything thrown across the floor. It looks like they got in through the back door, used some sort of pick. Thankfully there wasn't too much damage to the door though."

"Did you call the police?"

"No," said Clark.

"Thank goodness you weren't there. Who knows what might have happened."

He paused again and stared towards the window.

"Do you think it was the hard drive he was after?" he eventually said.

"I would guess so," said Clark nodding, "the computer was taken but I don't think there is anything on it to give away any detail of what I was doing or what I had found. I was working directly off the hard drive and taking some notes."

Clark paused. "Here's the thing though Jackson, the notes are missing too and I can't be sure what was in them."

Jackson rubbed his chin and stared again towards the window, focusing on the swarm of lunchtime hunters. After a moment he looked back at Clark.

"What did you learn from Milton?"

Clark took a deep breath and summarised his discussion with Milton, Jackson listening intently, nodding occasionally but not saying much. Jackson leaned back in the sofa and stared at the ceiling. He rubbed his temples with his fore and middle fingers, the heel of his right foot gently tapping on the floor. He closed his eyes for a fleeting moment and then turned to face Clark.

"This is all to do with the hard drive, Clark," he said, "What is on it that can be so important to someone?"

"I don't know Jackson, I'm working on it," said Clark.

"You are threatened the night before your first meeting with Milton, then he gives you something, and the night before you are to meet with him again your house is broken into. Why were you threatened? Why was your house not broken into before the meeting? Did he know you were going to meet Milton? Did he know Milton was going to give you something? Did he then know that Milton had given you something at the meeting?"

"I don't know Jackson. Don't you think I haven't already thought about all of this?" He sighed, "Maybe it is something to do with me working at the department at the time and having some link to this."

He paused for a long moment.

"Jackson, I really need to find out what went on five years ago.

Perhaps I feel guilty about leaving the department at the time, not really understanding, or trying to understand what really went on. I knew Declan Somerville. We worked well together. He died, Jackson, working on an audit project that I had started. I had suspicions at the time about his dying. But I did nothing about it. Not that I could have done much, but I did nothing. He left a wife and teenage daughter. I didn't even go and see them. I didn't even go to the funeral. Yes, this has been turning over in my head for a long time. And I am now involved in something that is in some way related. I want to find the answers. No," he said slowly, "I need to find the answers."

He leaned back in the sofa and covered his face with his hands. He sighed, relieved. He had shared at least some of his feelings with Jackson.

"I hear you," said Jackson slowly nodding, "I go back to the hard drive. It seems to be the key to resolving all of this. You need to keep it protected. Where is it now?"

"Don't worry Jackson, it is safe. And Ellie knows nothing about it. It is not at her place any more. I want to keep her out of it," said Clark as he discreetly slipped his hand into the deep pockets of his overcoat to check that the hard drive, along with the replacement notepad, was still there.

"Did Milton give you anything else, apart from the hard drive?"
Clark shook his head.

"There was nothing else in the parcel?"

"No," said Clark, "just the hard drive."

Jackson nodded. "What are you going to do now?"

"I want to go and look around the factory site."

Jackson nodded again. "Well, I need to get back to work. Be careful," he said as he rose from the sofa and left, leaving Clark alone with his cold, untouched coffee and blueberry muffin.

Clark descended the escalator and exited Victoria Square towards Cornmarket, one of many historic trading areas in the City. The area remained a major congregating point, people drawn to its central ornate structure. He passed the residential blocks of Victoria Square and glanced up towards Ellie's apartment, not quite able to see it, but nonetheless an instinctive glance. He thought about the Saturday night they had spent together and about their meal on the Sunday night. He thought about his leaving the hard drive discreetly in her apartment. He had been excited by what he was piecing together from its content, but was also conscious of Milton telling him it was the only one, and to be careful with it. He was conscious too of the confrontation on the Friday night outside his house. Someone, whoever it was and for whatever reason, knew where he lived. He could not know for sure if that incident and the fact that he had the hard drive in his possession were related. All things considered however he had felt it safer not to leave the hard drive in his house.

It was deceitful he knew, and now felt guilt for doing it. What if he had been followed and Ellie's apartment had been ransacked? How would he have explained that? The police would inevitably have been called. Other residents would have been concerned. No, Clark reflected, it had been a wrong move. Although the hard drive had remained safe it could have been so different.

He would have to tell Ellie. He would have to tell her something, if not everything. He decided then that he would. He had confided in Jackson. It would only be right to confide in Ellie. What did he have to lose? What was he afraid of? They were after all in a relationship, verging even on girlfriend status. Trust and honesty going forward he decided.

He returned his focus to the factory site.

Passing through Cornmarket he made his way along Castle Lane, turning left down Callender Street to Donegal Square East and the Metro Bus stop for the 9c service. He climbed aboard the waiting bus that eventually made its way towards the Lisburn Road from where he walked the final stretch to Ethel Street.

He went straight to his car, not even pausing to look at the house.

He already had the car keys dangling in his fingers as he left the bus. He was determined to see the factory, where it was, what it looked like, what was around it, what was inside it. He felt he could understand more if he could get a feel for the factory and its function. When all was said and done this was all about money, grant money that had been paid, grant money that was missing, grant money that could only have been paid following inspection of physical evidence. The factory was the only place the physical evidence could have been. Clark had to see the factory.

He fought to control his adrenalin as he pulled away from the kerb.

Mallusk was approximately six miles from the city centre, a journey that should take Clark no more than thirty minutes, allowing for congestion. He headed along Great Victoria Street, passing Millfield and eventually joining the M2 Motorway at York Street. The M2 Motorway at this point was reputed to be one of the widest in Europe with its eleven lanes, or so Clark had heard. He had also heard that the two lanes that eventually headed towards Mallusk climbed what was one of the steepest motorway climbs in all of Europe.

Clark's Toyota Corolla struggled against this climb, only just making it without the need to downshift gears. He left the Motorway at Junction 4 and entered the Mallusk Industrial Estate.

It was a sprawling estate, factories and warehouses of all shapes and sizes for as far as the eye could see. Clark drove aimlessly for five minutes, not really sure what he was looking for. He spotted two men sitting outside the gates of a large metal fabricated building on what looked like an electricity or telephone junction box. They were deep in conversation, forcing large chunks of sandwich into their mouths as they spoke. It was clearly lunchtime at the factory and they had escaped.

Clark pulled up alongside and wound down his window asking if either of them knew where the Dubai Wire and Cable factory had been. Both men laughed at once.

"You're a bit late mate, that place is closed," said the older of the two, a stout man with short curly greying hair and a ridiculously large thick black moustache.

The other younger man laughed heartily as if it was the greatest joke he had ever heard.

Workman humour thought Clark to himself, humour in the face of monotony, the only way to cope. Clark understood. He nodded and laughed along.

"Yeah, I'm just doing a bit of research and wouldn't mind seeing where it was."

"Are you writing for the papers?" asked the younger man, broad shoulders and thick arms barely contained within his overalls.

"No, nothing like that, I just want to look," said Clark, wondering if he looked like a reporter, whatever a reporter looked like.

The older man took over. "That place has been lying empty since those foreigners took off. It was a disgrace, milking all that money and doing a runner. We were all hopeful at the time of maybe getting a job. But no such luck. They just took the money and disappeared. Not one single job created. And that local guy who creamed off money into his own bank account. It was a disgrace. They should have hung him."

Clark smiled at this interpretation of events, although he could not provide anything substantive to contradict it, apart from the hanging he thought, that was perhaps a bit strong. He had however just learned that the factory had remained empty.

"Is it close to here?" said Clark in an attempt to get the conversation back where he wanted it.

"Yeah, sure. If you just follow this road and take the second on the left you'll see three factories beside each other with a big fence around them. The Dubai crowd were in the one to the left of the gates, the biggest one."

"Thanks a lot, enjoy your lunch," said Clark and gave a small wave before winding up his window and heading straight towards the second road on the left.

He looked in his mirror and seen the two men resuming their conversation, deep in laughter.

CHAPTER 12

The three factories were constructed of block and steel, three factories sitting at ninety degree angles to each other and each one considerably different in shape and size. They were set behind a twelve foot chain link fence with a wide entrance that led to a large communal yard, designed no doubt to accommodate a number of articulated lorries with full loaded wagons.

The large metal gates to the yard lay open. Clark drove in. Straight ahead was the smallest unit, perhaps twenty thousand square feet that contained a manufacturing business creating kitchen units and wooden furniture. To the right was a larger unit that housed a light engineering business. The largest unit was on the left, a fifty thousand square feet unit just as Milton had said. The unit was set well away from the other two and had a large parking and turning bay to the front. At the side was a raised loading platform extending to some seventy five feet. The unit was in a sorry state of repair. This surprised Clark given that it shared the area with other units, other units that were well maintained. He surveyed rusting fabricated sheets sitting atop moulding block work. He noted the long line of windows high up at the apex of the fabricated walls. Many of these windows were broken, shards of glass scattered around the parking and loading bays. Large metal shutters at the loading docks were bolted closed. Rust was flaking on the doors.

Clark spotted a large yellow rubble skip at the far side of the building. He parked tight behind it, the car well hidden from anyone driving past or emerging from the two occupied buildings. Clark did not want interrupted by some overzealous passing security guard or a police patrol responding to reports of a suspicious car.

He walked nonchalantly around the front of the building casually checking each of what looked like two visitor entrance doors, presumably leading to some form of reception area. Unsurprisingly both doors were tightly closed, secured with bolts and padlocks. Neither door looked like it had been opened in years. He relaxed when he rounded the corner to the side of the building, from where he could not be seen from the other buildings although would still be visible from the road. He would not totally relax therefore until he reached the seclusion of the back wall.

At the corner was a large door that Clark assumed led straight to the factory floor, most likely the worker's entrance. Beside this was a large loading shutter looking like it gave vehicle and forklift access. Like the front doors these doors were tightly locked. He climbed onto the loading platform and in turn checked the rusted shutter doors to each of the docks. He detected no movement, the doors seemingly welded shut. There were no windows at a level to allow him to look inside. All windows were at the top of the walls, letting light in but not letting the factory's inhabitants see out.

He sighed. He had wanted to see the inside of the factory. It was a fortress, all manner of security protecting it from intrusion. He contemplated what to do next. Maybe he should call it a day, go home and continue searching through computer files. That was after all what he was about. What was he doing at an abandoned factory? What did he really expect to see and what really would he do with anything he might see?

In the far corner he could see a single door, either an emergency exit or access to a small store. He thought he might as well walk the length of the rear wall and test the door. In any case walking full circle around the factory would take him back to where he had started, back to his car. He passed a row of long narrow windows, about eight feet off the ground, each encased within a metal security cage. The glass inside was shattered. Clark guessed these might be restroom windows.

When he arrived at the door Clark sighed again. It had been bolted and padlocked at the top and bottom with a central lock reinforced with a bolt and padlock. With nothing to lose Clark pulled on the handle of the door. To his surprise there was some movement. He pulled again, this time with more force. The door jolted towards him stopping only when the bolts held firm within their couplings. He pulled again, yet harder. He looked closely at where the bolts inserted into bore holes on the wooden door surround. He shook the door vigorously, watching the bore holes. The wood began to splinter. Clark was glad he was at the rear of the unit where he could not be seen. Behind him was a retaining wall almost to the height of the unit. He hoped this along with the nearby road traffic would help muffle the noise.

He used all his strength. He heard and felt the wood cracking. He was sure that if he pulled the door hard enough and for long enough it would give. He paused for a moment. Was this what he really wanted, to break and enter a locked building? He thought of Declan, of Milton, and of himself and the years of torment. He was now on a journey that would allow him to understand, to move on. He had to see this factory. How else was he going to get in? Who could he talk to who could let him in? Who would have keys? What story would he have to tell to get someone to agree to let him in? This wasn't a factory for sale or lease on the open market. This was government property. He could not simply pose as a potential investor and approach some commercial property agency. If he was to ask too many questions or develop too grand a story would the police be informed and show an interest given that the Dubai Wire and Cable money investigation was officially still open? No, he had to gain access there and then, and he had to do it this way.

He put his right leg against the wall to the side of the door surround and pulled. He muscles tightened, his teeth clenched and his face reddened. He heard another crack. He released his tension on the door and then gave one more pull. Small splinters of wood came towards him showering his face. He closed his eyes, grimaced tighter and kept pulling. There was a loud crash as the wooden door surround came away. He stumbled backwards, just managing to stay upright. The door swung towards him, the bolts still in a closed position but with nowhere to be. The surround had rotted, after years of being left to the devices of nature with no maintenance.

A cold dusty air hit him, closely followed by a rancid dank smell. He stared into an abyss. It was dark, but in the distance, as if at the end of a tunnel, he saw a chink of light. Not much light, but light it was, presumably emanating from the high windows above the factory floor.

He checked over each shoulder and slowly stepped into the building.

He found himself in a long, dark and narrow corridor with a low ceiling overhead above which he imagined there was the second floor, probably housing storage or offices. Somewhere there would be a staircase.

He groped his way along one side of the corridor heading towards the light. He took small careful steps, unsure of what might be underfoot. He stopped and listened. There was no sound.

He stopped at the end of the corridor and stared at a huge cavernous space. He saw long walls, perfectly straight that seemed to go on forever, and he saw high walls stretching right to the roof, perhaps fifty feet above, walls that were broken only by the line of shattered windows. A cold draught was blowing through the space. Clark was reminded of an old abandoned church.

One thing above all else struck him. There was nothing on the factory floor, no machinery, no bits of machinery. Clark reminded himself of why he was there, to try and establish some link between the factory and the grant payments. Machinery grants were paid, meaning machinery would have had to be present to pass any inspection. Where was it? Then Clark began to wonder if it had ever been there. Might there have been rogue inspections leading to rogue grants? Clark thought not as a rigorous audit process involving a lot of people would have been undertaken, a process too rigorous to allow uninspected and unaudited grants to be paid. However he could not be sure.

He moved into the heart of the factory. Light was streaming in from the overhead windows, creating sporadic spots of light on the floor. He turned and saw the stairs to an upper floor at the back of the building. Underneath the raised floor were what looked like rest rooms, beside which was a clearing with a number of tables and chairs. Clark assumed this would have been a refreshment area. He turned again to take in the expanse of the factory, his eyes dropping to the floor, a floor strewn with dust, debris and broken glass. He began pacing, hands in pockets, kicking at the debris.

His foot hit against something, something solid. He knelt and found a metal bracket fixed firmly to the concrete floor. He looked around further and found a number of similar brackets at equal distances from each other, and in a rectangle shape measuring some thirty feet by twenty. He moved back and forwards and to the left and right, gently kicking at the debris.

In total he found six sets of brackets, three on each side of the factory floor, brackets he considered served to anchor heavy machinery to the floor.

Clark climbed the stairs to the raised floor. There were three offices in all, two of which were a similar size that he assumed were designed as managers' offices and one much larger which could have been a support office for secretaries and administrators. Through the glass panelled walls he could see that the larger office and one of the smaller offices were empty. The second smaller office had an aging oak desk with drawers, but no chair. There were papers scattered across the desk.

The papers were mostly scrap, dog eared yellowing pages filled with doodles and scribbles. Some pages had letters and words on them, but nothing particularly legible or meaningful. He folded them and put them in the rear pocket of his jeans. There was an out of date road map of the City and a six year old trade magazine. He opened the drawers of the desk. The top one was empty. The bottom one was more interesting.

Clark removed a set of original architect's plans for the factory, plans for the factory when it was new and empty. He lifted them from the drawer and underneath was a photograph, one of the instant Polaroid photographs of yesterday. He removed it and stared, nodding, a smile coming to his face. It was photograph of the factory floor, but not an empty factory floor. He was looking at a photograph of six heavy machines, three on each side of the factory floor.

He put the photograph in his rear pocket along with the scraps of paper. He looked one last time in the drawer. A small piece of card caught his eye, trapped on the drawer's edge. He fished it out and turned it over. It was business card, with the name of Abdul Alim of Dubai International Corporations.

Clark put the card in his pocket and went down the stairs. He took a few steps into the floor of the factory and reflected on what he had found. It had been a useful mission after all. He now had proof that there had been machinery in the factory. Machinery grant payments were therefore legitimate. But where did the machinery go, and when? This he would have to consider.

He was startled by a noise from behind him. He spun around and was faced with a figure that had emerged from the dark corridor. All he could make out were broad shoulders and a shaven head, and was certain they were the same broad shoulders and shaven head that had been outside his house on Ethel Street three nights before.

"Hello Clark," the man said.

Clark froze as the man stepped forward into the light. He was smiling, hands in the pockets of his long Crombie overcoat. He stared at Clark. Clark stared back seeing the man clearly for the first time. He thought there was something vaguely familiar about him.

The man moved to within ten feet of Clark and stopped. Clark instinctively balled his fists. He was not a brawler but neither was he about to run like a frightened hen. He had nowhere to go in any case. He would end up looking and feeling pathetic running around the factory with the only exit blocked by the man he was running from.

"Who are you?" he said.

"It doesn't matter who I am Clark. I think you might have something I might want?"

"I have no idea what you are talking about."

The man emitted a low menacing laugh. He stood perfectly still with his hands in pockets. "That is a nice computer you have, or should I say had?"

He laughed again.

Clark began to question his own decision to stand firm. He had to think of a way out. He knew he was strong but the other man was the aggressor, and an unknown quantity. He was big, both tall and wide.

"I need the hard drive, Clark," he said.

"I have no idea ..."

The man's demeanour changed. He took a step forward and raised his voice.

"Clark, don't play games with me. I know you have it. I know you have looked at it. I have your notepad. I know you think you have found something but let me tell you, you have found nothing. Give it to me now."

There must be more on the hard drive, Clark thought. The man as much as said there was something there to find. This was a gauntlet thrown. Clark was determined to get away and get back to examining the drive.

The man had clearly not seen or searched Clark's car. Clark had taken off his overcoat and put it on the backseat. He had put the hard drive and the notepad in the glove compartment. He had to get back to it.

"I don't have it," Clark shouted and ran forwards, head down.

The man was quick for his size. He side stepped and grabbed Clark in a headlock, spinning him around and throwing him on his back to the ground. Clark fell heavily, the wind taken from him. The man held Clark's arms pinned over his head as he lay on his back and dropped a knee on his chest. Clark could not move. He had underestimated the strength and agility of the man.

"Clark, this is not the way it has to be," the man shouted, "I don't want to hurt you, but believe me I will hurt you if I have to. Where is it?"

Clark struggled. He could feel his right arm loosening from the man's grip. He wriggled and manoeuvred his body until the right arm came free. The man was taken off guard. Clark swung with all his strength, his fist meeting a hard granite chin. The man rocked backwards slightly but quickly regained his composure, and his control.

"Not good, Clark," he yelled and struck Clark across the face, first with his backhand and then his forehand.

"I said I don't want to hurt you but I will, make no mistake."

The man frisked Clark crudely and then abruptly got up, leaving Clark on the ground holding his face. He stood over Clark and smiled. Then he broke into a laugh. "Maybe that pretty girlfriend of yours has it?" he said grinning as he turned and walked casually down the dark corridor. "You should have left it alone Clark, you should have left it alone," he shouted over his shoulder.

Clark sat upright and tried to control his pumping heart and trembling legs.

He had to get to Ellie.

He had to warn her.

He ran down the corridor into the darkness. The rear door was closed. He pushed against it but it would not move. Something had been set against it. He pushed again but to no avail. He had to get out, and quickly.

Then he remembered the restrooms. He ran to the first door under the raised floor and pushed his way in. Above the stalls were the small ventilation windows. The glass was shattered in each one, the metal cages fixed to the wall from the outside. Clark climbed on to the cistern of the nearest stall. He covered his hand with his handkerchief and pushed out the remaining shards of glass. He pushed at the metal cage. It held firm but he sensed movement. He jumped from the cistern and ran to the next stall and lifted its cistern lid. He ran back to the first stall and hammered the cage with the ceramic lid. It began to give. He gave a full swing and the cage crashed to the ground outside. He squeezed and pushed until he was out to his waist. He pushed further and he fell to the ground, landing on his hands. He glanced to his right to see a scaffold pole wedged between the door and the retaining wall.

He picked himself up and ran to the corner of the factory, to where the loading platforms faced the road. He arrived just in time to see Jackson's car pulling away from the factory gates.

CHAPTER 13

Clark ran to the large yellow builder's skip at the front of the factory. His car was still behind it, unharmed. The man had clearly not ventured around that side of the building. Clark got into the car and checked the glove compartment. The hard drive was still there. He started his engine and pressed his foot to the floor, the Toyota's wheels spinning furiously before eventually finding traction.

His head was spinning. What had just happened? What was Jackson's car doing in the middle of it all? What was he going to do now? He had to figure it out. But first he had to call Ellie.

He stopped the car at the side of the Mallusk Road and fished the Nokia from the inside pocket of his overcoat.

Ellie answered immediately.

"Hi Clark, is everything okay?" she said knowing it was him from the caller ID, "It's not like you to call me at work."

"It's fine Ellie," Clark said, and then paused to correct himself. "No, it's not fine actually. I need to talk to you."

"What's going on Clark?" she asked slowly, her voice shaking.

"I'm in the middle of something right now Ellie, a data

investigation, and it's not turning out well."

"Are you all right? Has something happened? You sound a bit shaken."

"I'll be okay. Listen Ellie, it's a long story. I'll tell you about it later but the crux of it is this. I have a data unit that I am investigating and someone knows I have it and wants it. I have just been threatened."

"Oh no," Ellie said drawing breath, Clark visualising her with her hand over her mouth.

"Are you hurt?"

"No, nothing like that. Just a bit of verbal."

"Who was it? Do you know who it was?"

"I've no idea who he was," Clark said and paused.

"Ellie, as he was leaving he mentioned you, mentioned that I might be hiding the data unit with you."

"What are you talking about? What have you got me into Clark?"

"Nothing Ellie, I promise you. It was just a threat," he said hoping it was true, "I just want you to be careful, maybe stay away from your apartment for a few days?"

"What? Nothing to worry about? Just a threat? And now you are telling me to stay away from my apartment? Clark, you are frightening me. I don't like it."

He had sprung it on her. In the last couple of days he'd had a meeting with Milton White and had accepted an assignment, an assignment that would no doubt involve the police at some stage. He had confided in Jackson. But he had not confided in her. He had not wanted to burden her, he'd thought, but now she had become involved.

"I'm sorry," he said, I will tell you about it later. Can you come round after work and we can talk?"

"Okay," she said with a sigh, "but I'll be working later tonight, it might be nearer eight. I was going to call you anyway. As luck would have it I already have a bag packed for a few days. I need to go to Mum's. I have arranged with work to take some case files with me and I can always commute into Belfast if I have to. I'll call round with you on my way."

"Okay, okay. I'm sorry Ellie. See you later."

Clark hung up and dropped the phone onto his lap. He had messed up. Ellie was angry, and rightly so. She was heading off to her mum's for who knew how long. He would miss her, but he was relieved. At least there she would be safe. He did not want to let her go on bad terms. He would have to think of what he should tell her.

Clark drove home through the start of rush hour traffic. It was a slow journey, every traffic light conspiring against him. He was fortunate again to find a parking spot right outside his house. He made sure he had the hard drive and his coat with him and went into the house.

He could barely remember the drive home. His mind had been a blur as he had been trying to piece together what had happened. He sat on the burgundy club chair and put his head in his hands. After a moment he picked up the Gibson and began strumming a random blues progression. He thought it appropriate. While intuitively strumming he was running over and over in his head yet again what had just happened. It was certainly Jackson's car, of that there could be no mistake, a silver Vauxhall family saloon with a customised twin exhaust system and a *JK50 MOR* vanity plate.

He began to retrace what he had told Jackson, in some way to try and understand how and why he would have been at the factory. Of course he had told Jackson over coffee that he was going to the factory but why did he then show up? Clark thought through the events of the last few days and his conversations with Jackson.

And then he gasped, his heart and his stomach sinking as realisation hit him.

Jackson had invited him out of his house the previous night, drawing him away from the hard drive. He had encouraged Clark to delay going home by suggesting he go to Ellie's for another bottle of wine. Clark had seen him on his phone as he and Ellie left, his back turned from Tracey. When Clark had arrived home he found the house had been ransacked. That morning after he met Milton he happened to bump into Jackson who had acted strangely. At coffee Jackson had repeatedly brought the conversation back to the hard drive. He had said, 'Do you think it was the hard drive he was after?' Clark did not know how many intruders there might have been and had referred to 'they.' It was Jackson who had mentioned 'he.' And Clark recalled Jackson asking what else was in the parcel that Milton that given to him at the Palm House. Clark did not tell Jackson about a parcel. He was sure he had just said Milton had given him a portable hard drive.

Clark did not know how or why, but he knew that in some way Jackson was involved. He grabbed his coat making sure the hard drive and notebook were in its pocket, picked up his car keys from the fireplace where he had discarded them and headed to Jackson's house.

Clark fought to control his anger, but equally he was saddened. How could Jackson betray him? He was his longest and most trusted friend. He had trusted him with Milton White's story and he had trusted him with his own findings. He had trusted him over Ellie.

Rush hour traffic was in full flow, or not flowing at all to be accurate. Clark sat for twenty minutes on the Lisburn Road, moving only one hundred yards. Belfast was like that, a thriving commercial and business city where most workers commuted in and out from the surrounding suburban towns. The commuter routes were best avoided by non-commuters at commuter time. It was commuter time but Clark had no choice. He had to speak with Jackson. He had to face him.

He cut across from the Lisburn Road to the Malone Road and eventually arrived at Jacksons's house on Stranmillis' Sharman Road. It was a quaint semi detached house with a large bay window covering most of the ground floor, a bright yellow painted front door beside it. Windows belonging to two of the three bedrooms sat above on a white pebble dash render. The ground floor level was red brick. The red brick and the white pebble dash met just above the door and the bay window. There was a driveway, but no garage. The driveway gates lay open in the midst of a neatly trimmed hedge.

Clark turned into the driveway stopping just short of the front door. The silver Vauxhall was not there. Clark jumped out of his Toyota and closed the door with a loud bang. After a few long strides he was at the front door, thumping harshly with his fist.

Tracey came to the door, dressed in sports pants and vest. She looked magnificent Clark instinctively thought as he always did, beads of perspiration running down from her forehead to her neck and beyond to her chest. But at that moment he was too vexed to care.

"Oh, Hi Clark, I wasn't expecting you," she said, "It s not often you call around here out of the blue. Is everything all right? Jackson isn't here. He's not usually home until well after six o'clock. Do you want to wait? I've just finished up on the exercise bike. I was going to take a shower and change. I was going to make some dinner. I was thinking of doing some Cottage Pie. You can wait if you want."

"No, Tracey. I don't want to wait. And I don't care about what you are going to do. Frankly Tracey I wish you would just shut up for once. Close your mouth and listen. I need to see Jackson. Tell him I was here."

Clark turned and climbed back into his car leaving Tracey standing on her doorstep, open mouthed and speechless.

He reversed onto the road and sped away, not once looking back. A few minutes later he had arrived at the roundabout outside Stranmillis Teacher Training College and pulled into the public car park opposite the College. He had to calm himself. His heart was pumping violently, his anger unrelenting. He took deep breaths, holding them in for a few seconds and slowly releasing them. This was apparently a stress calming technique, or so Clark believed. It worked for him anyway. He got out of his car and stared aimlessly at the heavy stream of cars negotiating the roundabout. Cars were lined in every direction for as far as he could see.

He checked his watch. It was five thirty. Ellie was calling after eight. He had to see Jackson. But Jackson wouldn't be home for another hour. He needed to do something to take his mind away from the festering thoughts of what was going on, and of what Jackson had to do with it. Many scenarios were developing in his head, none of which he liked. He looked at his watch again. He might just have time to fight across the city and call on his dad in the Ulster Hospital.

He made it in less than forty minutes, the traffic flowing surprisingly free once he had weaved through the city centre streets and reached the Newtownards Road across the River Lagan, its two lane carriageway clearly paying dividends.

The visitor's car park was as busy as ever but he was fortunate to find a space on his first circuit. He pulled on his coat and checked the pocket, lifting the collar to protect against the dropping evening temperature. The light was dropping too, dusk settling, rain clouds accumulating overhead. Rain was inevitable in the Belfast climate but the trade off for Clark was the lush greenery nurtured by the wet and mild climate. He thought then of the garden and fields by the Lough where he had grown up, the long days spent playing, chasing and hiding with Amy. He'd loved the green fields, the freedom and open space of the countryside. He thought of his moving to the City, the lifestyle change in shared student accommodation and then in his own house in Ethel Street. It had been a major change, but he had liked it almost immediately. He liked the close proximity of friends and of places to go. He liked the freedom of going where he wanted, when he wanted, and with whom he wanted. He liked not having to explain where he was going, who he was going with, when he would be home, and how he was getting home. He missed Amy. He missed what they had. They were good memories but he, and she, had moved on.

His parents too held many memories for him, fond memories.

They were devoted to their two children, working hard to provide a good standard of living and always being around at school holidays. Frequent trips were made to the family holiday cottage in Donegal where the entire family would hike far into the hills and picnic, laughing and playing together. His mother would bake fresh soda bread on the cottage range and they would all sit around and eat with the butter instantly melting and running down their chins. They would all laugh at that, no recriminations. His father tried on many occasions to interest Clark in fishing, but try as he did it was not something he took to. He enjoyed however spending the time with his father, playing in rock pools by the sea or climbing trees by the lake as his father fished. Amy liked fishing. She would be the master of the fishing net, standing perfectly still beside her father and netting the catch. Clark enjoyed watching from his elevated position in the trees. His mother would often be sitting underneath preparing the lunch, boiling a kettle for the obligatory tea on the small portable gas stove.

These memories were going through Clark's head as he crossed the car park and entered the main hospital entrance where he found the direction arrows pointing towards the recovery ward.

His father was sitting up in the bed, assisted by the bed's own lifting mechanism. He was wired to a variety of machines, and had tubes going into and out of him assisting with the body's essential requirements. The portly nurse at the station had reluctantly let Clark in given that it was not visiting time and that his father although stronger was still very weak. She had said the doctor was due on his rounds at any moment. But at the end of the day there was little she could do to stop him going in. He was his son after all.

Clark went close to the bed and leaned forward just as his father turned. Clark stepped back, slightly startled, not expecting his father to be awake. His father smiled on seeing Clark.

"Hello Son," he said.

Clark felt a lump in his throat. He swallowed hard and rubbed his hand over his forehead to hide the moisture in his eyes.

"Hello Dad."

"Your mum will be here later. She went home for a rest."

Clark nodded.

"Your sister plans to come over for a few days."

Clark nodded again. He was afraid to speak, afraid his voice would let him down. He was glad he was there. He hadn't been there since Saturday afternoon and it was Monday evening. He was upset by his own inability to do what deep within him he knew he wanted to do. He was upset that he had allowed some sort of division to develop, and if he was honest he didn't really know what had created it. There was no incident. There was no major falling out. It was just Clark growing upwards and inwards, wanting to spend more time alone unable to communicate his true feelings, and for some reason being uncontrollably uncomfortable and embarrassed in his parent's company. There was no rationale for it. He found solace in his computers and eventually in a new group of friends. He began to feel more comfortable around people again when he moved away but the discomfort he felt around his parents remained. He couldn't explain it, but perhaps more importantly, he did nothing about it. Time went on and Clark's new life established despite his parents making regular attempts to engage him, even on occasion calling on Clark in Belfast. This was particularly uncomfortable for him, an intrusion into his new existence. Amy had sided with her parents, she too unable to understand or accept the inexplicable choices her brother had made. The wedge between him and his family grew.

He remained incapable, or unwilling, to publically show his true feelings.

"How are you Dad?" he managed to say realising it was a ridiculous thing to say in the circumstances but unable to think of anything else.

"Strong," his father said, "I hope to get home tomorrow."

Clark noticed the broad smile on his face, a familiar broad smile but one he had not seen in a long time. Then he knew his father was playing with him. His father used to be the king of wind ups when they were growing up Clark recalled. Clark returned the smile. "Yeah, good one Dad," he said.

Then they both laughed.

The portly nurse rushed in. "What's going on here?" she said, "Mr Radcliffe needs to rest."

"I'm sorry nurse," said Clark, "I'm going now."

"Humph," she said and pushed past him to check on the patient charts at the foot of the bed.

"Bye then Dad," he said.

"Bye Son. And thanks for coming. It was good to see you."

He paused and looked at Clark. "Come again, Son." He held out his hand. Clark hesitated and glanced quickly at the nurse. She was busy with the charts. He reached out and held his father's hand for a brief moment.

"I will Dad," he said again swallowing hard and then quietly left the hospital.

CHAPTER 14

It was dark by the time Clark was driving down Ethel Street. Seeking out a parking space he caught the outline of a figure sitting on his wall. He then spotted a silver Vauxhall saloon.

Clark parked on the opposite side of the street, a couple of houses down from his own. He climbed out of the car and checked his coat pocket before locking the door and stopping to glare at Jackson, to gather his thoughts.

Jackson stared back.

After a moment Clark approached the gate, Jackson rising to meet him standing tall, feet apart making his narrow frame as broad as he could.

"Just what is going on Clark?" he said, his voice sharp and clipped.

"Not here Jackson, inside," Clark said as he brushed past and turned the key in the door.

He led Jackson to the lounge and hung his overcoat over the back of one of the kitchen chairs. He turned but before he could speak Jackson stepped forward.

"I don't know what's got into you Clark," he said, his face red with anger. "What were you doing at my house?" What did you say to Tracey? She's upset, wouldn't tell me what you said, only that you had insulted her."

"Maybe I should be asking you what is going on."

Jackson raised his brow. "What are you talking about?"

"Why were you at Mallusk this afternoon?"

The aggression quickly evaporated. "I, I, eh, don't know what you are talking about."

"Save it Jackson, I saw your car, that very same car that is sitting outside my house now," Clark said pointing over Jackson's shoulder to the window. "You were driving away as I came out of the factory, no doubt with some bald heavy beside you."

"Oh, for goodness sake, Clark, you are making no sense."

"Am I not Jackson? And what were you doing today at Victoria Square? Just happened to be there did you? Doing some shopping were you? Do you do random shopping often Jackson?"

"I told you I was at a meeting …"

Clark held up his hand. "Hear me out Jackson, I haven't finished yet. How did you know Milton gave me a parcel? I didn't tell you. Can you answer me that? Why did you ask me if 'he' had found anything in the break in? Do you know more about this, who the 'he' was? Or maybe Jackson it was you who sent him?"

"Clark, I …"

Jackson lifted both hands and covered his face. He moved backwards to the brown leather sofa and sat down, his hands still over his face.

"Clark," he said quietly, "I've messed up. I should have been honest from the start. I guess I'm no good at this."

He looked up at Clark. "Any chance of a beer?" he asked.

Clark lifted two Coronas from the fridge and pulled the tops. He handed one to Jackson and sat himself on the burgundy club chair, beer in hand.

"I've been following you Clark," Jackson said, "ever since you told me on Friday night about being threatened outside." Jackson pointed over his shoulder with his thumb towards the window.

"What?"

It was Jackson's turn to hold up his hand. "Please, Clark, let me finish. Let me try to explain."

Clark nodded as he lifted the beer bottle to his lips, taking a long slow drink.

Jackson continued, "I was worried about you. When you told me you were threatened I was frightened for you Clark. I wanted to stay here on Friday night, just in case, you know, someone came back. But I didn't. You were adamant you would be all right. I was worried the more I thought about the story you told me, about Milton White and about Declan Somerville. You were obviously involved in something back then and it seemed to be raising its head again. Why was Milton calling you after all these years? Did he want to cover something up, tidy loose ends? Was the threat you got something to do with Milton?"

Jackson too took a long drink from his bottle. He said, "Maybe I should have asked you if you wanted me to go with you to see Milton, maybe I should have insisted. But I didn't. I just hid behind a tree and waited. I watched him arrive, I watched you arrive, I watched you and him talking, and then I waited after you left to watch him. I don't know what I was really thinking at that stage. I had no idea what you and he talked about but I saw him give you the parcel. I thought I might follow him, see where he went, and see if I might find anything out about where he might have been for the last five years."

Clark sat in silence. He had so much spinning around in his head he may as well listen, more to consider and analyse later.

"And then it got worse, Clark. I then got more worried about you and about what Milton White was up to."

"What do you mean, it got worse?" said Clark.

"After you left Milton sat on for what must have been ten

minutes. He was just staring at the ground, rubbing his hands together. Then from the other side of the Palm House, from behind the big dome, two people came towards him. They stood in front of him and had some sort of conversation. Then he got up and the three of them walked away together, in the opposite direction from you towards the Queens Sports Centre."

He looked at Clark. "The other two were a man and a woman. The woman had long blonde hair tied back in a ponytail and looked fairly young and delicate. The man however looked a bit older. He was tall and wide and wore a long dark overcoat. It looked like his head was shaved."

Clark didn't know what to say. He took a long drink from his bottle.

"I remembered you had told me the man outside your house the other night wore a dark coat, and looked like he had shaved his head," said Jackson, "and here was a shaved headed man talking with Milton."

Clark hadn't yet mentioned to Jackson his struggle in the factory with a man with a shaved head in a long dark coat. He would get to that. He wanted to listen to Jackson's story, to his account of things, and to piece it together with what he knew.

"I called you on Saturday night to ask how you got on," said Jackson, "and I don't know, but I think I might have wanted to tell you I had been at the Palm House that morning, that I had seen you, that I had spied on you. But I was embarrassed, Clark. What would you have thought of me, having crept around and spied like some child or amateur sleuth? I was ashamed, I have to admit. But I did see something that concerned me. I wanted to warn you, but just couldn't think how. I thought that if I invited you out of the house you would at least be safe for a while if anyone came back."

"So that's why you wanted me to go out on Saturday night?"

"Yes, and when you told me Ellie was coming over I thought at least there would be someone else there, not ideal but at least you wouldn't be alone."

"And last night?"

"I thought if we all went out you would be safe for another night."

"That's why you encouraged me to go back to Ellie's?"

"Yes. I realise now how it must have looked, like I was trying to get you out of the house for some ulterior reason. But I was genuinely worried Clark, and the longer it was going on the harder it was for me to tell you what I had seen."

Jackson's voice was quivering. He fidgeted with the label of the beer bottle, gradually picking it away. What he was saying seemed plausible to Clark.

Clark asked, "When Ellie and I were leaving Zen last night I looked back and you were on the phone. It looked a bit suspicious. You had tried to keep us there with after dinner drinks, and then you tried to send me and Ellie to hers. Then you called somebody, and with your back to Tracey? What were you hiding from her?"

Jackson looked confused. "I don't know what you are talking about," he said. "After you left I called a taxi. I might have turned away to hear or to get a better signal."

Clark nodded. "And this morning at Victoria Square?" he asked.

"Yes, I have to admit, I was spying on you again. Pathetic I know, but there you are. I suppose I just wanted to be there to provide some sort of protection if needed."

"But you didn't know about the break in to my house at that stage?"

"No, I knew nothing about it until you told me at coffee. I suppose I assumed the bald man had something to do with it, and that was why I had asked you what 'he' had found."

It seemed reasonable to Clark. He nodded and finished his beer. "Another one?" he asked Jackson.

"No, I'd better not, the car outside and all that."

"Sure," said Clark, "I think I'll have one."

Clark returned to the burgundy club chair with a second Corona.

Jackson said, "I was mortified when you caught me on this morning. I didn't know what to do or say."

"You did look and act a bit suspicious," said Clark and raised a smile. Jackson smiled too.

Jackson said, "You said you were going to the factory. I didn't know exactly where the factory was but knew it was around Mallusk somewhere. I thought I would go up there and maybe…, I don't know, in case you needed me. In case something happened. I don't know what I was thinking Clark, or what I was expecting, or what I thought I was going to do. I eventually found the factory after asking around. I couldn't see your car. All the doors at the front and side of the factory looked to be heavily bolted, so I guessed you had driven in and given up. So I just drove back to work."

He stopped fiddling with the beer bottle and looked again at Clark. "Why did you think I had a heavy in the car?" he asked.

Clark told him about the confrontation and struggle inside the factory, about the man virtually admitting it had been he who had broken into his house. He told him about being locked inside the factory and managing to break out just as Jackson's car was leaving.

Jackson was visibly distraught, having failed in his objective to provide assistance or protection.

"He knew my name, Jackson," said Clark, "and he knows about Ellie. Or at least I suspect he knows about Ellie. He didn't mention her by name but I guess if he knows me and where I live he knows about Ellie."

"Have you told Ellie?"

"Yes, but not much. At least not yet. She is on her way here now. She should be here anytime," said Clark checking his watch. "I did tell her not to go home to her place."

"How did that go down?"

"Not well as you can imagine, especially without an explanation. She had planned to head to her mum's tonight for a few days anyway, so it should be okay."

Jackson dropped his head and fiddled some more with his empty bottle. He was silent for a while.

"Clark, I'm sorry. I should have been honest. I just wanted to look out for you. You and I, we are like brothers, all that we have been through. You were there for me after Beth, and after Diana. I really appreciated it. I suppose I wanted to be there for you in this thing but I didn't know how. I got off to a wrong start and didn't do anything to make it better. Like I said, I messed up."

Clark stared at him. Yes, they had been through a lot, had been friends for a long time. Clark could understand Jackson wanting to be there for him. If the roles had been reversed Clark would have wanted to be there for him. Would he have done it any differently? He did not know.

It was Clark's turn to feel ashamed, ashamed at having doubted Jackson. He should have always believed in Jackson. What was it with him that he could doubt even genuine friends?

He rose from his chair and offered his hand to Jackson.

Jackson rose and offered his hand in return. No words were spoken.

The handshake became an embrace. "I'm sorry for doubting you," Clark mumbled into Jackson's shoulder.

CHAPTER 15

They both pulled away when they heard a key turn in the door. It was Ellie.

"Hi, Ellie, I was just leaving," said Jackson as she entered the room.

Clark nodded at Ellie and walked Jackson to the door.

"Jackson, let's talk tomorrow. It would be useful to talk through some of my thinking. Maybe bounce a few scenarios?"

"Yeah. I'll check my schedule in the morning and give you a call. And Clark, you might want to speak with the police. I get the feeling there is something still not right with Milton White and this whole thing."

Clark nodded. "I had intended to call them tomorrow," he said, "and Jackson, maybe apologise to Tracey for me?"

Jackson laughed, "You'll have to do that one yourself. Don't worry about it though. She'll get over it."

He waved as he dropped into his car and said, "Clark, be careful tonight. Give me a call if you need me."

Clark went back inside to face Ellie.

Ellie was standing with her back turned, both hands on the back of the kitchen chair.

"How was work?" Clark asked, standing well back.

She turned, her face cold and taut. "Why don't you tell me what is going on?" she said.

"Do you want to sit down?" Clark asked quietly and pointed towards the sofa.

She nodded and moved slowly to the seat. She was still in her work clothes, a light grey Ralph Lauren trouser suit and white blouse, low cut but dignified. She wore her Burberry sandals with high three inch heels, giving her the few inches she felt she lacked. Her short hair was tussled and she wore little makeup other than deep red lipstick and dark eyeliner. She readied her glasses on the bridge of her nose.

Clark sat on the edge of the club chair, clasped his hands on his lap and stared at the floor. "Ellie, something is going on," he said, "something weird with a job I am doing. Well, it's not really a job as such, more of a thing I am doing for someone."

"For goodness sake Clark, will you spit it out," she said.

"Okay, okay." He raised the palms of his hands to her in surrender, "You remember I used to work in the Department of Industry and Trade Development, back before I met you?"

She nodded, and sat forward slightly.

"Well," he continued, "there was a guy who worked there, Milton White he was called, you maybe remember something about it in the news, but he was accused of pocketing grant money that was supposed to fund some company investing here from overseas?"

She nodded again, "Vaguely," she said, her eyes fixed on Clark.

Clark was having difficulty maintaining eye contact with her, his gaze repeatedly shifting from the floor to her and back to the floor again. "It was me who found the evidence against him. His bank transfer details were buried in a program. I found it during a computer audit. Anyway he lost his job and disappeared. I moved into the freelancing around about the same time."

He looked at her and held her eyes for a long moment. "He contacted me last week and we met. He claims he was set up and he gave me a portable hard drive with what he claims are all the computer files relating to the incident. He asked me to take a look at it."

"And?" said Ellie, lowering her head slightly, looking at Clark over the top of her glasses.

"I said I would."

Her face tightened. She folded her arms abruptly. "Typical Clark," she said, "useless with people but can't say no to a computer."

"Please Ellie," he said, "there's more to it. This is something I have never mentioned to you but it is something that I have been unable to get out of my mind since it happened. I have had sleepless nights over the years. Every so often it would come to my mind and it would take days to shift it."

He lifted one hand and rubbed his eyes.

"Clark, are you all right?" she said sliding to the edge of the sofa and resting her elbows on her knees. She had shortened the distance between them. They were close enough to touch, if that was what they wanted.

He nodded. "Someone died in the office Ellie, apparently of natural causes but I don't believe it. He was working late one night on the audit, doing something that I had asked him to do. I don't know what he found, if anything, but the audit shut down right afterwards. I feel responsible, Ellie. He left a wife and child."

He looked up at her, his eyes filled with tears. He rubbed his nose and shook his head. She slid from the sofa onto her knees in front of him. She held both his hands to her face. She kissed each hand lightly.

"Oh Clark," she said, "It's okay."

She stood and Clark stood with her. They held each other tightly. For the first time in as long as he could remember Clark sobbed in the presence of someone else.

He kissed Ellie on her forehead and sat back on the chair holding both her hands in his. She stepped back and let the grip slip as she too sat.

"That's why I couldn't say no, Ellie. I have a chance to find out what really happened, a chance to understand, to finally move on."

"I understand Clark."

"But as it is I am no further in understanding. If anything the whole thing is getting more complicated. Milton White has told me what happened, at least his version of it. I believed him but now I am not so sure."

"What do you mean?"

"I'm still working it through in my mind Ellie. Things have happened. As I told you earlier on the phone someone threatened me, said they were looking for the portable hard drive, and said that maybe my girlfriend had it."

"So I am your girlfriend?" she said teasing, a gentle smile spreading across her face.

Clark too smiled. He was stupid. He should have known that of all the people in the world who he could talk to, and be himself and be happy with, it was Ellie. She understood him. And he had kept it from her.

Some details he did not yet want to share, for the best of reasons he thought. He did not want to concern her any further by telling her about the break in. He did not want to tell her about the man outside his house the few nights before, the same man who had earlier that day threatened him. The night the man was outside was the night before Ellie had stayed over. He did want to tell her either that the confrontation at the factory had got physical.

He did however have to give some detail to protect her, to warn her.

He said, "He knows my name Ellie, he knows where I live, so I have to assume he knows about you, and where you live."

"So you want me to go away for a few days?"

He nodded.

"It's okay," she said, "I was going to my mum's anyway so no harm done, but more importantly Clark, what about you? If he knows where you live will he not come here to carry out his threat, or to try and get his hands on the hard drive? Where is the hard drive anyway? And what about the police in all of this?"

"It's okay Ellie, the hard drive is safe. He will not get his hands on it. The police apparently, according to Milton anyway, have an open investigation but it has not progressed in the last couple of years. I intend to talk to them tomorrow, although I don't know what to tell them, or what they will do."

He looked away towards the fireplace and turned to face her again.

"Ellie, Jackson knows. I told him all about it earlier, just before you came. He is going to help me work through it, help me with the investigation, give me someone to bounce ideas off. He has offered to be here if I need him. I think Ellie I'll be okay. If need be I'll get Jackson over to stay."

Clark's face had reddened as he told Ellie he had confided in Jackson before her. There were of course reasons, that he had thought Jackson was involved. He had no intention of sharing that with her though.

As it turned out it was fine.

"That's good Clark," she said, "I'm glad Jackson knows. It is better you have someone to help you, someone you can trust, not just with the investigation but with looking out for you. You and he go back a long way Clark, it would be selfish of me to think you should put me before him, especially with something like this, something that started way before we met. No, I am glad you told Jackson. I am glad you have a friend as close as Jackson."

She paused, and looked at the ground. Her hands were clasped and she was circling her thumbs around each other. "Maybe someday," she said, "I will be your confident, a friend you will come to no matter what?"

She looked at Clark. He smiled, rose from the chair and walked towards her. She shifted along on the sofa and he sat beside her, draping an arm over her shoulder. She leaned back into his arm and nestled her head on his shoulder.

Clark said nothing. He kissed the top of her head and gently caressed her shoulder. She smiled. She knew Clark didn't have to say anything. She knew him. She was happy.

Clark ordered in pizza that they ate at the kitchen table, Clark washing his down with a Corona, Ellie with a glass of tap water. They talked about work, how busy Ellie was with conveyance cases despite the downturn in the housing market, and how Clark had a security report outstanding that he needed to get to Fabian Townsend at Chesterton and Williamson. He would need to get it finished and get it away. He needed to keep Fabian off his case. They talked about Ellie's mum and how she was responding to her treatment and Clark told her about going to see his dad earlier that day.

It was after ten o'clock when Ellie checked her watch. She put her hand over Clark's as it rested on the kitchen table.

"Do you want me to stay with you tonight?" she asked, "I can always go to Mum's first thing in the morning."

"Thanks," said Clark placing his other hand on top of hers, "I appreciate it, but your mum needs you. I'll be okay."

"If you're sure?"

"Yes, honestly. Go on. Make sure you stay in touch though."

They both stood and held each other tightly. They kissed long and hard. Ellie was first to pull away.

"I'd better go," she whispered.

"Yeah," said Clark. He stood still, maintaining his hold on her, arms tightly around her waist, staring into her eyes.

"I…, Ellie, I…"

She put her finger to his lips.

"I know Clark," she said, "I know."

Clark walked her to the door where they hugged again.

"Be careful Clark," she said and walked down the street to her car, the black Audi convertible that would take her the fifty miles to County Tyrone.

Clark smiled and shook his head as he waved her off. He moved back inside making sure the door was secured and stepped to the fridge for another beer, deciding it to be the last one of the night.

He retrieved the hard drive from his coat pocket and headed up the stairs to his study.

CHAPTER 16

Clark called up the files and folders to his Dell and began scanning them yet again. Nothing immediately drew his attention, at least not to the extent that the Dubai Wire and Cable and Inspection database files had intrigued him. He began opening each folder in turn, scanning through their contents for any title or naming convention of interest. Clark yawned loudly when he checked his watch and realised it was well after one o'clock. He hadn't found anything. But there were many more files to examine. He couldn't go to bed without progress, subconsciously thinking he would stay up all night. At least then he would be ready should there be any further attempted break in. It wasn't realistic of course. He knew he would eventually fade. He closed his eyes and thought through what he had already discovered.

He had found text fragments in two folders, fragments from deleted documents relating to meetings and inspections at the factory. Someone had tried to remove these documents for some reason. He thought how he might carry out a search of the hard drive specifically for other text fragments, text fragments that might indicate other documents that had been deleted. He could try a diagnostic search to interrogate the hard drive, perhaps apply one of the diagnostic tools on his Dell. He didn't think however they could deliver in their present form. He would have to re-write the program code.

He rubbed his hands together and whistled aloud. With Bruce Springsteen turned low on the small CD player in the study he went to the kitchen to fix a pot of coffee. Caffeine would be essential. He liked low background music when he was working with program code. He did not know why, just something that helped him focus. He had yet to get around to transferring his vast CD collection onto MP3. He eventually would, probably.

One hour later and he had written code to search all files in the hard drive and extract any text fragments. It would take a while to run, but how long exactly he didn't know. He decided to go to bed while the Dell continued with its work.

He awoke at seven thirty and made straight for the study. He stared at the screen on his Dell, rubbed his eyes and stared again. The diagnostic program had recovered over three hundred fragments. More coffee needed he thought, much more coffee.

Clark attached his inkjet printer to the Dell and ran off a hard copy of the fragments. Over three hundred single lines of code printed in double space ran to eleven pages. With coffee and pencil in hand Clark set to work, quickly establishing that his program had erroneously extracted a number of lines of print code, and also hardware and driver code. There was however, in the midst of it all, something that interested him.

It was a random set of letters that did not sit with the alpha numeric code around it, no numbers or spaces. He wrote the letters on a fresh page in his notepad.

forsetdallemer.

He looked at it again, and then again. He wrote it backwards. He broke it into syllables and wrote it different ways. He called up his internet search engine and fed it in. There were no hits. It did not look like any computer code he recognised, nor did it look like a word. He fed the letters into a search function on his Dell and explored the portable hard drive to identify where the letters were located within it.

He then found something even more interesting.

The same letters were displayed on the Dell's screen. However there were gaps between them, gaps of varying size. Clark reflected for a long moment, ruminating different options and scenarios, eventually concluding that what he had found were most likely word fragments; words that had been contained within a document file, a file that had been deleted.

His next challenge was to decipher the letters.

The letters appeared in three parts, *forset*, *dal* and *lemer*. The prevalent spaces were around the letters *dal*. There was little space between the letters *forset*. There was even less space between the letters *lemer*. This could mean anything he knew depending on the cause and extent of the error. However he felt a reasonable assumption was that the larger the gap the more was missing.

He wrote the letters again as they were on screen, replicating the spaces. He looked at it again, and again. He focused on what looked like one word, given it had the least space between the letters. *lemer*. The letters looked familiar, but from where? He ran the word over in his head. He said it aloud. He split in into two syllables and again said it aloud. He repeated this aloud, a flicker of recognition in his mind. He said it louder each time as he began to visualise where he had seen the letters before. He was sure he had seen the letters somewhere recently, somewhere within the hard drive.

He called up the folders containing the record of meetings and the Letters of Offer and Acceptance documents. He trawled through them carefully scanning for what he was looking for.

And then he found it.

He rose from the chair and paced the room, his heart racing. He would need to speak with Milton White. But he had no way of contacting him; all contact had come from Milton to Clark and the caller had withheld ID details. He would have to wait.

It was approaching ten o'clock, Tuesday morning. Clark showered, changed and took a simple breakfast to the sofa, catching up on the television news as he ate. He could however not focus. The plate rocked back and forth, lucky not to topple to the floor. He set it by the sink and lifted the landline phone, calling the police exchange and asked for Detective McArdle at Financial Crimes.

"McArdle," said a gruff voice.

"Yes," said Clark, "my name is Clark Radcliffe. I believe you have been involved in the Dubai Wire and Cable investigation against Milton White?"

"What? What did you just say?"

Clark repeated and waited. Silence, save for the rattle of a drawer opening and a rustling of paper.

"Who is this?"

Clark repeated his name again.

"Sorry. I can't help you." He hung up.

Clark sat on the club chair and thought through what he needed to do. He expected Jackson to call so they could get together. He needed to call Ellie. He needed to get something to Fabian Townsend at Chesterton and Williamson. But there was something else he needed to do.

He went to his random drawer and lifted a small telephone address book. He sat again on the chair and dialled a number from the book, a mobile number that he had seldom dialled.

"Amy, its Clark," he said when his sister answered the phone.

A long pause, "Yes Clark?"

"I..., I ..., went to see Dad yesterday."

"Oh, did you now?"

"He was sitting up. We spoke."

"That was good for you I'm sure," she said.

"He said you were coming over?"

"Yes, I'll be over. I want to see Dad. I want to be with Mum. How is Mum anyway?"

Clark closed his eyes tight and rubbed his temples, a thumb on one side and fingers on the other. He breathed deep, "I haven't seen her since Saturday."

"Humph. Have you called her?"

"No," he said, "I haven't."

He was about to give a reason, that he was too busy with an important work thing. But he didn't. What important work thing? What work thing should ever be more important than your family, especially in a time of distress and need?

"I wanted to Amy. I should have. I didn't … I couldn't."

"Save it," she said, "it's too late for all that now. Listen I need to go."

"Amy, when you are over maybe we can, you know …"

She hung up.

He returned to the chair and stared at the ceiling. Butterflies churned in his stomach. Tears came to his eyes. Why? Was it something to do with the memories that were coming back to him, memories triggered by his father's illness? Maybe it was something to do with the many nights he had lay awake with a head filled with images from the department and the fact that he was now on a journey to understand, to move on. Or maybe he should just phone his mother.

The telephone rang.

He shook his head, clearing his thoughts and reached for the handset. "Hello?" he said.

"Clark Radcliffe? It's McArdle. Detective Inspector McArdle, Financial Crimes."

Clark sat forward. "Yes?"

"Your name rang a bell. I checked you out. Seems you were the one who found that computer evidence against White?"

"Yes, that was…"

"Let's meet. Face to face."

Clark sat further forward and did not reply, at least not for a moment. "Sure," he said eventually.

"Midday, first floor lounge, Europa Hotel."

Clark looked at his watch. He didn't have much time. He stepped into his desert boots and pulled on his overcoat before running up the stairs and powering down the Dell and placing the hard drive and notes in his pocket.

He walked briskly to the bus stop on the Lisburn Road to catch the 9c service to the city centre.

CHAPTER 17

The Europa Hotel sat proudly on Belfast's Great Victoria Street. It was a tall imposing glass fronted building renovated to an exacting specification befitting of its four star status. It was a hotel that had been home to many guests over the years, from visiting sports stars and celebrities to American Presidents. Clark liked the Europa. He liked all that it stood for, a symbol of prosperity in the middle of the city centre for all to see.

He made his way from the foyer up the wood panelled staircase to the first floor lounge. A grand piano stood in front of large full length windows that gave views up and down Great Victoria Street, a place to sit and watch the world go by. The piano had no pianist.

Clark bought a coffee from the bar and took a seat at a small table affording a view of the outside as well as to the bar on the inside. After ten minutes two men came in, unmistakably police despite their attempts to dress casually. Detectives did not wear uniforms, but they might as well Clark thought. Both men wore grey shiny trousers, one in a navy tweed sports coat, the other in a navy flannel sports coat with gold effect buttons. They both wore ties that undoubtedly came free in packets of shirts. They had rubber soled shoes.

One was older. He was tall and round with a stomach protruding over his belt. His face was red, although Clark was not sure if this was his complexion or because he had just walked up one flight of stairs. He was cleanly shaven with neatly cut thick black hair. There was no greying. The younger man was equally tall but slim. He too was cleanly shaven and his hair was slightly spiked, with a shine from some applied product.

The older man approached Clark, the younger man taking a seat at the bar and watching.

"Radcliffe. DI McArdle," he said extending his hand.

Clark nodded and shook his hand, but did not rise from his chair. He noted the man had come straight to him. The man was indeed a detective, probably had called up his driving licence photograph at the station.

"Coffee?" asked Clark.

"No we're sorted. Campbell's organising coffee," he said pointing over his shoulder with his thumb, "Detective Constable Campbell."

Clark offered a feeble one finger wave and instantly regretted it. DC Campbell stared.

McArdle sat opposite Clark. He looked fresh up close even with the red face. Clark put him in his early fifties.

"What about White?" he asked. No messing about.

Clark took a deep breath and exhaled loudly. "Where do I start?" he said, "What's happening with your investigation?"

"You do the talking Radcliffe, I'll ask the questions."

Clark nodded. "Okay, fair enough. To get straight to the point then, there is something going on at the moment that I think has something to do with the Dubai Wire and Cable case and with Milton White."

"Oh yes, what's that then?"

Clark wanted to know what the police knew, he wanted to know why Milton was never prosecuted, and he wanted to know why the investigation had stopped but was still open. But he didn't want to tell much of what he was currently doing. Not yet at least. He decided on an approach that might draw some response and information from McArdle.

"I don't think Milton White did it. I think he was set up."

"Oh do you now?" said McArdle, "And here was me thinking I was going to hear something new and not some rehash of the same story White has been spinning for years. I'm sorry you have wasted my time Radcliffe."

He moved his seat back and began to rise.

"No, wait," said Clark. He needed to give something to hook McArdle.

"I have met with him, twice in the last week," he said.

McArdle stopped. "Where?"

"Here, in Belfast."

McArdle nodded and relaxed slowly into the chair. "Here in Belfast, you say. He was supposed to be away, living down in Sligo or somewhere?"

Clark lowered his voice. "He has come back to clear his name. He has given me a copy of something he wants me to look at. He says that as I had been so meticulous in finding the bank account stuff that implicated him in the first place then if there was anything else to find, something that may clear him, then I would find it."

McArdle nodded and after a moment said, "You found that bank account information in data files. Isn't that right?"

Clark nodded in reply.

"And he wants you to find something else, presumably in data files?"

"Yes."

"But you don't know what you are looking for?"

"No."

"And where might I ask are you looking for this something?"

McArdle had him. Clark couldn't divulge that he had the hard drive with copies of department files. There were data protection and security issues at stake. But on the other hand the police would have to know he had access, or potentially could have access to the files.

"Listen," said Clark, "if I was to tell you that I might, just might, be able to get access to files from the whole Dubai Wire and Cable thing and just might be able to find something relevant would you be interested?"

McArdle sat further forward and rubbed his chin. He glanced left and right before looking straight at Clark. "Hypothetically speaking, yes I would be interested. But what makes you think you can find something that we didn't find during our investigation?"

Clark now had him where he wanted. "To what extent did your investigation involve data mining? Who did you use? What skills did you have at your disposal?"

"Are you accusing us of sloppy work Radcliffe?"

"No, just asking. I do a lot of freelance work as you probably know, a lot of systems interrogation, a lot of corporate security work. I have a reputation. My services have been specifically requested. But I have never been asked to carry out any forensic data investigations for the police. So my question is who do you have?"

McArdle nodded. "We have forensic data specialists, of course we do. Probably not in your league though if all I have read about you is true. But sloppy we are not. The case against White was watertight."

"So that's why there was a successful prosecution then?" said Clark.

McArdle's face turned a deeper shade of red. "We had money transferring to his bank account Radcliffe, money from a fund that he had control over. We had him trying to hide the bank details in some computer system, but not well enough thanks to you. We had the money arriving in his bank account. And we had CCTV footage of him in the Isle of Man opening the bank account that the money went into. As far as we were concerned we had enough evidence to go to trial."

"But you couldn't prove he actually received the money? Isn't that right? It arrived into his bank account in the Isle of Man and then transferred out again. And there is no physical evidence that he has money in his possession?"

McArdle sighed, paused and nodded.

Clark had hit a nail on the head. McArdle had been sure he had all he needed to secure a conviction. The data investigation had been cursory at best, a process to tick all the boxes. The police had judged the other evidence to be enough. McArdle had been convinced, and remained convinced, that Milton White was guilty. He didn't want it to look like his case had been flawed by ordering a retrospective detailed data investigation after failing to reach prosecution. He had let it go.

"What exactly are you asking, Radcliffe?" he said.

"If you had a chance now to investigate the data further, would you take it?"

"We're still hypothetic right? … Maybe a deeper search might have found something."

"And hypothetically speaking, if I was to find something, you might be interested."

"Hypothetically, yes." McArdle thought for a moment and then leaned forward. "Radcliffe, I cannot condone anything illegal. I cannot use anything hacked, for example."

Clark laughed. "I'm no hacker. One more thing, did you check for any paper files?"

McArdle slowly shook his head "Okay, the less I know of what you plan to do the better. Stay in touch."

He handed Clark a card with direct contact details. "I'm not holding out any hope though. In my book White is guilty. I don't know what he is up to if he has come back to Belfast. I don't know what he is up to contacting you. But I will say this. Be a careful. He is a very clever man."

McArdle got up to leave and offered his hand again. Clark shook it firmly.

Clark did not mention the break in or the intimidation. To do so would have raised McArdle's curiosity. For the moment Clark had what he wanted. There was more he would need to ask, not least about Declan Somerville, but that would have to wait. Clark was satisfied that the police now knew he was involved in something and could give him cover or protection if required. He now knew the police investigation was still open as McArdle refused to close it, still regarding Milton White as guilty. And most of all Clark now knew that the police had not carried out any detailed analysis of the computer files.

"Could you do something for me?" Clark asked, "Could you try and contact Milton White through whatever channel you have, through Sligo or wherever, and have him call me. I need to speak to him."

McArdle didn't answer. He left along with DC Campbell. Two coffee cups were left untouched at the bar.

Clark stayed seated with his view across Great Victoria Street, answering his rumbling stomach by ordering lunch, Irish Beef Burger with red onion marmalade and sparkling Irish spring water. He hadn't heard from Jackson. Jackson had said he would call Clark when he had checked his schedule. Clark called him from his mobile phone. Jackson answered almost immediately.

"Clark, I was just about to call you," he said, the same way everybody says it when they hadn't called someone they were supposed to, "Are you at home?"

"No, I'm upstairs at the Europa. I've just ordered lunch."

"I don't suppose if I came around you could treat me?"

Clark laughed.

"Are you all right? Was everything okay last night? No prowlers?"

"No, no. Everything was good. I'm fine."

"Good. You know you just have to call."

"I know Jackson, thanks," said Clark. He paused for a moment then said, "Jackson, I've just met with the police."

"What? Did something happen?"

"No, it's not that. I'm fine. I met them to talk about Milton White."

"Oh right, did you learn anything interesting?"

"Are you free to come round for a bit?"

Jackson paused. "I'm a bit busy now Clark. I'll see what I can do. Will you be there for long?"

Clark checked his watch. "Probably an hour or so, by the time I get through lunch."

"Okay. I'll try and get round."

It was less than an hour when Jackson strode into the bar, spotting Clark and joining him at the table. Clark attracted the waitress's attention and ordered two coffees. She lifted his empty plate.

Clark told Jackson about his meeting with McArdle, DI McArdle. He told him that McArdle was fixated on Milton White's guilt and had assumed he'd had enough evidence to close the case. He told him the case had stayed open as McArdle was waiting for the moment he could finally prosecute Milton White. He told him the case had stalled because McArdle had no new lines of enquiry. He told him McArdle had as much as admitted that computer analysis formed little part in the investigation. And he told him that he had interpreted McArdle as having given him a green light to investigate what he was investigating but not get up to anything illegal.

The possession of the portable hard drive was a grey area.

"So, what now?" said Jackson.

"I found more text fragments this morning. I've been trying to figure them out, and I think I may just be onto something. But I want to check it with Milton."

"And you think all these fragments are left behind from some attempt to delete files or documents?"

"That's exactly what I think. Now I have to think who and why."

Jackson paused and sat forward. "There is of course someone who might be able to help you with that."

"Who?"

"Someone who was in the department at the time and who is still in the department now?

"No, I'm still not getting it."

"Someone who specialises in IT security?"

And then he realised. "Rob? Do you think I should bring Rob into this?"

"Sure, why not. You and he go way back to your time in the department. And Ed too. You never know. They might know something."

Clark nodded. While he had become good friends with Rob and Ed over the years he realised they rarely talked about work. Clark left the department to go into freelance and while there were wisecracks about his consultant's salary there was little else talk about his work. Similarly Clark rarely asked them what they were doing in the department, nor did they volunteer any information. Clark had contemplated at one stage severing ties with Rob and Ed, to minimise reminders. But as time went on it became less of an issue. Neither Rob nor Ed had any idea of what Clark had gone through. Rob and Ed were friends he could escape with. Good bar friends. Did he want to share any of this investigation with them? Did he want to admit that it had been haunting him? Did he want to admit that this investigation was a way for him to move on? Clark wasn't sure.

Jackson looked at his watch. "I need to go," he said, "But listen, Rob and Ed, think about it. They'll be able to tell you if any of the players are still there, give you an inside track. It's your call but if it was me, I would. What is there to lose? If they came to you, you would help them if you could, wouldn't you?"

He got up and fished his wallet from the inside of his suit jacket pocket.

"It all right Jackson. It's on me," said Clark.

"Thanks," said Jackson as he left.

Clark stared towards the window thinking Jackson was right. He should consider bringing in Rob and Ed. They were his friends after all. He was at their weddings for goodness sake. Yes, he would go and see Rob later.

But right then he had to get home and get back to work on the hard drive.

CHAPTER 18

It was half past three by the time Clark got home. He had just hung up his coat and taken the first step on the stairs towards his study when his mobile phone rang, an unidentified number. He turned and stepped to the lounge to answer it.

"Clark Radcliffe."

"Milton White will see you tomorrow morning, same place, same time," said the husky voice and then hung up.

By same place and same time Clark assumed half past ten at Victoria Square, and not the Palm House. He also assumed that the meeting was as a result of McArdle contacting Milton, as he had asked. McArdle had delivered. Clark read that as a good sign. As he still had his phone in his hand Clark decided to call Ellie. She answered after a couple of rings.

"Hi Clark," she said, "Is everything okay?"

"Everything's fine here. How are you?"

"Good thanks. Mum's doing well, she just depends on us to do a lot of stuff for her."

"Yeah," he said, "pass on my regards."

"I will do, thanks. Are you sure you are safe there?"

"Yes. I'm good. I'm keeping busy. I met with the police this morning. And I have another meeting with Milton tomorrow. There are some things I need to ask him."

"Oh," she said, "Was everything okay with the police?"

"Yeah, we just talked a bit about their investigation."

"Did you mention the break in?"

"No, I didn't want to draw attention."

"If you are sure Clark. What is it you want to ask Milton?"

"Just a bit of clarification. I might have found something in the hard drive but I need to check it with him. I'm about to head up now and look some more."

"Okay, be careful."

"And you too, remember what I told you. Stay safe."

"I miss you Clark."

"Yeah. I'll be in touch."

Clark rang off. He missed her too. He had seen her the previous night. But he missed her. He was worried about her but he took comfort that she was away, safe with her family. If only he could tell her how much he missed her, how she was always in his thoughts. Maybe he should try. Maybe she knew him well enough and he wouldn't have to. Maybe he should tell her anyway.

His mobile phone rang again. He checked the caller ID and grimaced. He could have ignored it. But he didn't.

"Hello Siobhan," he said.

"Hi Clark. How are you?"

"Good. Busy. And you?"

"Yeah, me too. Listen, sorry to be a pain but like I was saying the other day, there is something I would like your advice on?"

"Oh yeah?"

"Yes, a work thing. Some follow up work from the Qatar thing. There seems to be some error in the program. It's their program so there is no one here who knows much about it. I thought maybe you could take a look?"

She was tempting him with a programming problem, flattering him by saying he might be able to help.

"I like to think I'm always available to help with an IT problem Siobhan, but it's just I'm a bit busy, and will be for the next few days. There is no way I can get time to come to your office. Can it wait?"

"Unfortunately not Clark," she said. She paused and sighed. "Clark, what if run a screen dump and drop round the hard copy?"

She'd hooked him. While the likelihood of success with a screen dump analysis would be limited it would at least be a start. Clark liked computer problems. He nodded, and smiled. He wasn't sure he wanted her in his house though. It was probably something to do with the way he remembered she looked, the way she had sent an electric charge through his body when she touched him. It was probably something to do with the fact that Ellie was away. It wouldn't be right to invite another girl to his house with Ellie away, even if it was for a work meeting. No, he would have to decline.

"I'm sorry Siobhan, but I'm really busy. I've got to head out tonight."

He had planned to go and see Rob. He was glad he had a genuine reason.

"Okay, no harm done." Then she said, "Clark, I'm heading into the city centre later to meet a few friends. How about you and I hook up for five minutes somewhere and I can give you the screen dump?"

Clark thought for a moment, a brief moment. His reservation about inviting Siobhan to his house was no longer relevant, but there was still the guilt. But no, it is just a meeting about work, a meeting about work with a girl who used to be a colleague. If they still worked together a meeting to discuss a programming issue would be a regular occurrence. The guilt evaporated.

"It would have to be later," he said.

"What about ten o'clock in the Apartment Bar, where we met the other night. Keep it simple?"

"I'll try," Clark said and hung up.

He ran up the stairs before the phone could ring again. He scanned one more time through the folders and files looking for nothing in particular. He had a train of thought implanted in his mind, a train of thought that might develop after his meeting with Milton. He read again through the documents of meetings. He made more notes. After nearly two hours he was startled by a loud banging on his front door, a persistent pounding that sounded like it might bring the door off its hinges.

He jumped from his chair. "I'm coming now," he shouted, leaping down the stairs, three or four at a time. The banging continued.

He opened the door and froze.

The man with the shaven head and the Crombie coat stood outside.

"Hi Clark," he said and pushed past.

Clark followed him into the lounge. "Look I don't know what your game is," he shouted, "but you cannot push into my house. Get out."

"I can Clark and I just did," the man said smiling, "The computer hard drive? Perhaps you could give it to me?"

"I don't know what you are talking about," Clark said loudly and moved slightly in an instinctive move to block the doorway to the stairs.

"Where is it Clark, upstairs? In that little excuse for a study?"

He stepped forwards. Clark held firm and widened his stance. The man was quick. He grabbed Clark by his shoulders and spun him round, anchoring one arm across his throat. Clark gasped for breath. He tried to pull the arm away but it held strong. He balled a fist in his other hand and with full force aimed an elbow at the man's ribs. He connected. The man gasped and winced. The grip relaxed on Clark's throat, enough for him to pull free and spin around. The man was ready again, the blow to the ribs no more than an unexpected irritation. He smiled. Clark lunged forward, head down, and tackled the man round his chest. The man lost balance, but didn't have anywhere to go. They both fell against the fireplace, the mirror above crashing to the floor. The man was unfazed. He pushed Clark away. Clark stumbled back to regain his stance when the man came at him. He pulled Clark's head into a lock, spinning him round so his back was to the fireplace. Clark could not move, breathing heavily. The man too was breathing heavily.

Just then a loud shout from the doorway, "What's going on?"

Two men ran into the lounge through the front door, the front door that had been left open. They grabbed the man and pulled him off Clark, spinning him around and throwing him to the floor. They turned him over and locked his arms behind his back. The man was overpowered and in pain, his arms twisted behind his back. His face was contorted but he did not make a sound. One of the men continued to hold him while the other stood.

"Are you okay Clark?" asked Vince from next door.

"Yeah, I think so. Thanks." He nodded at Ryan who was maintaining his hold on the man.

"Think you might need a new mirror?" said Vince.

Clark managed an embarrassed laugh.

"What about him?" asked Vince, nodding at the man trapped on the ground.

"It's okay. Let him go."

"You sure?"

Clark nodded and Ryan released his grip.

The man stood and brushed himself down. He looked fleetingly at Vince and Ryan. He looked to Clark and held his eye for a few seconds. He then nodded and left through the open front door.

Vince and Ryan returned next door. They did not ask Clark any questions.

Clark tidied the pieces of shattered mirror to the back yard bin, satisfied someone else had broken it. It would be their bad luck.

He sat on the sofa for a moment taking deep breaths, trying to calm. He stopped abruptly, his heart pounding. The computer and hard drive? He jumped to his feet and ran up the stairs afraid to breathe.

They were fine. He let out the heavy breath he was holding and fell into the study chair, its castors taking him towards the wall. He did not know what would have happened if Vince and Ryan had not arrived, if the front door had not been left open. They were neighbours yet strangers. Maybe neighbours preferred to be strangers, or maybe they should be strangers. He didn't know, but he was nevertheless grateful.

Clark thought he should call Ellie. She answered almost immediately.

"Hi Clark, is everything okay?"

"Yes, everything's fine. I wanted to let you know the man came back, but it's all right."

"What, to your house?"

"Yes."

"Did he get the hard drive?"

"No, it's safe. It got a bit rough in here. Vince and Ryan from next door intervened. I don't think he'll be back in a hurry."

She gasped audibly. "Oh no. Is anybody hurt?"

"No, just pride and ego."

"Thank goodness for that."

"Ellie, he seemed to think the hard drive was here. I was wondering if maybe he might have searched your place first."

"I hadn't thought of that," she said, "I suppose I could call Hazel and ask her to check."

Hazel was a neighbour from the same apartment block. They held each other's spare keys.

"Yes," said Clark, "and you could let me know. Maybe if I had a spare key I could go and check?"

Clark didn't have a key to Ellie's apartment, although she had her key to his house. That was just the way it was. They regarded Clark's house as theirs. Clark could never see the need for a key to hers. It was her place of sanctuary and he only intended ever being there when she was. If he was honest he would say he liked the drama of being buzzed in from the street, riding up in the lift, and Ellie meeting him at the door. He liked to anticipate seeing her, how she looked, what she was wearing.

Ellie laughed. "So now you wish you had a key to mine, after all these years?"

"Yes, well, you know, so I can keep an eye on it, on you, you know," Clark said.

Ellie laughed again. "Aw shucks, you want to look after me. Bless you Clark Radcliffe."

Clark was glad Ellie could not see the colour of his face.

"Don't worry, I'll get you a key," she said, "I'll ring Hazel now and let you know if she sees anything. I'd better go back to Mum. Are you sure you're all right?"

"Yes I'm fine, really. Talk to you later."

Clark put his phone on the kitchen table and checked the time. Half past six. He wanted to go and see Rob, and he wanted to be back in time to go to the Apartment Bar for ten o'clock.

He powered down the computer, put the hard drive and notes in his coat pocket and gathered up his phone and keys.

CHAPTER 19

There was one thing he wanted to do on his way to see Rob. It wouldn't take long. He had upset Tracey, the partner of his oldest friend. Upsetting her was in many ways upsetting him. He wanted to make it up to her.

He decided he would apologise in person. That would be better than a phone call. He was sure there was something else that should be done in such circumstances. Flowers, yes flowers would help. He would stop at the garage on the way and pick up a bunch of flowers from the bucket beside the bags of kindling sticks and logs.

Clark pulled into the driveway at Sharman Road. There was no other car. Jackson would still be at work, and Tracey didn't have her own car. He didn't want Jackson there anyway.

He stood on the front step, flowers behind his back, and knocked. No answer. He knocked again, louder and waited. The door slowly opened, just a touch as Tracey's head appeared, hair wet and flat.

"Clark," she said coldly, "what do you want?"

No, she had clearly not yet forgiven him.

He forced his best smile and produced the bunch of flowers from behind his back. "A peace offering?"

Tracey looked from him to the flowers and back to him again. She shook her head, her face lighting up as she laughed. The door opened wide.

"You'd better come in I suppose."

Clark stepped into the entrance hall and Tracey pushed the door closed.

"Follow me," she said, "I better get a vase for those flowers. And some plant food by the looks of them." She was still laughing and shaking her head as she brushed past Clark and made her way towards the kitchen.

Clark tried hard to keep the scarlet glow from climbing visibly towards his face. He glanced towards Tracey, just out of the shower judging by the damp red hair not yet dried into its spiked style. She wore only a white tee shirt, its length to her upper thigh. Clark followed her down the hallway, not knowing where to look.

At the end of the narrow kitchen Tracey turned as she reached the sink, holding out her hand for Clark to pass the flowers. Clark obliged and moved back, leaning against the worktop than ran the full length of the kitchen. Tracey put the flowers in the sink and stood on her toes, reaching up to the wall unit. The tee shirt rose. She stretched some more. The tee shirt rose some more. Clark looked in the opposite direction but as if pulled by some magnetic force he looked back. The tee shirt had ridden to reveal a trim of lace.

"There we are," she said setting the vase on the worktop and adding water before arranging the flowers inside. She turned towards Clark. He returned his stare quickly to the floor.

"I'm sorry Tracey," he managed to say, "It was just some work stuff going on with me and Jackson. I shouldn't have let it annoy me. But most of all I shouldn't have taken it out on you."

She laughed again. "It's all right Clark. Jackson told me you had a bit of a falling out but you are all good again. It's fine. I understand. And besides, how could I stay mad with my lover's handsome best friend?"

She stepped forward. "Come here," she said an opened her arms.

Clark stepped forward and made to put his arms lightly around her shoulders, to plant the obligatory platonic kiss on her cheek. But she wrapped her arms tightly around him and pulled him close. She buried her head into his chest. He patted her on the back. She held on to him, perhaps too tight and perhaps for too long.

"I think I'd better go," he said and left without another word.

Rob Jeffery lived in Holywood with his wife Angela. Holywood was a small affluent town in County Down, on the shores of Belfast Lough and only six miles from the centre of Belfast. The rail line from Bangor to Belfast ran via Holywood. This helped to make it the popular commuter town that it was.

Rob and Angela lived in a traditional red brick box semi detached house in Holywood's Princess Gardens. The house was elevated with a short steep driveway to an attached garage. Rob and Angela had been married for over ten years, with no children as yet. Angela was a nurse at the Ulster Hospital, often working a twelve hour shift pattern. This allowed Rob to have his nights out with the boys without any conscience, unless of course Angela was off duty on a Friday night.

Clark parked at the bottom of the drive and climbed the path. He tapped the door lightly and Angela answered, opening the door with a wide radiant smile.

"Hello, Hello," she said, "this is a pleasant surprise."

"Rob darling, someone here to see you," she shouted over her shoulder and turned back to Clark with a finger over her lips. She clearly believed a visit from him was the surprise of the century.

Angela was small and round with plain features and a simple short hairstyle. Some might say she was frumpy but Clark preferred to say she was eternally happy. She wore a floral house dress that Clark had not seen the like of since he was a child at home.

Rob's head came round from behind the door to the lounge.

"Clark," he said coming to greet him, a wide smile on his face also, "it's great to see you. Come on in."

Clark grimaced against this show of pleasure in his unannounced visit. He sat on one of the two armchairs in the lounge. Rob and Angela sat side by side on the sofa. Rob was not tall, but not as small as Angela. He had a round stomach that sat proudly on top of his trouser waist band. They would often joke when they were out that Rob bought trousers based on his waist measurements below his stomach. Rob had a round face to match, sitting on a thick neck. Rob and Angela liked their food.

"How's Ellie?" asked Angela.

"She's good thanks," Clark said.

"And her mum, Rob said she is poorly?"

Clark looked quickly to Rob who was staring at the floor smiling, fiddling with his wedding ring. Clark gave Angela a quick summary of what he knew about Ellie's mother. He knew Angela's concern was sincere. He had to listen to a lot nurse related anecdotes.

Rob lifted his head, still smiling. "So what brings you here?"

"It's just a work thing. There is something I want to run past you, a security issue. I thought you might be able to help."

Clark stopped and looked at Angela. She too was still smiling, the silence however offering a clue that perhaps she should leave Clark and Rob alone.

"I'll just leave you boys to your work chat, then. Give me shout if you want anything." She left smiling, touching Clark lightly on the shoulder as she passed.

"So what's the problem?" asked Rob taking off his square framed glasses and cleaning them on his shirt fabric before putting them back on.

"You remember when I was in the department and that whole thing with Milton White and Dubai Wire and Cable?" said Clark.

"Of course I do, how could I forget? That was some carry on."

Clark gave Rob a quick overview of his meetings with Milton and his investigation of the portable hard drive. He didn't mention the shaven headed man, nor did he give any detail of what he had found. He focused on the fact that documents were missing, identified by text fragments on the hard drive.

He asked Rob if he could access the original folders and files on the department server and if he could identify through employee access data who had deleted them.

"I'm not sure, Clark. That's a big ask. I don't even know if the files are still on the server. They might be archived somewhere and that would make it very difficult. I would need a reason too. If I was to access the files then my user ID would flag up with the boss. I would need a cover story, especially if there is still an open police investigation."

"Yes I know Rob, just thought I would ask. I wouldn't want you to get into any trouble. There might be a way I can find the user IDs on the hard drive."

Rob shook his head. "No, the user IDs would be on a linked file. I doubt you would have that on the hard drive. Maybe I could take a look at the hard drive?"

It was Clark's turn to shake his head. "No thanks, I don't have it with me," he said discreetly checking his pocket to make sure it was there, "and besides if there is anything there I will find it."

Rob smiled and leaned forward. "Clark I said it was a big ask, and that I would need a cover story. I didn't say no. Leave it with me. I'll think of something. It'll make a change from the usual departmental problems I have to deal with, blocking spam and spyware and checking who is spending too much time surfing holiday websites instead of working."

Clark and Rob laughed together. There was always a lot of laughter when they were together. Clark enjoyed his company.

"Thanks Rob, I appreciate it."

"No problem, hopefully I'll give you a call tomorrow."

Angela came into the room with a tray which she sat on the coffee table between the armchair and sofa. She continued to wear her broad smile as she told Clark and Rob to help themselves. She had delivered coffee in china cups and saucers with French Fancies and German Biscuits on a two tier china cake stand. Clark nodded his thanks, thinking she must have mistaken him for the vicar.

She left the room and Clark said, "Rob, you remember those two women who worked with Milton White at the time, those two senior officials, Delores O'Reilly and Fiona Mitchell? Whatever happened to them?"

Rob nodded and reached for a biscuit. "Fiona Mitchell is still there. She's a Deputy Director General now, second in command in the department, responsible for finance and central services. It would be her I would work to, although she is so far up the chain we wouldn't see each other that much."

Clark already knew after Milton White had left there was a shuffle of Director Generals within the departments. To the best of his knowledge the Director General at Industry and Trade was a Neil Shaw, previously at the Department of Finance.

"So Milton left and she was promoted?" said Clark.

"Yeah, apparently her and Shaw are very close, or so I've heard." Rob gave a wink and slapped his own leg.

Clark laughed.

"I've no idea what came of that woman Delores," added Rob, "She left the department sometime around the Milton thing. There was some sort of controversy but I can't remember. But tell you what, Ed might know. Don't forget he did a lot of project work for her. It might be worth giving him a shout."

"Yeah, good idea, I had forgotten Ed worked with her," said Clark. He paused and looked at the ground, playing with his fingers. "Rob," he said still looking at the ground, "What did you make of the Declan Somerville thing?"

"You mean him dying?"

"Yeah."

Rob lifted another biscuit. "It was awful, very sudden and unexpected. And leaving a wife and daughter too." He too dropped his eyes to the floor.

"What do you think happened?" asked Clark.

Rob looked up. "What do you mean?"

"I don't know. Do you think there might have been more to it?"

Rob's brow furrowed. "I don't know. I suppose I haven't really thought about it. I just assumed it was just what it was, a fatal heart attack. Why do you ask?"

Clark looked up at his friend. "Rob," he said, "Declan was doing some follow up work on the Milton White bank account thing. He was doing what I had asked him to do. If I hadn't asked him he would not have been in the building that night. He might have been at home and maybe someone would have got to him in time."

Clark paused and thought of his father and what the doctor had said to his mother, that he was fortunate she was there when it happened.

He continued, "And not just that. We were looking for other incriminating evidence on the system. Rob, in all the time since it happened I haven't been able to shake the fact that someone may have benefitted from Declan's death. I don't know what if anything he had found that night."

He turned his head and looked away.

Rob sat forward on the sofa, crumbs falling to the floor. He lowered his voice. "Clark, I had no idea. You feel in some way responsible?"

Clark nodded, his head still turned away.

"Look Clark, it was an accident, a tragic accident. Nothing more. The police and coroner both confirmed this. His wife accepted it as far as I know. You have nothing to feel guilty about." He lowered his voice to a near whisper, "Clark, it was just his time."

Rob reached across the room, over the coffee table and patted Clark on his knee. Clark turned back towards him and allowed a smile. He nodded, appreciating Rob's words, both relieved and glad he had shared.

Rob passed a china cup and saucer to Clark who accepted and laughed, both in relief and at the ridiculousness of two beer buddies drinking coffee from the best china with handles neither of them could fit their fingers into.

"Have you ever spoken with his wife?" asked Rob.

Clark shook his head.

"Maybe you should. You might find it reassuring. I know that a lot of water has passed under the bridge since it happened but you never know. Ed has spoken to her a few times. Ask him what he thinks. He might be able to put you in touch."

"Thanks Rob." Clark drained the lukewarm coffee and stood, placing the cup and saucer back on the tray. He hadn't bothered with any cakes or biscuits. Rob could finish them. "Don't say anything to Ed until I get a chance to speak with him. And Rob, keep all this to yourself," he said.

"No problem Clark. I'll give you a call tomorrow if I can find anything."

He stood and held out his hand. As Clark took it Rob pulled him closer and put both his arms around him. Clark's cheeks flushed. But he was thankful. He nodded and left the house shouting his farewells and thanks to Angela in the kitchen.

CHAPTER 20

Clark checked his watch. It was too late to drive to Bangor to see Ed. He had an appointment at ten o'clock. In his car at the bottom of Rob's driveway he decided to phone Ed instead.

"Hello," said Ed.

"Ed, it's me, Clark. Will you be in tomorrow night? There's something I want to talk to you about."

"Yeah, sure. Is everything all right?"

"Everything's good Ed. There is just something I am working on at the minute and could use the opinion of someone still inside the department."

"Mm hmm, okay".

Ed was a man of few words. In many ways he was the opposite of Rob, always frowning and laughing sarcastically at Rob's humour rather than in appreciation of it. But it worked well, anyone in their company enjoying the trade off between Rob's jovial chat and Ed's droll retorts. He was a clever man and a good friend in his own way, once his foibles were understood.

Ed Delavergne was the son of a French immigrant. His father had settled in Belfast and established a successful French cuisine wholesale business before branching out into a thriving French restaurant on Belfast's Golden Mile. Ed was married to Caitlin and they had two young children. Caitlin worked as a supervisor in a supermarket in Bangor. She often worked late, dictated by shop opening hours, leaving Ed to collect the children from the childminder and spend the early evening with them. He was therefore not as regular a participant in their boys' nights out as he would have liked. He was a devoted family man.

"What time?" Ed asked.

"Maybe about seven? That'll let you get home from work?"

"Okay."

"Ed," said Clark, "let me ask you something in the meantime. Do you know what became of Delores O'Reilly, you remember the senior official in the department."

"I remember her, used to do a bit of work with her" Ed said, "but don't know what happened. She left around the time of that Milton White thing. I don't think she's in government anymore. Why do you ask?"

"Nothing. It's just her name came up in something I'm working on."

"Okay. I could ask about."

"Thanks Ed, appreciate it. I'd be grateful if you can keep a bit of a lid on it though. Don't be mentioning my name to anyone."

"Got it."

"Well, I'll see you tomorrow night. Have a good day tomorrow."

"Bye," said Ed and hung up.

Clark turned his car and headed home to quickly shower and change before his ten o'clock appointment.

He managed to arrive at the Apartment Bar ten minutes early. He always preferred to be first to arrive. He preferred not to have to scan the room for people. If he was first there he could watch the door. It was just easier.

He ordered a bottle of Corona and sat on the bar stool nearest the door, turning frequently to see who was leaving, and more importantly who was arriving. He didn't have long to wait.

It looked like she too had planned to arrive early. In she came, tossing her long hair away from her face. Perhaps Clark had one or two Coronas too many the first night he set eyes on her as while he remembered the stunning long brunette hair and the figure squeezed into a short dress he did not remember such natural beauty.

She saw him instantly and waved. Her face glowed as she approached him, the lights over the bar illuminating sparkling eyes, rose blushed cheeks, glistening thick lips and the perfect white teeth.

Clark sat tall in his stool, sensing all the other eyes from within the bar catching a glimpse of her entrance.

"Hi, Clark," she said, unbuttoning her Forzieri brown leather jacket.

"Hi. It's good to see you again. A drink?"

"Yes thanks, a glass of wine, Sauvignon."

Clark held his up hand to the barman to attract his attention. There was however no need for the theatrics, the barman was already on his way over.

They moved with their drinks to a corner table, well away from but facing the bar. Clark slipped onto the booth to leave the armchair opposite for her. But she slipped onto the booth beside him, moving close. She turned slightly to face him. Their knees touched.

She took off the leather jacket, sporting underneath a Vivienne Westwood sleeveless and loose fitting purple jersey top over tight Bastyan skinny jeans. High heeled Chloe mid length boots completed the look, an elegant and expensive casual look. Clark felt decidedly underdressed in his Hilfiger chinos and Giorgio Armani shirt. His trusty Hugo Boss leather Derbies were warm and comfortable on his feet. He had taken his overcoat off before she arrived.

"You look nice," she said and put her hand on his knee. She leaned forward. "And you smell nice too."

"Thanks," said Clark not knowing what else to say. "You look nice too," he managed. He looked at the hand on his knee, a perfectly manicured hand, nails a perfect length, perfectly filed and sparkling in the light. He was there for a business meeting, he told himself. People don't touch each other at business meetings. What was going on here? He had to admit this girl was attractive, no, beautiful. But so was Ellie. Ellie was smart, professional and understanding, everything he thought he could ever want in a woman. And Ellie was the same age as him, give or take. This girl was a decade younger. He told himself he shouldn't be there.

He put his hand on hers to remove it, but she was too quick. She put her other hand over his. A pulse shot through his body, an involuntary reaction to her touch. He felt warm. He felt good.

"I'm sorry Clark," she said, "I'm always being told I'm too touchy."

She smiled and released his hand. Clark sat back slightly, creating a bit of space between them. He relaxed.

"Chesterton and Williamson still keeping you busy?" she asked.

"Yes, very," he said remembering he had an outstanding obligation to fulfil to them. "What about you?"

"I'm still finishing up on the Qatar thing with Petersons Global. There should be more work coming out of it. So yes, I'm busy enough." A black strap slipped down her shoulder from beneath the jersey top, its subtlety stirring Clark. She leant forward. The loose neckline of the jersey top dropped to expose a full cleavage and black lace. Clark wondered if this girl had any idea of what she was doing, the sensuality she oozed. Everything about her was alluring, her hair, her features, her smile, her laugh, her smell. She wore the clothes of a model on the figure of a model. What was she doing talking to him?

This was a business meeting he kept telling himself, stick to the business. "Siobhan, do you have the screen dump?"

"Oh yes, of course."

As she turned to her Coach bag Clark's phone rang. He checked the caller ID. It was Ellie. He cringed. He shouldn't be there, even though he had earlier rationalised that there was no harm to be done by having a business meeting with an ex-colleague.

He held up his hand to Siobhan. "Ellie," he said answering the phone.

"How are you?" she asked.

"Good."

"I called Hazel. There is no problem at my apartment."

"Good."

"Is everything okay Clark?"

"Yes."

"Are you sure? You seem, I don't know, distracted?"

Siobhan placed her hand again on his knee. He looked at her and she smiled, a wide beautiful smile, her eyes gleaming. He fixed his eyes on hers.

"No, everything's good."

"Well, okay then. I suppose I could go?"

"Okay, I'll call you tomorrow."

Clark hung up.

"Was that your girlfriend?" Siobhan asked, rubbing her hand gently on his leg.

Clark stared, first at her eyes then down to her hand on his knee. He looked back to her eyes. Her expression had not changed, the warm smile fixed on her face. Clark wanted to be angry, to chasten this girl for her boldness. But he couldn't.

He smiled.

She laughed.

He laughed.

She handed him the pages from her bag. Clark took a quick look and shook his head. They were of no use to him.

"Siobhan, there is no program data here. This is all screen data."

"Oh," she said, "I must have run the wrong pages." She took a look at the pages herself. "No, how stupid can I be? And there's me with a deadline. Clark, there might be something you can do from my laptop? I have it at home if …"

Clark managed to shake his head. "No Siobhan. I really don't think so. As I said I am busy and probably should be getting back."

"Of course, I'm sorry," she said, "I shouldn't impose. Forget about it. Let's just finish our drinks."

Clark nodded. He was pleased with his rebuttal. But he was tempted, mightily tempted, not just by the girl but by the computer challenge. No, it was not appropriate. There was Ellie. He couldn't go when Ellie was away caring for her sick mother. He shouldn't go, probably not ever.

"Cheers," he said and lifted his bottle.

"So tell me, why did you leave the department?"

Clark was startled by this question out of left field. "Eh, an offer I couldn't refuse?"

"I remember something about you having something to do with that Milton White thing?"

Clark stared at her. "Look, Siobhan, what is it you want?" He slammed his bottle down on the table and grabbed his coat. He went to get up but couldn't. He half stood, knees bent and rear protruding. "I need to go," he said, "please let me out."

He looked down at her. The colour drained from her face. Her eyes moistened. "I'm sorry Clark, what did I say?"

All she had done was ask a question about something that happened when they had worked together Clark quickly processed. To her this was probably the last recollection she had of him in the department. It was possibly therefore a reasonable question. How was she to know that the Milton White thing was active? But still, he did not need mundane conversations about it.

"No, I'm sorry Siobhan," he said, "I really need to go."

She took a business card out of her bag and wrote an address on it.

"I'd really appreciate it if you can look at the laptop. I need to have it sorted by Friday. I'll be working in it over the next couple of nights. Maybe if you have an hour?"

Clark took the card glancing at the address, "I'll see," he said, "no promises."

Siobhan let him out from the booth and watched him leave the Apartment Bar and turn towards the taxi rank.

CHAPTER 21

Clark awoke early the next morning, Wednesday morning, having spent a restless night thinking over all that was going on. He was annoyed with himself for having gone to the Apartment Bar. What was he thinking? There was no answer. He had allowed himself to be lured, lured by flattery and by some primal urge. He knew there was much to lose should he capitulate. He was angry. And why had she mentioned Milton White?

He buried it all in his mind. He had to get ready to meet Milton at Victoria Square. He had to call Jackson and tell him about the meeting. And he had to call Ellie to make amends for last night's fiasco.

After a quick breakfast Clark lifted his phone. "Hi, Jackson, sorry to call so early."

"No problem, is everything all right?"

Clark told him about the shaven headed man pushing into his house the previous day and that everything had worked out. He told him he had arranged to meet with Milton again in Victoria Square.

"Right, okay, I'll be there. Somewhere."

"You don't have to be. I was just letting you know to keep you in the loop."

"Listen Clark, after the bald man's visit to your place yesterday I think I should be there. We don't know who he is or what he has to do with Milton. Don't worry. I'll stay in the shadows."

Clark laughed, an image in his mind of Jackson melting into the background like some CIA operative. "Okay. Let's maintain radio contact. We can rendezvous post event."

"Roger that," said Jackson and hung up not picking up on Clark's sarcasm.

Clark smiled. Café Nero in Victoria Square would provide a simple enough opportunity for Jackson to keep an eye on things. The coffee house was an integral unit within House of Fraser's ground floor, situated beside the men's clothing section. Jackson could easily linger among the formal suits and casual wear.

He called Ellie and as expected received a frosty response.

"Morning," she said. Silence.

"Ellie," he said, "Listen, sorry about last night. It was just that I was in the middle of something when you called… I went to see Rob… and…"

He thought not lying, just confusing the timeframe would appease his conscience.

"Yes, well, I suppose you had things to do, what with everything going on. No excuse for your rudeness though."

"Yeah, sorry."

Clark told her briefly about his visit to Rob and that he had asked for his help. He also told her he had contacted Ed and was going to see him later that night.

"I'm glad you are sharing this with your friends," she said, "Friends can help you know Clark, if you just open up to them."

She rung off telling him she was going to work through some case files at her mother's that day and they should call each other later.

Clark dropped the phone on his lap and rubbed his eyes. He still felt a pain from the night before, perhaps even more so as he had been economical with the truth. He had gotten away with it, but he would learn. Ellie was too special. He reflected back to when they had met. It had been four years ago at a lunchtime seminar run by the Government's Procurement Division for private sector companies interested in supplying Legal, Finance and IT services to the public sector. Fabian Townsend had asked Clark to go and represent him from the IT perspective, given that he was a specialist and also a former public servant. Ellie was there representing her firm from a legal perspective. When Clark had entered the room there was a spare seat beside her and he took it. If he was honest there were other spare seats but he was drawn to the elegantly and powerfully dressed woman sitting alone at the back of the room. Her welcoming and inviting smile as he approached helped. The seminar was also billed as a networking opportunity. Clark wasn't one for networking, not being any good at developing business contacts from mundane small talk conversations, so he was glad to be able to sit at the back and not draw too much attention to himself. Conversation with Ellie while stilted at first soon followed. They shared smiles and laughs. Eventually they exchanged business cards but they did not contact each other. They met again at a business meeting when he along with others represented the interests of Chesterton and Williamson, and she along with others represented the interests of Geddis, Kenny and Marshall. There was recognition and a brief conversation afterwards, but again that was it. It was not until some weeks later when they met unexpectedly on a night out, him with the boys and her with some work colleagues that they arranged to meet again socially. Just the two of them, on a date as some might call it.

Clark snapped out of the memories, happy memories, and checked the time. He showered and dressed, allowing time to check over his notes before the meeting with Milton White.

forsetdallemer. lemer

He looked at the letters again. He looked again at the list of fragments he had earlier printed from the hard drive. With elbows on the desk and his head in his hands he focused on the list. Then something struck him.

He hurriedly checked the program folders in the actual hard drive of his Dell, and not on this occasion on the portable hard drive. He scanned program files and the text structure of saved documents before focusing on one program file in particular. He compared it with what he had found on the portable drive.

He saw something familiar.

He nodded as the pieces began to come together.

There was no time to walk, no time to catch a bus. He ordered a taxi to collect him in ten minutes and take him to Victoria Square.

Milton White was already seated in the coffee house, despite Clark arriving early. A lukewarm Americano was again waiting for him.

"You wanted to see me?" said Milton.

That was it, no greeting, no comment on how he had received Clark's request for them to meet. It didn't matter Clark thought, Milton was there and that was what he has asked for.

"Yes," said Clark, "I need to ask you some questions."

Milton nodded.

"When you carried out the negotiations with Dubai Wire and Cable, where did the meetings take place?"

"I told you, at my office for the formal meetings and some informal discussions in the early days around some city hotels."

"And who was at these meetings?"

"Again I have told you, it was me, Fiona and Delores from the department and Abdul Alim, Anthony and Jennifer from Dubai Wire and Cable. Why, what is so important?"

"Did any of the six of you hold meetings outside of these group meetings?"

"No."

"Would any of you six have held formal meetings without the knowledge of the others?"

"No, there would have been no need. All discussions were carried out in plenary. It was safer that way. It allowed for clarity, no misinterpretation or misunderstanding. Why, what is on your mind?"

"Bear with me, did any formal meetings take place outside of your office."

Milton sighed, "No."

"Would any of the six of you have met off the record?"

"Not to my knowledge, why, what would have been the point…?"

Milton looked away for a moment. Something seemed to resonate with him. "What are you getting at, Clark, what have you found?"

"Please Milton, did any meetings take place in Dubai?"

"No."

"I'm no expert," said Clark, "but would some form of due diligence not have been required on the company?"

"Of course, but our overseas representative covering Dubai would have sorted that. There would have been a site visit, a check on the infrastructure, a check on the order book, a check on customers and suppliers, that sort of thing, all of which was routine. We would have received a report from the overseas representative. The finance and legal teams in the department would have verified all it back here with access to Dubai Wire and Cable's corporate reports and accounts."

"So there was no need for anyone from here to visit Dubai to verify, or for any other reason."

"No, as I said the verification came from the department's representative who was already there. It was a guy called Donald Benson, a good guy, served as a representative all over the world, spent a long time in the States. The representatives all tended to serve three year stints and then came back to the department. It suited Donald to keep doing the stints. He had no ties back here, and to be honest it suited us. He was good, reliable and diligent. He's probably retired now."

Clark nodded and took a mental note of Donald Benson's name.

"What about you Milton, did you ever go to Dubai?"

Milton looked at Clark, and with a puzzled look on his face said, "No, as I said, there was no need."

"Where did the Dubai Wire and Cable Company work out of?"

"I can't remember where exactly, only that Abdul Alim had an interest in a hotel in Dubai and he used a business suite there as his office, and also as his corporate business address."

"What was the name of the Hotel?"

"Le Meridien," said Milton.

CHAPTER 22

Le Meridien, *lemer*, *le mer*. Before he had left his house that morning Clark was certain he had found a fragment of an electronic diary. He was certain the error was as a result of failed links between the diary and documents electronically filed. He had studied the letters and the spaces between them hypothesizing *forset* as four September. He had already considered *lemer* as a possible location. He was sure he had a date and a location but why? The discussion with Milton White was helping to confirm something else, something he had given some consideration to earlier that morning. *dal. Al* could be Alim, Abdul Alim who had an interest in Le Meridien hotel, in Dubai. The *d* Dubai.

Could this be a diary entry fragment relating to a meeting with Abdul Alim? Possibly on the fourth September at Le Meridien Hotel in Dubai? Who had this meeting in their diary and why? Milton White had said it was not with him. Who had attempted to delete this meeting from their electronic diary?

It could of course have been a reference to a meeting arranged by Donald Benson, but that did not explain why it was deleted.

He didn't know how much to tell Milton. There remained some mystery around Milton, what his purpose was, where he had been and what exactly he was currently doing. Why when arranging meetings with Clark was some mysterious intermediary involved? And there was the issue of the shaven headed man. Who was he and what connection did he have to Milton?

Clark decided to go with instinct. Yes, Milton was a mystery but it had been he who had come to Clark and to date Clark had not found anything to contradict his story.

"I think," Clark said, "someone has been trying to cover up something that went on between the department and Dubai Wire and Cable. I think meetings have taken place outside of the formal meetings. I think someone went to Dubai."

Milton stared at him. "What? Who?" He shook his head. "I don't understand."

Clark outlined what he had found, the missing records of meetings and the suspected electronic diary entry. He told Milton about his visit to the factory but didn't mention the confrontation he had. He watched Milton closely for any signs that he might already have known, or been involved in any way.

"So you are confirming the machinery grants were genuine?" he said.

"That's what it looks like." Clark put his hand into the inside pocket of his coat and pulled out the photograph of the machinery. He set it on the table. Milton looked and nodded. A slight but noticeable smile came to his otherwise stony face.

Clark said, "There is no machinery there now. The factory is clear. The anchor bolt holes are there but nothing else. The factory is a mess. It looks like there has been no one near it in years."

Milton thought for a moment and rubbed his chin. "No, indeed. There was never any production there you know Clark."

Clark nodded.

"They said the negative publicity over the whole grant thing was damaging and they pulled out."

"But not before they got their start up and machinery grants?" said Clark.

"They would say they didn't get the bulk of the grants. The start-up grants were expended on the start up costs, establishing the factory, sourcing the machinery, that sort of thing. But the main monies to assist with the machinery they said they did not receive. Apparently I got it Clark, remember. I apparently still have it." He managed a broader smile. "Do I look like a man who has been living off a secret pot of gold?"

Clark shook his head. "What do you think happened Milton?"

"What do I think? Let me tell you what I think. Somehow the company got the money. For some reason their expansion plans in Europe fell flat, but they had already committed and signed a Letter of Acceptance. Machinery was on order and they were committed to paying for it. I think the Middle Eastern shareholders were appeased by being told the proposed venture into Europe was cost neutral. The grants would have been required for that story to wash."

"But why not just legitimately claim and receive the grants and move on?" asked Clark.

Milton shook his head. "It wouldn't have worked like that Clark. We would have reclaimed the grants back as a breach of the terms of the Letter of Offer."

Clark nodded, thinking through what Milton was saying. "So you think that somehow the Dubai Wire and Cable Corporation set you up as a patsy so they could get away with the money and appease their shareholders?"

Milton looked down at his coffee cup. He checked briefly over each shoulder. He lowered his voice further. "Yes, Clark, I do."

Clark didn't know what to think. On the face of it the story did sit with what he had found, but was it plausible? Was it possible? How could it have been executed? Who from the Dubai Company could have accessed the department computer and set up Milton's bank account as a recipient of the funds? Who could have removed the details of meetings?

"What about the bank account you opened in the Isle of Man?" Clark asked.

Milton managed a laugh. "Oh yes, of course, you have been talking to McArdle, he who is fixated on the guilt of Milton White."

He leaned forward. Clark leaned forward too in response.

"Clark, there is a perfectly credible reason for my opening that account. If you check the dates and minutes for the Council of Ministers' meetings you will see I was in the Isle of Man at a meeting along with the Industry Minister. I simply took the opportunity during a walk one lunch time to open an account. For no real reason I hasten to add, just somewhere else to store a few pounds as I was preparing for retirement. It was all perfectly above board. I thought I may as well maximise the opportunities for return on my savings. Also I was in line to receive a considerable lump sum payment as part of my pension. Why not put it away where I can get more from it? I was in the Isle of Man so why not?"

Milton sat back with a slight smile still on his face, seemingly pleased with his justification. Clark had to admit again it was credible. Clark knew of the Council of Ministers, where Ministers from the devolved countries in the United Kingdom and its Isles, including the Isle of Man, met periodically to discuss issues of common interest. He knew the meetings rotated around the different jurisdictions. He knew it would have been usual for Ministers' Director Generals to accompany them. Clark could of course check it out.

"There is a sting in the tail however Clark. The account in the Isle of Man remains frozen. I can thank McArdle for that. There wasn't much in it however, just the initial deposit, I think five thousand was the minimum opening deposit. I never got round to adding to it. Although McArdle would say I embezzled much more through it."

Milton smiled again. Clark thought he was enjoying telling the story, or perhaps he was relieved that he was sharing it, and with someone with whom he felt had a level of understanding and trust?

Clark asked, "Why did you not contact Abdul Alim and challenge or confront him with all of this?" He put his hand again into the inside pocket of his coat and pulled out the business card he had found in the factory. He set it down in front of Milton.

Milton looked at it closely, fixing his eyes on it for a few moments. He lifted his head and looked at Clark. "I tried," he said, "but his numbers were unobtainable. So were Anthony's and Jennifer's. I tried the Company direct but they couldn't, or wouldn't put me through to them. I even got Donald Benson to call on the Company but he met with a wall of excuses. He went to Le Meridien and again hit a wall. Nothing, Clark, there was nothing. There was no more I could do. Once the police got their claws into me as a prime suspect there was definitely no way I could pursue contact with Dubai Wire and Cable."

"Did McArdle follow any of this up?" asked Clark.

Milton shook his head. "Not in any detail that I am aware of. He thought he had me in the bag and went for a quick prosecution. He said he checked with Dubai Wire and Cable and got nothing but denials. I think he tried a few phone calls and that was about it."

That Clark considered consistent with his own interpretation of McArdle's investigation. He had gone for a quick headline prosecution but had not been as thorough as he might have been. McArdle now realised this but did not want to admit it, and to show him or his team up as not being as meticulous in their investigation as they could have. McArdle had let the case drift. He could not close it as it would have to be closed as unsolved. He did not want an unsolved case on his or his team's record. Nor did he want to dig too deep and uncover evidence that he should have uncovered the first time around. That too would have shown him and his team up in a bad light.

It seemed to Clark, yet again, that McArdle wanted Clark to find something, something that he himself could not necessarily have found no matter how thorough his investigation had been. He wanted Clark to find something that would allow him to close the case, no doubt claiming credit for Clark's involvement and findings if it was to his advantage, and similarly denying all knowledge of Clark if it suited his interests. Clark took the speed at which McArdle had set up their meeting with Milton as a signal.

"What about Fiona and Delores, Milton? What came of them?" said Clark.

Milton smiled. "I went to see Fiona last week. She's a Deputy Director General now. She's s lovely woman, a beautiful woman." He looked away, his smile widening. He caught himself on. "Sorry yes, I went to see Fiona last week. It was just a quick meeting in her office. I wanted to tell her I had come back to Belfast and wanted to see if there was anything I could do to help myself. It was her, Clark, who reminded me of you."

Clark raised his eyebrows. "Oh, did you get anything else from her?"

"No, nothing. She was a bit distant. She didn't want to talk much about it. To be honest short of saying I should contact you there was very little else said about it. We just sort of caught up, about her family, my family, that sort of thing. She said she had another meeting to go to so I left quietly. It was the first time I had been in Adelaide House since I left so I kept my head down, didn't want to draw attention to myself. I had been away for so long and had cut off contact with everybody there. I had no idea if Fiona was even still in the department any more. I just took a chance and called and asked for her. The girl on the switchboard put me through."

"And Delores?" said Clark.

"I think I said to you the other day Clark that I had heard many years ago that she had left the department shortly after me. I asked Fiona about her but all she said was she had left and she didn't know where she was. If I remember correctly she then quickly changed the subject."

"Do you think maybe I should talk to Fiona?"

"You could try Clark, certainly. I would appreciate that. It was her who named you so I don't see why she wouldn't at least take your call."

"Okay, will do. Milton, there are a couple of other things I am still looking at. I may need to get in touch with you again?"

Milton nodded. He lifted Abdul Alim's card from the table and took a pen from his pocket. He wrote a number on the reverse of the card. "Send a text message to this number. Someone will get back to you."

He then sat back and folded his arms. The meeting was over.

Clark put the card and photo back into his inside pocket, and checked his front pocket for the hard drive. He nodded to Milton and walked towards the men's clothing section of House of Fraser.

He spotted Jackson surveying a range of grey business suits. He held his phone up and pointed. Jackson gave a slight nod. Clark went out the back of the store onto the first floor concourse from where he walked to the escalator and went up another floor to a spot beside a pillar where he could lean on the railing and see the rear exit to the House of Fraser. His phone rang.

"He's still here," said Jackson, "He keeps looking around and checking his watch as if he is waiting for someone. Hold on, there's someone coming towards him now. I'll call you back."

Clark waited. He reflected on the conversation he just had. Milton was convincing. But was he being played? He didn't think so, but there was always that doubt.

His phone rang again.

"Clark, it's him again. The big guy with the shaven head that I seen at the Palm House. He's on his own this time. He and Milton are talking. Hang on a minute."

Clark waited, wondering again what was going on.

"They are coming out the back door Clark, where are you?"

"I'm opposite the back exit up on the next floor. I can see the

168

door."

"Right, keep an eye on the door, I'm on my way. I'll get past them, they shouldn't know me."

"Roger, Roger. Over and out," said Clark shaking his head and smiling to himself.

He saw Jackson coming out of the door and head towards the escalators. Clark kept watch on the door. Jackson came up beside him.

"Well anything yet?"

"Nothing yet Nighthawk," said Clark jabbing an elbow into Jackson's ribs.

Jackson then realised Clark was fooling and looked round smiling. They both laughed.

"Here they come," said Jackson, "They must have stopped off for something."

Milton came out first and held the door open. A tall broad shouldered man with a shaven head came out behind him. The man pointed towards the escalator and Milton followed him.

Clark slowly shook his head.

"It's not him Jackson, it's not the guy who was in my house."

CHAPTER 23

"That guy's younger. The guy bothering me was more like our age, maybe older. That guy down there looks in his twenties. His hair is close cropped. My guy is literally shaven to the wood."

Jackson looked at Clark and said nothing. Clark watched the two men as they went down the escalator to the ground floor. Jackson turned his head to watch also. The two continued on the escalator to the underground car park level and disappeared from sight.

"Coffee?" said Clark.

At Costa Coffee they sat on the same leather sofa as before with large Americanos and blueberry muffins. Clark summarised his conversation with Milton.

"So, what do you think?" said Jackson.

"I've come to think Milton is right in what he says. Yes, I have a few niggles and doubts. But the fact that we have established that the big guy with Milton is a different big guy then one of my doubts is addressed. I still don't know why he is so mysterious about me contacting him though. Maybe he just wants privacy."

"So what now?"

Clark thought for a moment and said, "I think I'll might try and contact Fiona Mitchell at the department."

"Yeah, that sounds like a plan. Good luck. And be careful. We still don't know who is after the hard drive."

Jackson got up from the sofa and left for work. He paused momentarily to rest his hand on Clark's shoulder, an unspoken message of support to which Clark nodded his appreciation.

Clark asked the barista for a phone directory and called the switchboard at the Department of Industry and Trade Development. He was put through straight away.

"Fiona Mitchell's office," said a polite female voice.

"Hi, my name is Clark Radcliffe. I'd like to meet with Ms Mitchell please."

"Certainly, and what is it in relation to?"

"It's, err, a personal matter."

"I'm sorry, but Mrs Mitchell's diary is full for the next few days. Perhaps if I can take a message and have her call you?"

So it was Mrs Mitchell thought Clark, not really sure why it mattered. He was in the midst of reciting his mobile phone number when the secretary interrupted.

"Hold on a second, Mrs Mitchell has just come into the office."

There was a muffle as if a hand was being placed over the mouthpiece. Then a different voice came on, equally polite and well spoken.

"Hello Clark? It's Fiona."

Clark was surprised at the familiarity of her tone. "Hello, yes", he said and then didn't know what else to say.

"Did you want to come in for a chat?" she said rescuing him from the silence.

"Yes, if at all possible."

"What about twelve thirty? You can keep me company while I eat my sandwich?"

Clark checked his watch. He could make it. "No problem. I'll see you then."

At Adelaide House Clark made himself known to the ground floor receptionist, the first time he had been in the building in five years. It looked exactly the same, Groundhog Day. Thank goodness I got out he couldn't help but think. He was given a visitor's pass to clip to his coat and asked to take a seat. After a few minutes a young man in track trousers and a sports tee shirt approached him.

"You here to see Fiona Mitchell?" he said.

"Yes thanks," said Clark rising from his plastic chair and following the young man as he assumed he was supposed to do. The young man was clearly a low grade administrator exploiting government's perennial lack of dress code to the extreme. Clark could never understand why people could have so little respect for themselves when it came to dress, never mind the lack of respect for their employer.

There was no such issue when he was led into Fiona Mitchell's outer office. An officious secretary rose to receive him, shaking his hand and at the same time dismissing the young escort. She was well presented in a pin striped business trouser suit. She wore it well. She led Clark into a large corner office with sofas and a conference table with seating for eight. In the distance was a large ornate desk completed with banker's lamp. From behind it appeared a tall fair haired woman with hand extended.

"Clark, Fiona. I'm pleased to meet you."

Clark accepted her hand and nodded.

"Would you like coffee?" she asked

"Yes please."

The secretary then left silently.

Clark sat on one of the sofas as instructed. Fiona sat on the sofa opposite. She placed a wrapped sandwich on the low coffee table between them. She was indeed a lovely woman, a beautiful woman as Milton had described her. She was one of those women of indeterminable age Clark thought, extremely well groomed and presented, her hair perfectly cut, coloured and set. She wore a knee length business skirt and white sleeveless blouse. There was no doubt a jacket to match the skirt hanging somewhere. She had a figure that confounded her age, an age that Clark assumed had to be somewhere in her fifties. As she sat and crossed her legs Clark had to stop himself from looking.

"So Clark, what can I do for you?"

Where do I start, he thought? "I believe you put Milton White my way?" he said.

"Yes, he came to see me last week. I hadn't seen or heard from him in what must be five years. Not since… I was surprised to be honest. Things have moved on in the department and all that went on then is well behind us. I hadn't expected to see him again, and certainly didn't expect him to raise questions about the incident, you know the Dubai Wire and Cable thing."

"Why did you think that?"

"I don't know. It was just as I said. It was long ago. We had moved on. I assumed Milton had moved on too."

"What do you think happened back then?"

She looked at him. "Clark, let me be clear. I think it happened as everyone assumes. I think Milton benefitted in some way from the project. I don't know what or how but if you are asking me, I am telling you it was him."

Clark was surprised by this vehement standpoint. "But you worked closely with him on all the negotiations, didn't you?"

"Yes, but who knows what he was up to when I wasn't there?"

"Sounds like you have suspicions?"

"Not suspicions as such," she said, "just not surprised. Milton was, and no doubt still is, a complex and private man. You never really knew what was going on inside him, what drove him. Some might think he did what he did for some sort of financial gain. But I don't think so. I think he was motivated by the challenge, to see if he could do it. Maybe he was motivated by some perverse rationale that it was a worthy exercise, to test the robustness of the system."

Clark nodded and reflected. That was an interesting scenario and one, if he was honest, had a degree of sense to it. But what was he doing coming out of the woodwork now? What was he trying to prove?

Then something struck him, something that Jackson had said a number of days ago, something about Milton engaged in some sort of elaborate hoax to clear his name with Clark as his patsy. If Clark could find evidence of his innocence, and the police could be convinced of his innocence, then they might close the case. Milton would have gotten away with it. His hiding for five years could have been part of the plan all along. It was all running through Clark's head. The early doubt he thought he had suppressed began to resurface.

"Are you okay Clark?" asked Fiona, disturbing his train of thought.

"Yes, sorry, yes. That's interesting stuff. But tell me this, why did you ask Milton to contact me?"

"Clark, I'm sorry. I am guilty of using you as a decoy. Milton was fishing. He was asking questions I could not answer. He was asking me about meetings and things that went on at the time. I could not remember. I don't know if he expected me to still have the files or something but there was clearly nothing I could do for him. He started asking about Delores. But I didn't want to get into that with him. Delores had her problems, let's just leave it at that. So to give him something, I gave him you. I told him you had left the department and had carved out a nice reputation and career for yourself freelancing and that as you had been involved in uncovering him in the first place than maybe you could remember something. I don't know, maybe there is something you could tell him to appease him."

She had inadvertently brought him into it. Milton had already copied the files onto the hard drive before he left the department. He had been sitting on the hard drive since. Fiona had told him about Clark's expertise and independence. The fact that he had been involved at the start gave Milton a reason to approach him for information, but also to have him demonstrate his expertise in finding something in the files, something that may help him, something to use to prove his innocence.

Clark thanked Fiona for her time and said he would see himself out. They shook hands and he left her to her sandwich. He passed the secretary on his way out organising a tray with cups and biscuits. He ignored her and made for the lift and out of Adelaide House.

He stood outside the building leaning against the wall staring at the sky. His head was spinning, a pendulum swinging towards Milton White as a devious and calculating man, as oppose to Milton White the victim. Clark questioned his own integrity, his gullibility, his naivety. He had come this far, he decided. He would keep going, keep an open mind.

Delores remained a loose end. Nobody knew what had happened to her. Fiona at least intimated that she knew something but was unwilling to share. Clark needed to tie up any loose end before he could make a final judgment on Milton. He would play fair. He then remembered he had asked Ed to check up on Delores. He had told Ed he would call to his house later. Clark couldn't wait until later. Ed worked in Adelaide House. Clark was standing outside Adelaide House.

He called Ed.

"Ed," he said, "Any luck on the Delores thing?"

"Yeah, a bit. I'll tell you later."

"Actually Ed, I'm outside Adelaide now. Do you want to go for a walk?"

"Okay," Ed said and hung up.

Ed and Clark walked down Adelaide Street towards Zen.

"Well?" said Clark.

"Nancy said Delores had some trouble with her husband."

Clark had no idea who Nancy was. He assumed she was a colleague but it didn't matter. He listened. Ed was talking, which was something in itself.

"It was a messy one. Apparently he came to reception and shouted obscenities, called her a harlot. That's what Nancy says anyhow. Apparently Delores went home that night and never came back."

"Sounds like fun," said Clark. "So no idea where she went?"

"No."

"And nothing more from the husband?"

"No. Well, Nancy says she knows him, or knows of him. Someone called Thomas, Thomas O'Reilly. He worked in the Shipyard in some management job and had a reputation as a bit of a loud mouth. The last Nancy heard they were divorced. Why, what's all this about?"

"Ed, keep it to yourself if you would. I'm in the middle of something. I'll tell you about it later."

"Are you still coming round later then?"

"Yeah, if that's all right. I'll give you the details later."

"Okay, see you later" said Ed and went back into Adelaide house. They had walked a full circle from Adelaide Street to Linenhall and Clarence Streets and were back where they started.

Clark walked briskly towards the City Hall to catch a bus home. For some reason he wanted to try and find a contact number for Thomas O'Reilly.

CHAPTER 24

Walking down Ethel Street he saw a figure sitting outside his house. He could just about make out the pot belly protruding from the navy tweed jacket.

"Afternoon Radcliffe," said McArdle.

"Afternoon McArdle," said Clark.

"It's Detective Inspector McArdle."

"And it's Clark Radcliffe."

McArdle laughed and put out his hand. "Fair enough," he said, "Clark it is."

They shook hands and Clark led him inside. "Thanks for contacting Milton White for me," he said.

"No problem. So what have you got for me?"

Clark didn't know what to say. Should he tell McArdle all of what he was thinking, some of what he was thinking, or none? After a quick deliberation he decided on giving him something. He at least deserved that.

He said, "I think documents may have been deleted from the department's server, documents of meetings when the final details of the Dubai Wire and Cable project were discussed. I think there might be something in these documents that show someone other than Milton was involved in making final arrangements. I think something might have been discussed that Milton was not aware of."

Clark did not mention the broad shouldered shaven headed man. He told McArdle of his visit to the factory and finding an empty office but found evidence that there had been machinery installed. He told him he thought the grants had been legitimately paid. He told him that he believed some person or persons between the department and Dubai Wire and Cable had conspired to siphon the money, and with some success given that it was still missing.

"Yes, exactly," said McArdle, "and all the evidence points towards Milton White."

"Suspend your disbelief for a moment," said Clark, "try and presume Milton is not involved. Who else was part of the negotiations? There was Fiona Mitchell and Delores O'Reilly from the department and those three from Dubai Wire and Cable. To what extent did your investigation examine them?"

"Look, of course we made all efforts to interview relevant parties. We are not from Keystone you know."

"Made all efforts? Does that mean you did?"

"I'm not going to go into details of our investigation."

"Okay," said Clark, "Let me ask a couple of questions. What did you make of Abdul Alim when you met him?"

"He made a good account of himself."

"Did he look suspicious in any way when you met?"

McArdle looked away and did not answer.

"I think it might be fair for me to say then that you spoke with him but did not actually meet him face to face? A phone call? Was that it?"

"We got what we needed," said McArdle.

"Did you go to Dubai?"

McArdle shook his head.

"What did you make of Delores O'Reilly?"

"What are you onto Radcliffe?"

"You couldn't find her, could you?"

McArdle looked at Clark but didn't say anything for a moment. "Okay," he said, "we met with the husband, a hard nut living in some big house in Marlborough Park. He told us they had some falling out and she had gone to live with her sister over in York. We made a few tentative enquires but to be honest she wasn't really a person of serious interest. All the evidence pointed one way."

"Did Fiona Mitchell tell you that she believed Milton was capable of pulling this off, possibly with him even justifying it as a laudable act?"

He nodded.

"And did she twinkle her eyes at you?" Clark asked raising his eyebrows and smiling.

McArdle also smiled and said, "I hope you are not trying to insinuate anything Radcliffe?"

They both laughed.

"Okay Clark," said McArdle, "you are right. Listen carefully. DC Campbell is waiting for me in the car. It's just you and me having this conversation. Am I making myself clear?"

Clark nodded.

"We could have done things differently during the investigation but we didn't. Yes, Milton White was a slam dunk. I will not however accept any criticism that we were slack. We made every attempt to speak to everybody we had to speak to. We followed process. All the evidence pointed to Milton White."

"You had opportunity, but did you have motive?"

"Look Clark, I'm trying to level with you here. Save me the Colombo act. It was a way for him to get money pure and simple, more money, no matter how much people have, believe me, it is always about getting more money."

"So if I find something that points in a different direction, a direction away from Milton White you will be interested?" said Clark.

"I've already said I'd be interested, but it's just you and me remember. If I am not around you sit on anything you find. I will decide what to do with it. Do you understand?"

Clark understood fully. It was exactly as he had surmised. "Two quick things if I may," he said.

"Fire away."

"Milton White had a legitimate reason for being in the Isle of Man and for opening the bank account there."

McArdle nodded and grimaced, a sign that Clark read as perhaps being one reason why the evidence did not reach prosecution.

Clark continued, "What about Declan Somerville, what did you make of his untimely death in the midst of all this?"

"Nothing at all Clark," he said, "it was an unfortunate accident. There was nothing more to it. Let that one drop Clark."

Clark saw McArdle out and offered a polite wave to DC Campbell sitting in the unmarked police car across the street. DC Campbell ignored him.

Clark found a phone directory in one of his kitchen drawers. He looked for a T O'Reilly of Marlborough Park, the address that McArdle had inadvertently but helpfully given him. He could only hope Thomas still lived there. He found the number and wrote in has notepad. He would call later, after work hours.

Clark had some time. He could not put if off any longer. He called Fabian Townsend at Chesterton and Williamson. Charlotte, Fabian's secretary put Clark through.

"Clark, I was just thinking about you. What time can you drop in the report?"

"I'm sorry Fabian, but something else has come up. I haven't got round to writing up the report yet."

Clark held the phone away from his ear. He knew what was coming next.

"What?" yelled Fabian.

Clark could imagine the whole staff on the floor turning to stare into his office.

"Not good enough," he said again, "I have a client waiting. I am waiting. I am starting to question your commitment, your loyalty Clark. Good work comes your way from me. Have you forgotten that?"

"No I haven't. And I appreciate it Fabian. It's just something personal."

"Look, I have a personal life too Clark. I have a wife. I have children. I have elderly relatives. I have golf. But I also have clients. My clients are your clients. We need to satisfy our clients Clark. Everything else can wait. That's my motto. That's the Chesterton and Williamson way. You are either in or you are out. Do you understand?"

"Yes. Believe me, if it wasn't important …"

"What are you going to do about it Clark?"

"I was going to suggest sending in my notes and outline findings. I think they are fairly comprehensive, and hopefully fairly clear. Maybe one of the trainees can formulate them into a report?"

"That's not the way I would expect a sub contractor to work Clark. They are my trainees, not yours. Send it in."

He hung up.

Clark went to his study desk drawer and found the CD ROM he needed. Thankfully, like all the other CD ROMS, it had survived the break in. He loaded it onto his Dell and spent the next thirty minutes tidying up his notes and findings. He emailed them to Fabian.

He went back downstairs and sat on the club chair. He thought he might call Ellie. He could not shift the guilt from the previous night, despite constantly reminding himself that he had nothing to feel guilty about. It was just a business meeting. For every thought of justification there was a questioning thought. There was something drawing him to Siobhan, something he had capitulated to yet something he had equally resisted when he was with her. She was still

181

on his mind no matter how he tried to dismiss her, no matter how guilty he felt.

He called Ellie.

"Hi, Clark. Twice in one day? A girl might think you miss her?"

He smiled. "I'm just working through some stuff and had a minute, thought I would give you a call."

"Aah, that's nice."

They talked about Clark's progress with Milton White, Clark not giving too much away. They talked about Ellie's work and about her mother."

"What about your dad and mum?" Ellie asked.

Clark said nothing. It was Wednesday afternoon. He had not seen his dad since Monday. He had not seen or spoken with his mum since Saturday.

"Yeah," he said, "I'd better give Mum a call."

"Yes, you'd better," said Ellie.

They said their farewells and Clark dropped the phone on his lap. He picked up the Gibson and began strumming mindlessly, his thoughts with his dad and with his mum. Yes he should call. He should have called earlier. He should have been calling regularly. This was one of the many problems in his relationship with his parents. And he knew it. But he did nothing about it. He didn't call when he should have called and time passed by. Time passed so quickly that it became too late to call. So he didn't.

But despite it all he missed his mum and dad. And he missed Amy.

He put the Gibson back on its stand and picked up the phone, having to consult his address book to remind himself of his parent's phone number.

"Hello?" said his mum.

"Hi Mum, it's Clark."

There was silence on the line.

"How's Dad?"

"Breathing."

"Come on Mum, I'm asking how he is."

"Are you now? Why don't you go and see him then?"

"I was there..."

"Yes Clark, you were there on Monday apparently. For about ten seconds I hear. Where have you been since? I have been there two or three times a day. I have driven myself back and forwards to the hospital. Evelyn from next door has taken me when I was getting tired. Where have you been?"

Clark began to think his call was a mistake. But then again he wanted to help, to offer some support. He just didn't know how. Surely a phone call no matter how uncomfortable is better than no phone call at all he thought? He was trying.

"I know Mum, I'm sorry. I, I have tried. I have been thinking about Dad since it happened. I have been thinking about you. It's just you know ..."

"No Clark I don't know. But since you're on, I hope to have your dad home tomorrow. Your sister is going to try and get over tomorrow."

"That's great Mum. Maybe tomorrow I could..."

"Whatever," she said and hung up.

Clark threw the handset on its cradle. Although upset, he was also happy. His dad was getting home which meant he was getting better. He had spoken with his mother, however uncomfortable it was. And Amy was coming over. Maybe he really could make an effort tomorrow. He hadn't been to his parent's home in years, his childhood home with the many happy memories.

He checked his watch. Thomas O'Reilly should probably be home from work.

He dialled the number.

CHAPTER 25

"Hello?" said a deep voice.

"Thomas O'Reilly?" said Clark.

"Speaking."

"Hello, my name is Clark Radcliffe. I'm sorry to bother you. I'm doing some follow up work with the Department of Industry and Trade Development on the Dubai Wire and Cable project."

"What? What are you talking about?"

"I'm sorry Mr O'Reilly, I understand this may be difficult for you but I have a few questions regarding your ex-wife?"

"After all these years you want to drag that all up?"

"As I said, I am sorry."

"Who are you?" O'Reilly barked.

"I'm a freelance consultant doing an independent closure assessment on the case file," said Clark not even sure himself if what he had said made any sense. But it seemed to work.

"All right," said O'Reilly sharply, "as I said it was a long time ago. I've moved on. I'm in a better place now, got married again, and am very happily married. So in hindsight that dragon actually did me a favour. What is it you want from me?"

"What do you remember of Delores and Dubai Wire and Cable?"

O'Reilly sighed heavily. "I remember it was their fault. I blame them for everything. Delores and I were happy enough, ticking along, or so I thought, and then that crowd arrived. She got so engrossed with them that I rarely seen her. She was always going out to meetings at night, to dinner meetings."

He took a deep breath, "Now I am not a suspicious man, why would I have been. We were married for over twenty years. Delores had a successful career. She was often away at conferences, at meetings and what not, sometimes abroad, sometimes for days at a time. But this was different. She was continually out with the Dubai lot."

Clark was suddenly interested. Milton had mentioned they had informal meetings in different hotels in the early days but Clark did not get the impression they were frequent.

He was about to ask a question when O'Reilly continued, "I followed her one night. I am ashamed to admit it, but I followed her. I followed her to the Ramada Hotel at Shaw's Bridge. She sat a table for four. I remember there was some guy wrapped in a sheet, a fat woman and an older guy with a bald head and a comb over. It all looked very cosy.

"I watched for a while and the man in the sheet and the fat woman left. Delores and baldy stayed. They laughed together. At one stage I even saw him hold her hand. I was furious. I suppose I could have confronted them then but I didn't. I just went home"

He paused for a moment and took another deep breath. "Delores arrived home in the small hours of the morning. I ignored her, pretended to be asleep. The next day when she was at work for some reason I went to her office and began shouting in the reception. Not my finest hour, but there you are. That's what I did."

O'Reilly went quiet.

Clark asked, "And what happened then, Mr O'Reilly?"

After a moment he said softly, "I went home and she came home shortly afterwards. We had a huge row. She accused me of not trusting her. She insisted she was at a business meeting. We must have shouted and rowed for the rest of the day. In the end she said I had humiliated her so much that she couldn't go back to work. She packed a bag and said she was going straight to the airport. She said she would wait for a flight to her sister's in England. She would take some time there."

Another pause and then he said, "I never saw her again. There were a few emails asking how I was and some attempt at an apology but I generally ignored them. We eventually divorced two years ago. All communication from her came through a solicitor. As I said I never saw her again."

"Thanks Mr O'Reilly for your candour," said Clark, "My interest is in the Dubai Wire and Cable project. Delores was a key negotiator and she hasn't had an opportunity to contribute to any follow up enquiries."

"Well all I can say is this; she was indeed involved in negotiations, too involved."

"Thank you for your time Mr O'Reilly. I am sorry to have troubled you."

Clark hung up. His head was spinning, and not for the first time since he started his investigation. From the records of meetings and from what Milton had told him all formal meetings were group meetings when Milton and Fiona were also present. Yes, Milton had mentioned initial informal meetings but he did not infer that these would have been attended by only one of his negotiation team.

There were a couple of things he would have to check. He phoned Ed's mobile phone.

"Ed, find out for me when Delores actually left if you can?"

"Okay. I'll try," said Ed and hung up.

He called back after five minutes.

"Nancy doesn't know exactly. But she said it was in the early summer, probably June. Don't ask. She remembers these things."

"Thanks Ed, I'll see you later."

June thought Clark. He thought back five years. It was in May that he had performed the computer audit that exposed Milton White. It was in May that Declan Somerville died. Milton White left the department in June. Clark too left in June. He couldn't recall any scandal surrounding Delores when he was there. Milton said he did not know what had happened to her. It must all have taken place therefore after Milton and he had left. Clark remembered that Milton had gone before him.

He remembered that at the start of his deliberations he had developed a timeline of meetings between the department and Dubai Wire and Cable, a timeline he had written into his notepad, the notepad that had been stolen. He remembered from that timeline that there were a number of meetings over a twelve month period, and after that there were the missing records.

He went to his study and called up the details of meetings again from the hard drive. He made another note of the dates. The meetings ran from January to January. The Letters of Offer and Acceptance were signed in April. The final negotiations, with the missing records, therefore would have taken place between January and April. The Letters of Offer and Acceptance stated the factory was scheduled to open in June.

If what Thomas O'Reilly had said was true, why was Delores having frequent informal meetings with the Dubai Wire and Cable representatives throughout the course of formal discussions and why was she at the Ramada Hotel fraternising with them in June, the month the factory was due to open, and in the month after the exposure of Milton White?

Clark needed to speak with Milton.

He sent a text message to the number Milton had written on the back of Abdul Alim's card.

The husky voice called back after ten minutes, "Milton White will see you tomorrow morning, same place, and same time."

"Thank you," said Clark, "But I really need to speak to him now. Just a question. It is very important"

There was silence, and then a different voice.

"Clark, tomorrow morning. Not on the phone," said Milton.

"I'll see you tomorrow morning. Just answer yes or no for now. Did Abdul Alim always wear a Kandura?"

"Yes."

"Was Jennifer Maitland fat and did Anthony Tobias have a comb over?"

"Yes."

"Would there have been any circumstance for one of your negotiators to meet with them privately alongside your formal negotiations?"

"No, Wh…?"

"We'll talk tomorrow."

Clark hung up. He held his head in his hands. He was seeing something in his mind, something that might just make sense.

The mobile phone rang. It was Rob.

"Clark I managed to trace the user IDs for who deleted those documents."

"What, oh, yes, sorry Rob, I was miles away there."

"There were documents deleted by different users. But Clark, all the missing records of meetings were deleted by the same person."

He took a deep breath.

"It was Milton White."

Clark froze, literally. He couldn't move, couldn't speak. No matter what progress he thought he was making suspicion always seemed to arrive back at Milton White. Yet for some reason he continued to believe him.

Eventually he managed to say, "Thanks Rob. I don't know how you did it but thanks."

"No problem. The files were archived but I was able to call them up, a perk of having IT Security Specialist access. I can pretty much go anywhere in the department's servers. Actually, I still have the file access data in front of me now."

Clark remembered something else.

"Rob, there was a file fragment in the folders that read *forsetdallemer*." Clark spelled it out. "I think it was from an electronic diary. Can you check who deleted it?"

"Yes sure, if I can find it. I just need to run a cross check on the original folders. Here we go … yes, found it, right, now I need to run it through the file access data. Here goes… got it. Now, I need to run the user ID through the staff database. Bingo."

He took another deep breath.

"It was removed by Dolores O'Reilly."

"Thanks Rob, I'll be in touch."

"Good luck Clark. Be careful."

CHAPTER 26

Clark sat in his study staring at the wall. He began mind mapping thoughts on his notepad. After a few minutes he startled when a car door slammed. Moments later there was a knock on his door. He rose from his computer chair leaving the computer running and the hard drive connected, and went to look out of the bedroom window at the front of the house.

Parked across the street was Jackson's car. 'Good,' he thought, 'I could do with a chat with Jackson. Maybe make some sense of this if we talk it through.'

He bounced down the stairs and opened the front door.

It wasn't Jackson.

Tracey stood in his doorway. She stood in silence, staring at him. Her lips quivering and her eyes moist. Mascara was running down her cheeks. She dabbed her eyes with her fingers.

Clark didn't know what to do or what to say.

"Tracey, are you all right?" he managed finally, a masterstroke of compassion and understanding.

She stood still, sobbing. And then began to cry loudly.

The penny finally dropped with Clark. He stood back.

"Tracey, come on in," he said.

She slipped past him into the lounge, sitting herself on the sofa. Clark found some tissues in a box on the kitchen worktop and handed them to her. She accepted and slowly regained her composure.

Clark sat on the club chair.

"I'm sorry Clark," she said, "Can I use your bathroom?"

"Sure."

She was gone for a while. Clark had no idea what was going on. He had never experienced Tracey, or anyone else for that matter, in the sorry state she was in. He supposed he should offer some form of consoling gesture. He was trying the figure out what that might be when she returned.

Clark stood to face her. She had stopped crying and looked better. Fresh mascara had been applied. Clark then noticed the short summer dress she wore. She carried no pullover or coat. It was cold out. Maybe she didn't feel the cold, or maybe she just liked the dress. As inappropriate as it was Clark could not help but notice her toned, taut physique.

He watched her as she sat, watched as she crossed one leg over the other. His gaze lingered as the dress rode up. His eyes slid down the length of her leg to the black Roman sandals, their straps criss-crossed on her calves.

"Are you okay?" he asked.

"I'm sorry," she said again, "I just had to come and see you."

"What is it Tracey?"

"It's Jackson. Something is not right. He is not himself lately. He is working late most nights and has started going out at weekends. I don't mean out with you and the boys. I know about that, the Friday nights. No, on Saturday and Sunday he disappears. He tells me he is going to work. But he is not at work. I had a client in this morning for a cut and highlights. She was in for two hours. We talked some."

No surprise there thought Clark.

"She works with Jackson. She told me he stays late the odd night but is not in at weekends. She said Jackson's team doesn't work weekends, at least not regularly.

"He went out today on the bus, told me he might grab a drink on the way home. That's why I have the car."

Clark nodded.

Tracey said, "I don't know, I think the worse Clark. I think he has someone else. I had to come and see you. I had to ask you if you know anything. After you were all out last Friday night you called him and he came here. Or at least that's what he said. I just don't know anymore."

The tears began to fall again.

Clark found it hard not to laugh aloud. Jackson with another woman? No, that could not possibly be the case. Clark knew Jackson. He had known him for long enough to know that he was hopelessly devoted to Tracey, besotted, head over heels. And why wouldn't he be thought Clark as he looked at her again. She was beautiful. She was good fun to be with, if incessant. She cared for him. She had made his house their home, a home with a heart, a home Jackson relished returning to every night.

Clark told Tracey all this, in his own way.

"What else can it be?" she asked.

"I don't know, but you know he has been helping me over the last week. In fact he was with me this morning. Maybe his catching the bus was just so he could meet me without having to worry about parking the car. We are working on a bank security audit, top secret it is, even his colleagues in the bank wouldn't know. Maybe that's all it is." Clark hoped this mix of truth and embellishment would placate her.

Tracey smiled. "Yes, I'm probably being silly. Thanks Clark."

Clark did wonder however what Jackson was doing if he was away as often as Tracey said. He certainly hadn't been with him.

"Cup of tea?" he asked recalling that was something his mother would have said in such circumstances. He walked to the kitchen, flicked the kettle and turned around.

Tracey was right behind him, very close behind him. She put the palms of her hands to his chest. He had nowhere to go. She buried her head in his shoulder. He didn't know what was happening. He didn't know what to do. He put both his hands on her shoulders and patted. He patted her on the back like he had before. Maybe that's all she wants he thought, a bit of reassurance. She lifted her head towards his. She looked into his eyes, her glowing eyes drawing him towards her. His head dropped to meet hers. She was waiting for him. Their lips met lightly at first, then harder. Clark's hand slid down her back, over her spine, and around and down her hips. Still his hands slid. They found the bottom of her dress where they gripped the fabric and began to rise again. He caressed her under the dress and pulled her closer. She pushed herself further into him. He was trapped. He could feel every contour of her body against his. He could feel her breathing. He could hear her gently purring. Her hands dropped from his chest to his thighs, and slowly rose.

He pulled away, lifting his hands and letting the dress fall. "We shouldn't," he whispered.

She looked at him and smiled. "I know." She stepped back, "but it felt good."

Clark didn't speak. He nodded.

"Thanks Clark." She moved slowly backwards to the sofa, picked up her bag and smiled again before letting herself out.

Clark did not move.

Eventually he pushed himself away from the worktop. What he was doing, what he was thinking. The guilt he had been enduring over Siobhan was nothing compared to this. This wasn't just betraying Ellie, it was betraying Jackson. It was betraying his own integrity, his trustworthiness, his honesty.

It was her, not me, he kept telling himself. That, at least for the moment pacified him.

He went back to his study. The chair had moved. He was sure the notepad with his mind mapping thoughts had moved to the opposite side of the computer from where he had left it. His computer he was sure was on a different screen. He had not locked his screen when he had gone downstairs.

His heart skipped, his attention focusing on the right hand side of the computer. He then breathed easily.

The hard drive was still there.

There were black smears on the desk. Clark nodded. Tracey must have sat at his desk to reapply her mascara, no doubt with some compact mirror from her handbag.

He powered down the computer and lifted the hard drive and his notes. It was time to head to Bangor to see Ed. He would stop off on the way for something to satisfy his hunger.

Ed lived in a narrow three storey terraced house on Dufferin Avenue in central Bangor. Many of the neighbouring properties had been converted to flats and bedsits, but that had never bothered Ed. He liked its location. He was ten minutes walk from the train station where he could take the train to Belfast, a distance of some thirteen miles. The train line ran through Holywood. Ed and Rob would frequently travel home together by train after their nights out.

There were no driveways on Dufferin Avenue, only small front gardens. But the house had five bedrooms. This allowed each of Ed's two children to have a bedroom each. It also allowed them to have a playroom, and for Ed to have a study.

Clark parked on the street outside and walked up the short path to Ed's front door. He heard the excited screams and shouts of young children from inside. Ed came to the door in answer to Clark's knock.

"Come in," he said, and turned to shout over his shoulder, "Conor, Francois, keep it down please."

Clark was greeted in the hall by seven year old Conor and three year old Francois. Two beautiful kids thought Clark, Conor taking after and named in accordance with Ed's Irish Colleen wife, and Francois still looking strikingly Irish but named in accordance with Ed's heritage.

"Go and play, Daddy needs to talk to Uncle Clark," Ed said leading Clark into the front lounge.

Uncle Clark. He liked that.

They sat in armchairs at either side of the bay window, Ed in silence waiting to hear whatever it was Clark was going to say.

Clark gave him the overview similar to that he had given Rob the previous night, focusing primarily on the missing files and that he had asked Rob to find out who had deleted the files. He told Ed that Rob had said it was Milton White who had deleted the records of meetings. He also told Rob he had uncovered what he determined to be an electronic diary record that Rob had found was deleted by Delores O'Reilly.

Ed listened and nodded periodically. He said nothing.

"You worked with her didn't you Ed?" Clark said.

"Yes. On some project stuff, but in reality I didn't see much of her."

"What did you make of her?"

"She was all right I suppose, always rushing about, always busy. She was away quite a bit."

"Away where?"

"Don't know."

"What about the Dubai Wire and Cable thing?"

"Don't know, wasn't involved."

So there it was thought Clark, nothing more to be gained here. Ed had exhausted his usefulness in talking with Nancy. Or so Clark thought.

He shared his feelings on Declan Somerville. Like Rob, Ed said it was an accident and Clark had nothing to feel responsible for.

"Clark, trust me," he said, "Nobody ever did or ever will put any blame on you. It was an accident."

Ed looked to the floor for a moment and then back to Clark. "Declan's wife Emily still lives in Bangor. Caitlin and Emily have been friends for years, from way back before Declan died. They still get together. I see her sometimes. Trust me, she accepts it was an accident."

Clark swallowed. He appreciated what he was hearing. He appreciated the reassurance that Ed was giving. He thought for a moment of all the years he had been dealing with Declan Somerville in his head, and that all this while he had known Ed yet had not known Ed knew Declan's wife. Maybe if their friendship had been more than the social convenience it was he would have known. Maybe it was time to develop his friendships. A tear came to his eye. Ed seen it and looked away.

"I didn't know Clark," was all he said. He shook his head and dropped his stare to the ground. After a moment he lifted his head. "Would it help if you met her?"

Clark said nothing. He eyes fixed on Ed. In his mind he was running through the last five years, the guilt he had felt, that he hadn't even gone to see Declan's wife and daughter, hadn't even gone to the funeral. He swallowed again and nodded.

Ed said nothing and rose from his chair. He placed his hand gently on Clark's shoulder and too nodded. He left the room.

Ed came back some minutes later with a mug of instant coffee which he handed Clark and nodded again before once more leaving the room.

Some time later he returned and sat on the seat opposite Clark. He leaned forward. "Glenda, Declan's wife, is at home now. Caitlin has just phoned her and said you were here and would like to meet. Glenda has said to come over."

Clark didn't know what to say. This is it, he thought, an opportunity to meet with Declan's wife, something that should have been done many years ago, something that has been put off ever since. He knew what he wanted to do, he knew what he had to do. The instant decision was just what he needed, given too long to dwell and he would have found a number of excuses.

He nodded to Ed and rose from his chair. Ed rose too. They embraced.

Glenda lived in a compact semi detached house on Primrose Street, not far away from Dufferin Avenue. Ed helped Conor and Francois with their shoes and coats and they all walked the short distance, Francois holding Clark's hand. No words were spoken.

Glenda was at the door waiting. She was tall with greying shoulder length hair, casually dressed in house leggings and oversize tee shirt. She had clearly not planned to have guests. She hugged Ed warmly and ushered the children into the house with a promise of sweets. Ed introduced Clark and stood back. Clark looked at her and could feel the lump rise in his throat, his eyes dampening. He did not want to speak, conscious his voice would break any time. He nodded and extended his hand. Glenda looked at him, she too saying nothing, her eyes also moistening. She looked to Clark's hand and ignored it. She looked up into his eyes. She stepped forward and threw her arms around him and held him tight, tears streaming down her face.

Ed sat at the kitchen table entertaining Conor and Francois with paper and pens that Glenda had produced. Glenda and Clark sat in the lounge, on separate armchairs facing each other.

"I'm glad to finally meet you," she said, "Declan spoke very highly of you."

Clark said nothing and fought hard to maintain composure.

"He was always saying how smart you were and how you were wasting your time in the department. He often said you were going places. I think he was in awe of you, and would have done anything to impress you."

Clark reddened. He had not realised. He remembered Declan as a conscientious worker, enjoying challenges and seldom getting distracted with the nonsense of office politics. He remembered

Declan always willing to help him, even volunteering to help him, but he had not read anything into it. In many ways this did not help Clark in coming to terms with what had happened. It seemed Declan was working late that night in Adelaide House to help Clark, to impress him. Clark didn't' know what to make of that.

"I'm sorry, Glenda," he said, "for not coming to see you before now, for not even coming his funeral. He was a good man, conscientious and capable. I don't know, I think I felt responsible. He was working late to help me. If only I had …"

"Clark, please. Don't beat yourself up. Declan was ill. He had a weak heart. The doctors had told him to take it easy, to slow down, to change his diet, to stop the smoking. He defied them all Clark. It was not your fault, it was not anybody's fault."

She choked back a tear. "It was just his time. There was nothing anybody could have done. If it had not happened in work, it would have happened here."

"But if it was here, you would have been here."

"Clark, you don't know that. You can't think like that. You have nothing to feel guilty or responsible for."

"Thank you Glenda for saying that. It means a lot," Clark said softly.

He paused and said, "I… I… don't want to dig up anything that may upset you, and I know it was a long time ago, but, do you know what he was actually doing that night in the office? I mean, routine work generally meant routine hours?"

"It's okay Clark, I don't mind talking about it. In fact it is good to talk about it, even after all these years. I loved him Clark. I still love him. There has been no one else. When Declan died Louise became my priority."

She walked to the sideboard and returned with a photograph which she handed to Clark. Clark took the photograph and fixed his attention on the beautiful face surrounded with long blonde hair that looked up at him, the shining blue eyes, long lashes and a stunning smile, dimples in the cheeks. Clark choked.

"You must be very proud," he said.

"Yes, Louise is in her last year at Durham, studying Computer Science. She was sixteen when her dad died. She too loved him very much. I think her decision to study computers was her gift to him, recognition of her affection."

"Declan's legacy," said Clark fighting back the tears.

"To answer your question," she said, "No, I don't mind talking about it. He thought he was onto something. I don't know what though, nor do I know what exactly he was working on, what the project or whatever it was he called them, was. I did know however he was helping you. He phoned me to say you had gone home and he would work on to find out more. I think, Clark, he wanted to have something to give to you the next day, something you would have been proud of him for finding."

Clark smiled warmly.

"But alas," she said and shrugged her shoulders.

Clark stood, and she stood. They hugged like long lost friends. Maybe they were thought Clark. He was glad he had met with her. He had received reassurance. He could start to put it behind him.

But he couldn't help but wonder if Declan had actually found anything the night he died.

CHAPTER 27

Back at Ed's house Clark sat in the lounge with Francois on his knee. He read her a bedtime story, something about a mouse that scared away a monster with its shadow. Afterwards Ed took her to bed and Clark played a game of Trumps with Conor. Clark was happy. He had addressed a recurring nightmare, something he should have done a long time ago. He had not known that Ed knew Declan's wife. But then again why would he have known, they never talked about personal matters, nor did they talk about work matters. Sure Declan was at Ed and Caitlin's wedding too, and Clark surmised Glenda and a young Louise would have been there too. But he would not have known them. He might have been introduced, but he did not remember. And Glenda did not show any signs of recognition.

Ed came into the room just as the front door opened. It was Caitlin returning from her evening shift. She and Clark exchanged a warm greeting and she took Conor to bed, diplomatically not asking how things had gone with Glenda.

It was time too for Clark to go. He stood and faced Ed.

"Listen Ed, I'm glad you now know …"

"Yes, I know."

"And … Glenda … I really appreciate …"

"I know," said Ed.

Nothing more needed to be said. Clark and Ed shook hands firmly, holding tightly to each other's forearm. With the warmth and satisfaction that he was feeling Clark wondered why he had not been more open with Rob and Ed before.

As he was leaving Ed called his name. Clark turned.

"If there is anything you need Clark, anything at all …"

"I know Ed. Thanks. I will."

Clark drove slowly back towards Belfast. He was enjoying the moment. He was as happy as he had been in a long time. The nights he had lain awake feeling guilty and responsible were finally behind him. He allowed himself a smile. He allowed himself to laugh out loud. He felt good.

Siobhan came to his mind. He did not know why. He was heading towards East Belfast. Siobhan lived in East Belfast. He remembered from the glance he had given her business card in the Apartment Bar. He stopped the car on the hard shoulder just past Holywood and fished the card from his wallet.

Kerrsland Drive, he read thinking, 'I could drive past Kerrsland Drive on the way home.'

He stopped outside Siobhan's house. It was an attractive three bedroom semi detached house with a large front bay window. It was dark outside. The inside of the house was lit brightly. The curtains were open. Through the bay window Clark saw Siobhan sitting at a desk surrounded by paper. She was reading from a laptop computer, chewing on a pencil as she read. Her hair was tied back tightly showing the full length of her neck. She wore a tight white vest top. She sat back in the chair and dropped her arms to her sides. She stretched, pushing her chest forwards.

Clark stared.

She sat forward and began rotating her head and massaging her own neck and shoulders.

Clark moved to open his car door. He had come to help her. Or had he? Why had he come? He thought of how readily she had entered his mind, his positive and contented mind. He looked at her again. She was alone. She needed help. Clark wanted to give her the help she needed. He thought of Tracey. He thought too of Ellie.

Siobhan took the band off her hair and shook her head backwards flicking the hair with both hands and continuing to massage her neck underneath the hair, the pencil protruding from her lips.

Clark started the car and drove home.

Back in Ethel Street he hung up his coat and set the hard drive and notepad on the kitchen table. He sat on the club chair and picked up the Gibson. He strummed a few chords of Dylan. He set the Gibson back on its stand and put Dylan's Greatest Hits on the CD player. He sat on the chair with his head in his hands. He reflected back on the rollercoaster of emotions that had been the last few hours, the visit from Tracey, the visit to Ed and his family, the visit to Glenda, and the aborted visit to Siobhan.

His life should be simple he thought, he had a family, he had friends, he had a girlfriend. Why did he let so many complications enter the mix? He didn't know. Why could he not focus his attentions on what he had? His openness with his friends had brought him satisfaction, and his openness with Glenda had brought him joy. There were rewards out there to be achieved. And there would be other rewards out there if only he could, or would, seek them out. He thought of his mum, his dad, his sister Amy. He thought of Ellie. Ellie meant a lot to him, of that he had no doubt. Why then was he tempted by others, others who could give him nothing more than Ellie could? He had all he needed to secure the comfort he sought.

He needed to focus his attention on securing that comfort.

He rose from his seat and turned off the CD, locked up the house for the night and went to his study with the hard drive and notepad to prepare to meet with Milton the next morning.

He thought for a moment that he might call Jackson and tell him he was meeting Milton, given that Jackson had been present in different guises at all previous meetings. He decided against it rationalising that the risk of the shaven headed man had passed. In reality however he felt guilty about Tracey's visit earlier. He didn't want to face Jackson. 'Here I go again,' he thought to himself, 'I have just sat on a chair and motivated myself to make a concentrated effort, and here I am sticking my head in the sand again.'

He sat at his desk with his notepad. He began to revise the links he had found between the department and Dubai Wire and Cable, the correspondence, the formal meetings, the informal meetings, and the personalities. He was reflecting on his conversations with McArdle when his mobile phone buzzed on the desk in front of him.

It was a text message from the number that Milton White had given him. The text message was terse, simply telling Clark to meet the next morning at nine thirty, earlier than the usual ten thirty.

He was tired. He knew it was late and it was not really the time but he folded down his barbell bench and completed a set of reps. He powered down the computer and stored the hard drive and notes in his desk drawer before climbing into bed.

He woke early. It was Thursday morning. He dressed, had a breakfast of cereal and orange juice. The coffee would wait until he got to Café Nero. He left to catch the bus to the city centre, repeatedly checking the pocket of his coat as he was walking.

Milton was waiting for him. The café was just opening. Milton had not yet received any coffee but told Clark he had ordered.

"Thanks for coming. Tell me more about what you were asking on the phone yesterday?" said Milton.

Clark leant close and lowered his voice. "I went to see Fiona yesterday."

"And?"

"She gave nothing away about Delores. As you had said she

203

seemed to dismiss the subject."

Milton sighed.

"But," said Clark, "I spoke to Delores' husband, or should I say ex husband."

"What? How? Who…?"

"Never mind, I tracked him down and spoke with him."

Milton nodded and smiled at Clark, apparently impressed.

"According to Thomas, her ex-husband, Delores was having regular meetings with the Dubai team, meetings outside of the formal meetings that I have seen records of and that you have told me about."

Milton shook his head.

Clark continued, "Thomas said she was going out regularly at night right through the project, even after the Letters of Offer and Acceptance were signed. He followed her one night to the Ramada and saw her with Alim, Anthony and Jennifer. Alim and Jennifer went and left Anthony and Delores together.

"He was angry, understandably. The next day he went to Adelaide House and caused a fracas in reception. Delores went home and according to Thomas has not been seen since, although he did receive correspondence and eventually finalised a divorce through her solicitor. Apparently she went to England to stay with her sister."

Milton was still shaking his head. "I had no idea…"

"Milton," said Clark, "this happened in June, five years ago, after you had left the department. Delores met socially with the Dubai team after you were exposed. The question is why? Not only why was she meeting with them, but why were the Dubai team in Belfast.

"McArdle had said he spoke with them only by telephone as they were in Dubai. I interpreted that as there no longer being a requirement for them to be in Belfast."

Clark paused and looked at Milton. "And that's not all. You told me all meetings were held in Belfast and that the only meeting in Dubai was when you sent your overseas representative to carry out a due diligence check."

Milton sat perfectly still, listening.

"I found a file fragment on the hard drive that came from an electronic diary, from an entry that had been deleted. It would seem a meeting was scheduled in Le Meridien Hotel in Dubai with Abdul Alim, the September before the factory was due to open. That would have been in the midst of your formal discussion and negotiation period."

Clark paused again for a moment and said, "Milton, it was Delores' electronic diary."

"Right," said Milton nodding slowly, "So something was going on between an official from the department and the Dubai Wire and Cable officials, even after I was implicated. And the police investigation did not pursue this with any vigour."

He looked at Clark and said quietly, "It looks like Delores was involved in some way in something and the police did not pursue that either."

It was Clark's turn to nod. "Yes," he said.

"This is just as I thought Clark," Milton said.

He put his hand in his pocket and produced an envelope that he set on the table.

The barista arrived with the coffee.

Clark looked at the envelope.

"After your call yesterday," Milton said, "I got to thinking. There is an avenue that needs proper investigation, an avenue that has not yet been properly explored.

"Clark, I want you to go to Dubai and talk to Abdul Alim and his team. I have tickets in this envelope.

"You leave tonight, six o'clock from Belfast and connect at Heathrow. You will arrive in Dubai tomorrow morning at eight o'clock and stay two nights in Le Meridien. Abdul Alim will be there. I have checked. You will be back in Belfast again nine o'clock on Sunday night. We are meeting earlier this morning to give you time to prepare."

Clark looked at Milton. "You can't be serious," he said, "I can't just drop everything and run to Dubai at a moment's notice just because you want me to."

"What have you got to drop Clark?"

That was a good question he thought. He was involved. He had been involved for almost a week. He had found inconsistencies. He still had questions he could not answer. As the week had progressed he'd found some answers to some questions. But others remained. He was curious about the police's apparent ambivalence towards investigating Dubai. He thought of Abdul Alim's business card he had found in the factory. He was curious about Delores' role.

Milton was indeed a mysterious person, but despite the negative character references from Fiona Mitchell and from McArdle, Clark believed him. He had come this far. He wanted to go further. Dubai seemed to be a logical step.

"Why can you not just phone Alim?" Clark asked.

Milton shook his head. "He still won't take my calls. Even after five years. All I get are excuses and promises of call backs from his staff.

"My suspicion is he has something to do with this, something about recouping the cost of a failed strategic venture into Europe. And you have just told me that he was seen in the Ramada Hotel after I had left, and at the time the factory was due to open? Why did I not know this? Why did the police not know this? Why could I not have met and spoken with him when he was here? Why could the police not have met him when he was here? Was he deliberately avoiding us?

"As you can see Clark, it is all very curious. I got someone to call his office in Le Meridien with some cover story. He will be in his office all over this weekend. In Dubai the working week is usually Sunday to Thursday, but he will be there working through. I would like you to go and make every effort to meet with him face to face."

Clark could not disagree with anything Milton had said. He lifted the envelope. It's only a few days he thought.

"I'm not sure, I'll let you know," he said and stood, pocketing the envelope.

Milton nodded and Clark walked away through the men's clothing department of the House of Fraser. He rode the escalator to Costa Coffee where he sat on the usual sofa with a fresh Americano. He had much to think about.

He needed to speak with Jackson. He wanted Jackson's counsel. He would have to stem his guilt and speak with him. He called Jackson and told him he needed to see him urgently.

CHAPTER 28

Jackson was there in fifteen minutes, his office being nearby.

Clark told him he had just met with Milton and made an excuse as to why he hadn't told him in advance. He gave him a brief overview of the meeting but did not mention Dubai. He took the envelope from his pocket and set it on the table, beckoning Jackson to look at it.

Jackson lifted the envelope slowly and read through its contents. His eyes widened. "He wants you to go to Dubai? Tonight?"

Clark nodded.

"And are you going to go?"

Clark shrugged.

Jackson thought for a moment. "There's still a danger you know. We still don't know who the shaven headed man is or who he is connected to. But I understand you are committed to this. You want to see it through. Clark Radcliffe will not be beaten, isn't that it?"

Jackson smiled and Clark gave a slight nod. He was right of course. Clark had lived with it for so long. He had found a measure of comfort and reassurance the previous night when he met Glenda.

But he had more to do.

"Clark," said Jackson, "I think you want to go… I don't want you to go, at least not on your own. You don't know what is there, what involvement these guys have. You have no idea if you will be safe. But, as I said, I understand why you have to go."

He looked at Clark. "I'll go with you."

Clark looked at him. He smiled gently. It meant a lot. Jackson, his friend, was offering to help him. Clark knew he would need the help. He would need someone with whom he could at least to talk through his thinking, if not someone to look out for him. Jackson was a good friend. He shook the thoughts of Tracey from his mind. He would have to deal with that eventually.

Clark held out his hand. He couldn't find the words. Jackson understood. They shook hands.

"What about work? What about Tracey?"

"Tracey will be fine. When I tell her I am helping you on an overseas investigation she will find it exciting. Besides Clark, she thinks the world of you. If she thought you would need any help she would be glad that we could provide it."

We, thought Clark. Jackson had referred to himself and Tracey as one. He had said that Tracey thought a lot of him. He grimaced.

"And don't worry about work. It's only the rest of today and tomorrow. According to these tickets you will be back on Sunday night."

Clark nodded and sent a text to Milton saying he would go to Dubai on condition that Jackson Morrow go too. He included on the text that Jackson was a friend and confidant who could be trusted and was also a computer analyst.

They waited for thirty minutes and Clark's phone rang.

"It's sorted. Tickets for Morrow can be collected at the City Airport. Milton White will see you as usual on Monday morning," said the husky voice. She hung up.

"That's it," said Clark, "We are good to go. See you at four thirty at the airport. Go and do what you have to do."

Jackson hurried away and Clark called Ellie. She was still at her mother's working through a case file. Clark told her briefly of his meetings since they had last spoken and that it looked like there was a finger of suspicion pointing towards Dubai. He told her Milton wanted him to go to Dubai and he had agreed to go but with the condition that Jackson go too.

"What," she said, "Are you serious? You are going to Dubai, just like that?"

"Yes, that's the way it is Ellie. I'm as shocked as you but in truth I am not surprised. Dubai needs to be investigated."

"Listen to yourself Clark, Dubai needs to be investigated? Who are you to investigate anything? Is it not a police matter? Why are they not investigating?"

She was angry, but he was going to do what he had to do. She would have to live with it. He had not told her he had met with the police and that in his mind he had their approval to keep doing what he was doing. He would not tell McArdle however that he was going to Dubai.

"Ellie, I need to do this. You know I was involved in this five years ago. I found something then and I have found something now. I need to finish this."

She sighed, "I know you well enough Clark. I know you lock yourself away in that study of yours for hours playing with your computer stuff. I know you will never give up. I admire that about you. And honestly, I'm proud of your commitment. Go if you have to. I'll be fine here in the rain."

Clark had difficulty in telling if she was being genuine. Maybe she was annoyed he was going with Jackson and not her, he thought.

"There will be no time for pleasure," he said, "We leave at six o'clock tonight and arrive there at eight o'clock tomorrow morning, their time. We leave again on Sunday morning at nine o'clock. There's a bit of a layover in London on the way back, we can't get a connecting flight from Heathrow back to Belfast. We have to bus it from Heathrow to Gatwick to connect back here. We are due back in Belfast at nine o'clock on Sunday night, our time."

"Whoa, you'd better get going then ..."

"And Ellie," he said interrupting her, "I would prefer if you stayed at your mum's until I get back. I still don't know any more about the break in, and I don't know what connection if any it has to what I am doing ..."

"Okay," she said abruptly, "I'll call you later. I need to go now."

There was something else that Clark needed to do, and he had little time. He checked his watch. It was after eleven o'clock. He needed to be at Belfast's City Airport for four thirty. He ran from Victoria Square to the taxi rank at City Hall and took a taxi home. He took his keys from his pocket but didn't go into his house. He jumped into his car and drove quickly down Ethel Street, around the one way system to the Lisburn Road and made his way to the shores of Strangford Lough, to his childhood home, a house he had not been in for many years.

The journey took about forty five minutes, the traffic relatively light and his journey further assisted by the absence of tractors and other agricultural vehicles that frequented the narrow rural roads from Comber towards the Lough. The scenery was stunning, the rolling drumlins across open green fields on both sides, and the blue glistening shimmer of the Lough in front. Clark was in a hurry. He was not appreciating the location or the view. His mind was elsewhere, on what he had to do before he went, and what he had to do when he got there.

He drove through Ardmillan village and onto the Ballydorn Road. The Lough came closer. Familiar surroundings came closer, the bungalow, the large garden with its trees and low hedges with green fields, and the Lough shore beyond. He turned into the driveway and parked beside a large silver Land Rover Discovery. It could have been his parent's car. He didn't know. He had no idea what they drove. He went to the front door and rang the bell. His mother came to the door. She looked pale and drawn, the signs of worry and lost sleep. She looked at Clark but did not speak.

"Is he home?" Clark said.

His mother stared at him with cold steely eyes. She did not blink. Clark did not move, did not say any more. He did not know what to say, or what to do. His mother's eyes began to glaze. She held her head steady, but the tears dropped on her cheeks.

His mother shook her head. "No, not until next week at the earliest. He is strong but it probably was premature to expect him home within a week of his attack."

Clark nodded.

His mother stood firm.

"And how are you?" he eventually asked.

"So you do care?"

"I'm sorry Mum it just that…"

"Just that you have been busy, or are you going to give me some different reason this time?"

"I am busy, yes. And I have to go away for a few days. I won't be back until late on Sunday night."

His mother folded her arms across her chest and sighed. "So why are you here?"

"To see him. And to see you."

"Well, he's not here. You can call into the hospital if you must. You have seen me. You go now to wherever you have to be."

She stood blocking the doorway.

"And Amy?" Clark asked.

"She's on her way."

Clark looked around him, briefly taking in the scenery and the tranquillity. He drew a deep breath and exhaled slowly. "Mum," he said, "Can I come in?"

She stood for a moment with arms still folded, and then stepped back giving him room.

Clark brushed passed her into the hallway. "It's a long time since I've been here," he said, "is it okay if I look around?"

"Suit yourself," she said, and walked towards the kitchen.

Clark looked into the lounge and dining room and walked past the kitchen down the long corridor towards the bedrooms. He made for the room that had been his.

The room had barely changed, his old computer desk and chair still there, the metal framed single bed and mahogany double wardrobe and chest of drawers also still there. There was a photo framed on the desk, a picture of Clark when he was a young teenager standing in the garden with a basketball. He was smiling broadly. Beside him, looking up at him, was Amy, her long fair hair shining in the sunlight. She too was smiling, smiling at her brother. Clark smiled at the photo. He remembered it being taken, even though it must have been over twenty years ago.

He opened the drawer of the desk. Inside were pens and pencils and scraps of paper, scraps of paper that had incredibly been untouched since Clark had left home. He looked out the window over the hedge to the field beyond. He lost himself in memories from a long time ago.

Eventually he turned back towards the desk, it's drawer still open. He put his hand into his coat pocket and pulled out the hard drive. He put it in the drawer and closed it shut. He walked to the door and turned to look back around the room. He nodded and smiled to himself.

"Well?" said his mum when he went to the kitchen.

The kitchen had been modernised. Indeed most of the house had been modernised from what he had seen, except for his old room.

"Brings back memories," he said.

"Humph. Do you want a sandwich?"

"Thanks Mum, but I need to get going. I will come back early next week to see how things are."

"Only if you can spare the time," she said.

"Mum," he said, "take care."

He walked out to his car and reversed in the driveway. He saw his mother standing at the door. He thought he could see more tears.

She waved at him as he drove away.

CHAPTER 29

The journey home took him past the Ulster Hospital. He didn't have time to stop. He would see his father when he got back. His mother had said he was strong. Clark took comfort from that.

He arrived home and quickly packed what he thought he would need. He went downstairs and made an instant coffee. He would eat later at the airport. He was tidying the kitchen when he heard a rattle in the door and turned to see Ellie struggling into the lounge, her arms filled with store bags.

"Hi, pet. I've brought you a few presents for your trip," she said.

Clark smiled, pleased to see her.

"I'm only going to be away for a couple of days, most of which will be on a plane," he said.

"You still need good summer clothes."

"I don't think I'll be seeing too much sun."

She dropped the bags on the sofa and he went towards her.

They held each other tight and kissed for what seemed like an eternity. Clark's pleasure at seeing her was in part to erode the guilt from the last couple of days. He pulled her tighter towards him. She buried her head in his chest.

"Oh, Clark, that's nice," she said.

Very nice indeed thought Clark but said nothing. He felt warm inside, safe, secure and happy in Ellie's embrace.

"What happened to your mirror?" she asked.

Clark didn't answer.

She broke away and fished in one of the bags, producing a keyring holding two keys.

"Present number one," she said, "one for the lobby door to the building and one for my door."

Clark laughed.

"We really are moving this relationship into serious territory," he said.

She laughed too and produced a Hugo Boss tee shirt, shorts and sandals from another bag. Then came Ralph Lauren linen trousers, short sleeved light blue shirt and a pair of boating shoes.

"To travel in," she said.

Clark was pleased. He would only be away for a short while, and he had thought he already had what clothes he would need, but he appreciated the effort she had gone to.

"When do you go?" she asked.

"I meet Jackson at the City Airport at half past four."

She looked at her watch.

"Better make sure everything is packed then," she said and lifted the bags before climbing the stairs.

Clark finished tidying the house downstairs, not that it took long given its size, and sat on the sofa to wait for Ellie.

He waited and waited. There was no sign of her, no sound from upstairs. He opened the door and called her name. There was no response. He began to worry. He climbed the stairs cautiously. The door to his study was open, but the bathroom and bedroom doors were closed. He knocked on the bathroom door. Again there was no response. He slowly pushed open the bedroom door.

Ellie was sitting on her knees on the bed wearing only a bright red silk mini chemise, her glasses perched on the end of her nose.

"I thought you'd never come," she said," This is your real present."

Clark smiled and kicked the bedroom door closed.

Ellie drove Clark to the City Airport, a short distance from the city centre on the road to Holywood and Bangor beyond. It was a rush but they made it. In the drop off area they again held each other close and tight. They kissed. They were glowing from the experience they had just shared, hurried as it was. It was passionate and memorable, and complete when they had showered together. Clark had dressed in his new clothes. He had left his overcoat at home, convinced he would not need it where he was going.

"I'd better go," he said.

They kissed again.

"Be careful," she said, "both you and Jackson. I'm sure he's had an earful from Tracey. He's probably looking forward to the break."

They both laughed.

Clark watched her as she drove off and walked towards the airport building.

Jackson was standing in the middle of the departures lobby watching and waiting. He waved an envelope at Clark when he seen him. His tickets, no doubt.

Tracey was standing beside Jackson. It was the first Clark had seen her since she had left his house the evening before. She was dressed demurely in loose fitting trousers and blouse. Clark grimaced. Tracey must have sensed his discomfort, or maybe she felt the same. She came to meet him, to intercept him before he reached Jackson. She stood on her toes and put both arms around his shoulders. She leant close.

"Clark, it's okay? We're all right aren't we? We're good?"

"Yes," Clark whispered in reply, "We're good."

She kissed his cheek and they looked at each other, holding the look for a long moment. They both nodded in unison. She led him by the hand back to Jackson.

"I was just telling Clark to make sure he looked after you," she said to Jackson.

Jackson laughed. "Can I have her back now Clark?"

Clark looked away as Jackson and Tracey kissed and said their farewells.

Tracey stepped forward and looked at Clark, rolling her eyes towards Jackson and then back to Clark. Clark read this as a sign to find out what Jackson was up to on the weekends he said he was working.

Clark nodded and he and Jackson headed towards the baggage check and the flight to London's Heathrow Airport.

The flight to London was uneventful. Clark and Jackson could not secure seats together and spent the short one hour flight flicking through the onboard magazines reading reviews of the airports the airline serviced and looking at pictures of tax free perfume and varying sized plastic models of the airplane they were in. Clark had no idea who would ever purchase such pointless and overpriced models. Maybe a collector, he thought, a collector with little else to do.

There was little time between the flights. Clark and Jackson had less than two hours to collect their baggage, change terminals and check in for the Virgin flight to Dubai International Airport.

They made it with minutes to spare and were allocated seats beside each other at the rear of the plane, where there were only two seats on the window aisles. This was good, there would be no need to either ignore or engage in futile small talk with a stranger for the duration of the seven hour flight.

Jackson took the window seat and Clark the aisle. It was an overnight flight and they both knew they had a busy couple of days ahead of them, although they were not really sure what those days would entail. All Clark knew was he had to try to speak with Abdul

Alim. Where, if anywhere, the journey took them after that he had no idea.

Their flight time disappeared through half watching romantic comedy movies, eating a series of rubber snacks and meals, and sleeping.

Seven hours later they touched down in Dubai, right on schedule, the Captain informing that local time was eight o'clock in the morning.

CHAPTER 30

Dubai International Airport was less than twenty miles from the Le Meridien, or more specifically Le Royal Meridien as Clark determined from his tickets as there appeared be more than one Le Meridien in the hotel chain.

They quickly passed through immigration, stifled by the heat but impressed with the complimentary bottled water. The immigration staff were all male, all golden skinned and handsome and all adorned in the traditional Emerati long white cloak Kandura and Guthra headscarf with an Egal black rope to keep the headscarf in place. Everyone was polite and officious, and made Clark and Jackson feel very welcome.

They took a taxi from the airport to the Le Royal Meridian, a journey that took over an hour given the heavy early morning traffic. The amount of traffic surprised Clark, although he did not really know why. He supposed he thought that as he was in the desert there would be camels and Bedouin campsites everywhere. How wrong he was. The cars were in the main high end luxury cars weaving in and out of the lanes with some skill, or careless audacity depending on your point of view. The construction was incredible. Swarms of Asian workers milling around building sites, building sites that rose high into the sky, cranes for as far as the eye could see.

Clark peeled off the Dirham notes to pay the taxi fare, notes that he had exchanged at the Travelex in Heathrow Airport. They retrieved their bags from the taxi's trunk and stood looking at the Hotel entrance.

An immense round tower welcomed them, inviting them. They were received in a monumental marble floored entrance lobby filled with opulent furniture and fittings. They looked around in awe, in admiration, and in excitement. At the reception desk stood two men and a woman, all dressed in typical western clothing, one man in a navy business suit, the other in a hotel emblazoned tunic, and the woman in a cream loose fitting blouse. Her hair was tied back tight into a bun. The woman called Clark and Jackson to her as they waited in line for service. She welcomed them warmly and checked their documents and passports. Clark and Jackson smiled gormlessly.

"Your room is ready. You will be sharing a twin Club room in the Club Tower," she said in perfect English with a slight accent, handing over two key cards.

"Would you like me to make a reservation for dinner?"

Clark had no idea what restaurants were in the hotel, or what the dining etiquette was. "No thanks," he said, "We'll just get our bearings first."

She smiled and bowed her head, pointing with a full hand in the direction of the Club Tower. Out of nowhere came a bellboy, or bellman, dressed in the same hotel emblazoned cream tunic that was presumably the hotel uniform. He lifted the bags and led the way.

Their room was on the sixth floor. The twin beds appeared large and comfortable, adorned with soft pillows and light duvets. The room had an outsized sofa allowing for a relaxing view across the pools, gardens and beach.

Clark tipped the bellman and he and Jackson took in the view before deciding to explore the hotel grounds.

It was nearing midday and the sun was strong. They each sat on a sun lounger by the landscaped swimming pool, parasols overhead to protect from the strong morning sun. To their right were the bedroom and corporate blocks, three separate buildings including their Club Tower building, all of which afforded magical views across the pools and beach to the Persian Gulf beyond.

In front, at the end of the pool, was an outdoor and swim up bar. Numerous staff were anxious to be of assistance. Over the pool was an arched walkway bridge, ornate yet practical in shortening the journey towards the beach.

Clark was taking it all in when Jackson nudged him and pointed to the far side of the bridge. Two girls were coming towards them. Clark looked and stared. Both girls were brunette, bronzed and clad in the smallest modesty covering bikinis imaginable. They walked in unison to a clicking sound. Clark's stare was drawn to the sound. On their feet they wore three inch high heeled shoes. He could not believe what he was seeing. It was something out of a music video or magazine shoot he thought. Jackson's jaw dropped. Both girls looked their way and laughed provocatively, flicking hair from their faces.

And then a man came behind them, a middle aged pot bellied man with a forest of chest hair. He walked between the girls and put an arm around each of their waists. The girls reciprocated and the three of them walked together towards the hotel.

"This really is the stuff of dreams," said Jackson, his eyes following the unlikely three.

"Welcome to Dubai," said Clark.

"Can you imagine if we were here with our girls," said Jackson, "and the two of them parading over the bridge like that?"

Clark smiled and looked back to the bridge. In his mind he pictured Ellie leaning over the rail in a scant bikini and high heels and beckoning him with a teasing finger. But his mind did not stop there.

He thought too of Tracey in a similar pose, teasing him, luring him. His mind lingered on the thought. He shook his head in an attempt to lose the image. This is not right he thought, not least that Jackson was sitting beside him. He concentrated his mind back to Ellie, and to her present to him the day before. He was glad he did. He relaxed, a contented smile spreading across his face.

Then his mind switched again, to an image of Siobhan in her Louboutins, with white swimsuit and shimmering skin, tossing her hair, laughing, coming towards him, the bridge like a catwalk, with Clark as her prize.

"Clark, can you hear me?"

It was Jackson waving his arms in front of Clark's face.

"I'd thought I'd lost you there."

Clark rubbed his eyes. "Sorry, I was miles away," he said, bringing his focus back to Ellie, the red silk lingerie, the send off.

"I'm serious Clark, we should think about bringing the girls." He paused. "There is something I was meaning to talk to you about."

Clark looked at him, his heart skipping a beat.

"It's Tracey …"

Clark swallowed hard.

"This is different from before," said Jackson, "I am thinking she is the one, Clark. I was thinking of asking her the big question, to get engaged. What do you think?"

Clark exhaled loudly and said nothing, but was thinking plenty. He thought of Tracey, her quirks, and of the way she demonstrated a devotion to Jackson. But he thought also of his growing feelings towards her, feelings he was trying to suppress, and of the feelings she had shown she had towards him. What exactly were these feelings? Was it any more than physical attraction, any more than lust? Was it okay to find the partner of a friend attractive? It probably was, but probably not okay to have lustful thoughts. And certainly not okay to act on those thoughts. He took some comfort from the fact he had eventually resisted her. He thought of their embrace at the airport, the words exchanged and the unspoken acknowledgement that passed between them, an acknowledgement that they had different directions to go in. His direction was with Ellie. Hers was with Jackson.

Jackson was happy. He seemed to Clark to be asking for his approval. Despite all Clark was sure that Tracey was right for him. Jackson was his friend. He wanted to share in his friend's happiness.

"Yes, go for it," was the extent of what he said.

A waiter from the outdoor bar approached them with lunch menus. They each ordered cheeseburgers, fries and a bottle of whatever beer they had. They would let the barman decide. Clark signed the bill to their room, thinking they might as well run up an account while they were there and give the receipt to Milton when they got home.

After lunch they went to seek out the corporate suite of Abdul Alim of Dubai International Corporations.

The girl in the main lobby, the same girl who had checked him in earlier looked at Clark strangely when he asked where he could find Abdul Alim.

"The corporate offices are in the Tower," she said, "on the top floor. Do you have an appointment?"

"No," said Clark, "I would like to speak with him."

The girl raised a hand to her mouth to hide a laugh. "Well good luck with that," she said still laughing.

Clark did not know what to make of that. He assumed that what she referred to as the Tower was the high building on the other side of the hotel. The building he and Jackson were staying in was the Club Tower, similar in appearance but not as tall.

Clark and Jackson headed to the Tower and rode the elevator to the top floor. Clark told Jackson to hold back and he approached a central reception area where he asked where he could find the offices of Abdul Alim. A man in a smart tailored business suit stood to face him.

"I'm sorry sir, but you cannot go through to the suites if I do not have you registered."

"How do I register?"

"You would need to make an appointment with his executive secretarial staff and they would sanction the registration."

"Okay, let me do that then."

"I'm sorry sir, but I cannot let you through to his executive offices."

Clark sighed. He had met bureaucracy before but this seemed to defy logic. "Look," he said, "I just need to speak with the man. What do I have to do?"

He handed Clark a card with a telephone number on it. "Call this number. Thank you, sir. Have a good day."

Clark took the card and walked back towards the elevator shaking his head at Jackson and waving the card. They went back to the main lobby and ordered coffee, taking a seat on a large sofa.

"Now what?" said Jackson.

"This isn't going to be as easy as we thought. I suppose all we can do is phone and see what happens."

"Oh, I almost forget," Jackson said and produced a small package from his pocket, "I got this for you at the airport. It's an international sim card for your antique phone, all prepaid. So now you can use your phone over here, and we can stay in touch if we need to split up. My phone is already good over here, and I would like to think so the price I pay for my contract."

Clark nodded. He hadn't thought of that. He might need his phone to contact Milton, or Ellie. And he would need some form of communication channel with Jackson. He smiled to himself when he recalled Jackson's sleuthing earlier in the week. He should have known Jackson would have thought it through.

Jackson set Clark's phone up for him and he called the number for Dubai International Corporations. He handed the phone to Clark.

"I would like to arrange to see Abdul Alim," said Clark when a well spoken and softly accented female voice answered his call.

"Certainly sir, and what corporation or embassy do you represent?"

Clark raised his eyebrows to Jackson. "Actually none," he said, "My name is Clark Radcliffe and I would like to speak to Abdul Alim about his business interests in Belfast."

"I'm sorry, I am not aware that his Excellency has business interests in Belfast."

His Excellency. Clark began to think they had underestimated the importance of Abdul Alim. He wondered if Milton knew and if so why had he sent him to Dubai? He wondered if McArdle knew of Alim's position and if that had anything to do with his reluctance, or inability, to pursue his investigation in Dubai. But then again, thought Clark, Alim had spent considerable time in Belfast. He was seen in the Ramada Hotel. He had left a business card in a factory in Mallusk. He could not be that aloof.

Clark thought he might try a degree of truth. "I represent an enquiry into Dubai Wire and Cable's European distribution centre. I would like to speak with him about funding transfers..."

"I'm sorry sir," she said cutting him off, "His Excellency is a busy man. Good day to you," and she hung up.

"We need a plan," said Clark to Jackson.

CHAPTER 31

They deduced that Abdul Alim could not stay in his office all day. Of course they did not know if he would have his own elevator of if he would use the general ones at the corporate lobby. There would take a chance he would use the lobby. They had nothing else to go on so they might as well watch and wait. They waited in the ground floor foyer of the Tower, not wanting to attract the attention of the man in the corporate lobby who had dismissed Clark. They agreed upon a combination of waiting together and splitting into shifts, keeping in touch by phone as required.

In the ground floor foyer was a notice board showing pen pictures of all Directors of the Le Royal Meridien. Abdul Alim's picture was there, at the top and considerably larger than the other pictures. They knew what he looked like, and therefore who to watch out for.

It was nearing seven o'clock. They had been sitting inside waiting for over five hours when one of the elevator doors opened and three black suited men stepped out and took up positions, one looking left, one right, and one straight ahead. Out then came Abdul Alim, fully bedecked in Emerati Kandura and Guthra, a middle aged well built man with a shining groomed moustache. He had striking eyes and flawless complexion, a handsome man some might say. Behind him came more entourage, two men dressed the same as Alim but smaller with a less commanding posture, and two women hidden within full body covering Abayas.

Clark urged Jackson to stay back and he approached Alim alone. The three dark suited henchmen sensed his advance and blocked his progress.

"Abdul Alim," called Clark, "Could I have a word?"

Alim walked on, head down behind the human wall. He ignored Clark's approach.

"Abdul Alim, I need to talk to you about Dubai Wire and Cable's factory in Belfast," Clark called louder this time.

A number of guests stopped and looked towards Clark.

Alim lifted his head and looked over his shoulder. He fixed his eyes on Clark. He kept walking, calling one of the female entourage towards him and pointing towards Clark whispering in her ear. She nodded and looked towards Clark. The three henchmen raised their hands to Clark as Alim slipped through a side door. Clark looked towards Jackson and tilted his head towards the door Alim had exited. The henchmen walked slowly backwards keeping their eyes on Clark. Clark held his hands in surrender and nodded what he hoped would be interpreted as an apology. He too walked backwards for a few steps and then turned and walked out the main front doors to the garden and pool beyond.

The henchmen turned and followed Alim through the side door. Jackson followed them nonchalantly and from a distance. He arrived at the door in time to see three black S Class Mercedes pulling out in convoy of what was a covered car park.

Clark went back into the Tower just as a hotel employee dressed in the cream tunic uniform was crossing the lobby.

"Excuse me, but was that Abdul Alim who just left there," he said to the man and pointed towards the side door.

"Yes sir," the man said bowing his head servilely.

"Is he back tomorrow?"

"That I don't know sir."

"What time is he normally here in the mornings?"

"If he is here he will be here by seven." He bowed his head again and scurried away.

Jackson came back into the lobby. "They're all away in a fleet of Mercedes, including the three goons."

"So much for the plan," said Clark, "I think we need to assume he will be back tomorrow morning and we need to be ready with a better plan."

Jackson nodded and they headed to the Seabreeze Sports Bar on the ground floor of their Club Tower building. They each sipped a draught Fosters lager and after thirty minutes thought they had the makings of a plan, a plan that involved Jackson needing a business suit. He hadn't brought one with him. Clark asked the barman where he might buy a suit and was advised there were a number of shops in the Walk at Jumeirah Beach Residence at the rear of the Hotel, shops that remained open until eleven o'clock each evening.

Clark dispatched Jackson to the Walk while he had another Fosters, a change from his usual bottled Corona but the beer choice was limited, and expensive. He assumed he had to tolerate the pricing and the choice given he was in a country where alcohol was not encouraged or freely available.

Jackson returned thirty minutes later with a navy linen suit by an Italian designer Clark was unfamiliar with but he admired the quality, a white shirt, red tie and black oxford brogues. He said they would sort out the cost when they got home but Jackson said he needed a new suit anyway. Clark ordered a Fosters for Jackson and another for himself, together with two club sandwiches. They clinked glasses and settled into their barstools.

"Have you ever wondered what Milton does for money?" asked Jackson, "I mean he didn't seem to have any problem organising this trip for us?"

Clark read that Jackson still had some doubts whether Milton had indeed profited from the Dubai Wire and Cable project. While Clark had a sense that Milton was honest Jackson had never spoken to him. His opinion was based only on what Clark had told him.

"I don't know," said Clark, "but I suppose if he was able to leave the department with his pension intact he would have an income more than twice average income, and that is without any lump sum or other investments he might have accumulated. He was the Director General remember, the most senior and highest paid official in the department. I think he is okay financially."

That seemed to satisfy Jackson. Clark looked around the bar. There weren't many other guests there although it was still early, just after nine o'clock, most guests would be in one of the hotel's restaurants and might perhaps come through to the bar later. There were two men in a corner table sharing a bottle of wine and in another corner was a young family of four, two young children looking bored as their parents were trying to enjoy cocktails. No doubt they would soon be heading to their room, the children exhausted and the parents wishing they could stay longer in the bar.

"Have you thought anymore about what I said earlier?" asked Jackson, "About Tracey?"

Clark looked and him. He nodded. "Yeah, if you think it's right then why not?"

"Thanks for the vote of confidence," laughed Jackson.

"I have to admit you and Tracey are good together."

"I know, I really look forward to seeing her, even after all this time."

It was Clark's turn to laugh. "All this time? It's been, what, a year? Ellie and I have been together for four years."

"I know but look at you two, separate houses, separate lives, coming together when it suits you," said Jackson teasing Clark.

"It works for us."

"I think I'll ask Tracey the question when we get back."

"Yeah. I am pleased for you Jackson, you are a lucky man. She is a lovely girl, and very attractive I have to say, even though she talks nonstop but you know, I find that quite infectious."

"Steady on Clark," Jackson said laughing, "I think I'll have to keep an eye on you two. She's always talking about you, saying how handsome you are and how it's a shame you have not settled down. You know, you took her those flowers the other day and she hasn't stopped talking about them. I think I need to make sure I don't leave you two alone in a room together."

Clark smiled and looked away.

"Maybe you and Ellie will take the plunge? Maybe even a double wedding?"

Clark managed a look at Jackson and forced a smile. "Maybe."

"I'm only teasing Clark." He held up his glass and they clinked again. "Clark, I would like you to be my Best Man."

Clark nodded and excused himself to the restroom.

They finished their club sandwiches and had another beer before heading to their room. They had an early start the next morning.

They were up at five thirty. It was Saturday morning, and exactly one week after Clark had first met Milton White at the Palm House.

They showered and dressed, Clark in light coloured Hilfiger chinos, white short sleeved Armani shirt and the new Ralph Lauren boating shoes Ellie had bought. No socks. Jackson wore his new suit. He wore it well thought Clark, he looked the part. They headed to the Tower to wait for Abdul Alim.

Clark walked through the side door to the covered car park and found his way to the main car park entrance. He was able to sit on a small wall in the gardens and watch the entrance, but from a position keeping him hidden. Jackson waited in the Tower lobby for Clark to call him.

At six thirty a convoy of three black Mercedes pulled into the car park. Clark watched and followed the cars, keeping a safe distance.

He saw the three henchmen first, one climbing out from each car. Abdul Alim emerged next from the middle car. The remaining four from the entourage then gathered, the two men from the first car and the two women from the last car. They all made their way to the side door.

Clark called Jackson.

"He's on his way, the three goons to the front, the other four followers are behind him. Right… one goon is opening the door… another is approaching the door now, Alim is right behind him. Go, Go."

Jackson walked towards the door as casually as he could. With the door open he stepped out bumping into the goon.

"Oh, sorry," said Jackson.

"I beg your pardon," said the goon.

Jackson nodded and stepped back against the wall to let him pass. Alim came behind him. Jackson was then right beside Alim.

"Your Excellency, Abdul Alim, how are you?" asked Jackson and walked alongside him. The rest of the entourage came through the side door, with Jackson then positioned among them. The door closed securing the group from the car park.

Alim stopped and looked at Jackson, appearing impressed with his professional and purposeful appearance. He nodded. Jackson put out his hand.

"Jackson Morrow, International Banking, Corporate Development." He handed Alim one of his Ulster Bank business cards from his other hand.

Alim accepted his hand and shook. He pulled away and took the card, beginning to read. The entourage had stopped and allowed the exchange to take place, Jackson seemingly unthreatening to them.

"I am pleased to meet you at last," said Jackson, "I have spoken many times with your people about arranging to meet. I am exploring investment opportunities in the Middle East and have a series of meetings in the next couple of days. I was hoping maybe we could meet formally to discuss options?"

Alim read the card and looked at Jackson. He looked again at the card. Perhaps it was when he focused on the Belfast address but his face changed. He looked to one of the male entourage and handed him Jackson's card. He nodded at his bodyguards and started to walk. He did not speak.

"Please step aside sir," said one of goons, the one Jackson had earlier bumped into.

Clark was watching through the small window panel in the door from the car park. Jackson turned towards him and shook his head. The ruse was failing. Clark knew he had to do something, and do it quick. They had come all the way to speak with Alim. They had seen him twice but had yet to have a meaningful conversation. They were going home the next morning. Clark threw open the door.

"Abdul Alim," he shouted. The entourage all stopped and turned. Clark stopped also and raised his hands in front of him and softened his stance. He did not know what authority the bodyguards had. He did not want to find out.

He lowered his voice and said calmly, "My name is Clark Radcliffe. I have been trying to speak with you about Dubai Wire and Cable. I represent the investigation into the Belfast project. The investigation is ongoing. The police have increased their interest in you personally Abdul Alim, and will be actively pursuing you for financial fraud ..."

Clark had more to say but Abdul Alim came towards him, recognising him from the previous night. The entourage watched closely but let him approach.

"Not here," said Alim, softly spoken and cold, "my office in one hour." He turned to one of the female assistants and spoke in her ear. She looked at Clark and nodded. Clark assumed she was acknowledging that she would make it happen, that he would have the clearance he would need to progress beyond the reception on the top floor.

CHAPTER 32

"Not quite the way we planned it," said Clark, "but at least we are getting to meet him."

"I thought I had him for a moment, but maybe I am flattering myself."

"Jackson Morrow, the undercover specialist."

They both laughed.

"I'll let you take the meeting on your own Clark," said Jackson, "You know all the detail and I'd just be sitting like a lemon. I'll keep an eye on things from out in reception and let you know if anything is out of sync."

"Yeah, good idea, let's get a coffee. We can get breakfast later."

One hour later and they were in the Tower elevator on route to the top floor. Jackson had changed out of his suit, exposing his long gangly legs in cream three quarter length cargo jeans, and sporting a red golf tee shirt and sandals. Clark groaned when he seen him returning to the lobby.

The man at the corporate reception desk was the same man from the previous day. He smiled when Clark approached.

"Good morning sir," he said.

"I have an appointment to see Abdul Alim."

"Yes sir. I have been told to expect someone. Please wait."

He turned and whispered into the phone. A moment later the female assistant who had earlier nodded to Clark appeared and led him down a long corridor.

Jackson smiled at the man and took a seat on a large sofa beside the elevators where he could see the full length of the corridor. The man looked Jackson up and down with a look of distain.

Clark was led through a series of outer offices where a number of staff were working, heads down. He saw the two men and the other woman from the entourage, but they did not acknowledge him. There was no sign of the bodyguards. The woman led Clark into a large office, as grand an office as he had seen. There were two large leather sofas, a solid yew conference table with seating for twelve and a commanding central bureau behind which sat Abdul Alim, clothed in his full Emirati regalia.

"You may leave us," Alim said to the woman who nodded and left, walking backwards with her head bowed. He pointed at one of two leather armchairs that were placed in front of the bureau.

Clark nodded and sat.

Alim looked at him and said nothing. He placed his elbows on the bureau and clasped his hands under his chin. Still he said nothing. He kept looking at Clark. After a moment a door to his right opened and a short fat woman with greying hair came into the room and sat on the chair beside Clark. She had squeezed herself into a grey business trouser suit.

Clark looked at her.

"Jennifer Maitland," said Alim.

Clark nodded. She nodded in return.

"Tell me," said Alim, "Who are you?"

"My name is Clark Radcliffe. I'm an independent computer analyst and have been asked by Milton White to look into Dubai

Wire and Cable's failed factory venture in Belfast. I also consult to the police," he said slightly embellishing his role.

"Ah, Milton White, of course. The man who tried to blame the Company, and to blame me, of doing wrong."

He looked at Jennifer. She remained silent, her face hard and cold.

"The man was caught fair and square," continued Alim, "and the last I heard the police were satisfied as to his guilt. I recall speaking with the police at the time and to the best of my recollection they did not see any requirement for further discussion. And now you are here accusing me, threatening me with a police investigation?"

He raised his eyebrows to Clark. Clark made to speak but Alim raised his hand. He hadn't finished, didn't want to be interrupted.

"Mr Radcliffe, you may or may not know who I am. I have been appointed Chief Operating Officer of Dubai International Corporations. This is a very important position. I control companies across the world. I control many investments in Dubai from overseas companies and governments. And I represent the ruling Al Maktoum family's interests in international and domestic commerce, including oil. So you can see I am a busy man, what you might call an important man."

He paused. "So you can see Mr Radcliffe, I cannot afford any negative publicity. I cannot afford to be associated with any police investigation. I will ask what you want from me. I will give you thirty minutes of my time. I will tell you what I know and then I will ask you to go home and tell your police to leave me alone. Am I clear?"

Clark nodded. He read the ensuing silence as his cue. "Milton White maintains he is innocent. He states he was set up. I'm not sure if you know but the case did not go to trial. There was insufficient evidence. The case sat on the shelf and Milton moved away a shamed and broken man.

"I used to work in the Department of Industry and Trade Development and it was me who uncovered evidence of Dubai payments going to Milton's account. He is an ill man and claims he wants to clear his name before, well...

"He asked me to carry out an investigation of computer files from back then claiming he valued my expertise. I must say that investigation has brought me here. I believe there is something to what Milton White claims."

"Continue," said Alim opening his palms to Clark.

"Why did the factory not open in Belfast?"

Alim took a deep breath. "The factory in Belfast was an important opportunity for the Company. Our initial research indicated that the domestic and industrial construction markets within parts of Europe were showing signs of marginal growth, despite a global downturn. The Board saw that as an opportunity to establish a presence in Europe. We tested many potential locations and were particularly impressed with the support offered by your Government. The Board agreed to establish in Belfast. The Board are a very sensitive Board, Mr Radcliffe. They did not take kindly to the negative publicity generated by the incident. News bulletins associated the name of Dubai Wire and Cable with embezzlement. These news bulletins and press reports were spreading around Europe, the Company's potential market place. The Company could not afford that. We tried to suppress the negative reports as much as possible through our public relations. I believe we were successful in this.

"However the worsening condition of the global economy at the time, and in particular a reverse of the forecasted growth of construction within Europe did not help. The Board decided to halt all expansion plans and refocus on growing existing markets. There was nothing sinister, Mr Radcliffe."

"But you received grants, did you not have to repay them?"

"No, Mr Radcliffe, we did not receive grants remember. Someone else got them. Yes, we were provided with an advance factory and some assistance with start up costs but we had to arrange and lease our own machinery. The grants were to assist with that. We did not receive the grants."

He leaned forward. "To be honest we just wanted out and the Board agreed to cease all communications and to meet any contractual penalty clauses. As I recall there were not any. Over time there appeared to be a mutual understanding that the project had run its course and both parties drew a line."

Clark nodded. "But you were seen in Belfast after the factory was due to open?"

"Yes, at the time I was a Board member. It was my role then to deliver the message that we would no longer be pursuing our European expansion plans in Belfast. As I recall my last visit was a brief one to a hotel."

He looked to Jennifer and she nodded.

"Who did you meet in the hotel?"

It was Jennifer who spoke for the first time, a well spoken English accent with a European slant, the accent of someone who had spent many years travelling. "It was Delores O'Reilly. The meeting comprised His Excellency, Anthony Tobias, myself and Delores."

Clark looked at her. "What came of Delores?"

"That I cannot say. You would need to speak with Anthony Tobias."

"And where is he?"

"No longer in our employ," she said, "I can arrange for you to meet with him if such a meeting will assist in completing your investigation? Tie up any loose ends?"

She raised her eyebrows towards Clark.

He nodded. "Thank you. I leave first thing tomorrow."

She nodded in reply. "Leave your contact details with the staff."

Clark turned to Alim. "I found your business card in the factory."

It was Alim's turn to nod. "That would be so. I was an onsite representative of the Board, remember."

"You verified the machinery on site?"

"That I did."

"And then what?"

"I don't understand what you ask? I verified the machinery on behalf of my Board. Someone else verified the machinery for the grant."

Jennifer added, "The Company only received clearance for a first instalment grant. Other instalments would have been due once production started. But of course, as you know, the company didn't actually receive any of the grant money."

"Milton White disagrees," said Clark.

"And well he might," said Alim. "As I recall he was a very competent man, a clever negotiator. Why would he not try and spin suspicion elsewhere? What exactly did he tell you he thought I was guilty of?"

"That the Company got burned in the deal and wanted to recoup costs in a way that would not result in claw back of grants."

Alim laughed. "Mr Radcliffe, I can assure that while the expansion project in Belfast failed and a cost was incurred, it was a negligible amount of money. Perhaps you might want to check later the net worth of Dubai International Investments, the parent company of Dubai Wire and Cable. You will see the cost to the company of the Belfast project would be only a minuscule number in the research and development budget alone, never mind the overall company budget. Forgive me but that scenario is preposterous, and I don't mean to sound patronising by demeaning the value of the monies offered by your Government.

"You might well ask if our net worth was so great why we were attracted by financial incentives. My only answer to that is that it was business. We considered a number of packages and offers from around Europe and the Belfast package was favoured."

Alim paused and thought for a moment. "And how does Milton White think we would have achieved what he claims? All administration for the project was carried out by his teams. It was his legal team and his IT team that were involved from the start to the finish. Our role was only to sign documents. We put full trust in the integrity of the systems his department put in place."

Jennifer nodded in agreement.

The man painted a good picture, Clark thought, but then again he had thought the same thing when Milton had told him his view of how Alim and Dubai Wire and Cable were involved. He was hearing yet another account of Milton White's intelligence and shrewdness. Despite all his attempts and desires to believe in Milton's innocence there was always a finger pointing in his direction. Maybe he needed to consider the evidence against Milton with the same vigour and belief that he considered the counter evidence presented by him.

"Did you negotiate with anyone other than Milton and Delores?" asked Clark, in a way just to test them.

Jennifer answered. "There was another woman representing the department. Fiona Mitchell was her name. Towards the end of the negotiations two other men joined us. They were from the finance side of the department and took us through the detail. I believe their names were Terry Davidson and Charlie Cappelli."

Clark thought she had a very good memory or more likely had spent the last hour reading her files to prepare for the meeting. This appeared to be her role, to provide the detail.

"Where did the meetings take place?" he asked.

"Predominantly in Milton White's office. There were some preliminary meetings in the early days at various hotels and restaurants," said Jennifer.

"Did you meet socially as a group outside of these meetings?"

"No."

"Did you meet socially with any individual members of the department's negotiating team on a regular basis?"

"No."

"But you have already said you met with Delores at the hotel in Belfast," said Clark, proud he had directed the questioning to where he thought he had tripped them.

"That was the only time," said Jennifer, "As I understand Milton

White had left the department by that stage and Fiona Mitchell was engaged on personal business. Delores was empowered to represent the department in closing the project."

"And what happened to the machinery?"

"The machinery was on lease. Yes, it was designed especially for us but it was then leased. The supplier was to provide all maintenance to what were very specialist and complicated machines. The missing grant was in fact a refund of the first lease payment."

"So the supplier would have reclaimed the machinery?"

"I imagine so. That would have been arranged by the department as part of project closure."

Clark nodded. That was something Delores was possibly covering at the meeting in the Ramada. He could check with Fiona Mitchell.

Clark was spent. Alim and Jennifer made a robust account of themselves and the Company and Clark was finding it difficult to find anything worthy of challenge. He looked from Jennifer to Alim.

"Will that be all Mr Radcliffe?" said Alim.

Clark nodded.

"Jennifer will show you out to my executive team. They will arrange for you to meet with Anthony Tobias. I take it that you and I are finished."

It was a statement, not a question. Alim did not rise or offer any handshake. Clark got up from his chair and followed Jennifer to the outside offices.

CHAPTER 33

Clark and Jackson ate breakfast in the Brasserie in the main lobby. Clark recounted the conversation with Alim and Jennifer and that he found it difficult not to believe them. He said he had clearly misunderstood the scale of the Dubai operation and was drawn to their version that the grant monies under investigation were virtually irrelevant to them. Clark said he was finding it difficult to picture a scenario where Dubai Wire and Cable would have manipulated the grant system to the extent they would have had to. He told Jackson they were on standby to meet later with Anthony Tobias and that they might get some answers on what happened to Delores O'Reilly.

In the meantime there was little for them to do.

They decided to take some time on the sun loungers by the pool, where they could watch the comings and goings over the bridge. After an hour of quiet reflection and uneventful people watching Jackson turned to Clark.

"Have you spoken with Ellie yet?" he said.

"No, not yet," Clark said. He had forgotten. He quickly drafted a text in full English sentences asking how she was, and how things were with her mum. He said nothing about himself other than he was busy and warm. He hit the send button not knowing if the message would even be received.

"There's no point in me calling Tracey yet," said Jackson, "it isn't even time to get up back home."

Clark nodded. He hadn't thought of that. Ellie would have a text waiting for her when she awoke.

"I'll call her later," said Jackson, "I'm sure she'll have plenty to tell me."

They both laughed.

"You know Clark, a lot of people think she's just an empty airhead full of nonsense conversation but she's a smart one. I know she talks plenty but she takes a great interest in me, and in my job. I enjoy her questioning me, and challenging me. You would not believe how much she knows about banking, about politics, current affairs, everything really. She watches all the politic programmes on television and would you believe even reads The Times a couple of days a week.

"She says she has a lot of well connected clients and likes to engage them in meaningful conversation, not just the usual holiday and soap opera chat, although she can do that as well."

They both laughed again.

"She even has clients from your old department. She says some of them know Rob and Ed. She can tell me what's going down in the world of local industry and trade even before it's on the news. Those women sure know how to gossip."

Clark wasn't sure why Jackson was telling him this. He assumed he wanted him to know more about why he had fallen for her, that there was more to her than met the eye. Clark however did not need to be convinced.

He then remembered he had something to ask Jackson, but needed to find a way of asking it.

"How's work these days," he asked, "getting much overtime?"

"Quite a bit, I'm very busy at the moment."

"And weekends?"

"Yeah, the last few weekends have been busy."

Clark didn't respond. He looked at Jackson. Jackson looked back at him, shifting slightly on his lounger, beads of sweat forming on his brow.

"I suppose I might as well be honest with you Clark. I haven't been able to tell Tracey this yet but I will. I will need to be honest with her, especially if I am going to ask the big question."

Clark nodded.

"You know Yvonne in my team?"

Clark nodded again but had no idea who Yvonne was. Perhaps he had met her before, perhaps Jackson had spoke of her in the past. He couldn't remember.

"She has been having some trouble at home and has sort of been confiding in me. I've been giving her an ear to listen. Things seem to be getting better for her. I have wanted to tell Tracey but I didn't know how she would feel. She doesn't know Yvonne. I didn't want her to get the wrong end of the stick. I suppose with hindsight I should have introduced them but I didn't. Maybe Tracey might have been able to help. In truth Clark I feel a bit ashamed."

Clark nodded yet again. He wasn't the only one feeling ashamed then, although he thought Jackson's shame paled into insignificance compared to his. He should have known that whatever Jackson was up to it would have been for the betterment of others. Jackson's role in life was to be helpful, loyal and trusting. Clark recalled that in the last week he had questioned Jackson's friendship and loyalty. That added to the shame.

"Go ahead and tell Tracey," he said, "I'm sure she will be good about it."

It was Jackson's turn to nod.

Clark felt his phone vibrate in his pocket. It was a text, an anonymous text simply saying "Al Mahara, Burj Al Arab, 8.00pm."

"Looks like we're going to the Burj tonight," he said to Jackson, "to meet with Anthony Tobias."

"Whoa," said Jackson, "the Burj? That's supposed to have some of the world's best restaurants. And it's supposed to be expensive."

Clark laughed. "We have two choices then. Either have a sandwich here before we go or invoice Milton."

Jackson laughed too. "A sandwich it is then. We wouldn't want to exploit Milton now would we?"

Jackson wanted to walk along the beach to take in the sights. As tempted as he was, knowing what sort of sights Jackson wanted to take in, Clark declined saying he wanted to rest. He positioned the parasol and lay on the lounger, closing his eyes and listened to the sounds around him, the piercing shrill of exotic birds as they hovered overhead, the sound of families splashing in the pool, the drone of adult conversation and laughter, and the sound of busy hotel waiting staff scurrying around the patrons taking orders and offering complimentary water sprays. The heat was taking his breath away, but he loved it. This was a heaven. 'Yes,' he thought, 'Maybe I will come back. Maybe I will bring Ellie.' His mind drifted to the conversation he'd had with Alim and Jennifer. He began to reflect on what he had heard. He drifted into a deep sleep.

It was mid afternoon when Jackson woke him. They had a poolside meal of grilled chicken and fries washed down with a draught Fosters. Jackson told him he had spoken with Tracey and she sent her best wishes. He didn't say if he had told her about Yvonne.

Clark remembered he had sent Ellie a text. He checked his phone and found a reply waiting for him. It was a short text, 'Take care. Miss you.' Clark smiled to himself and agreed. He missed her. It had only been a couple of days but it seemed longer. He was what seemed like a million miles away in a place of luxury and yes; he would like to have her there with him.

An afternoon of lounging and it was time to taxi to the Burj. Clark was impressed with Jackson's choice of evening attire, a light blue

Gucci casual shirt, navy linen trousers, and leather boating shoes similar to his own. Clark wore the Ralph Lauren linen trousers and shoes that Ellie had bought him, together with a finely striped red Hilfiger short sleeved shirt.

They did not have to wait long for the taxi, and it did not take long for the Burj Al Arab to appear in front of them. An impressive building it certainly was, it's iconic sail shaped structure sitting proudly on its own island, the Arabian Gulf as its backdrop. It looked as Clark had imagined, fully justifying its status as one of the world's most luxurious hotels.

The taxi stopped at a traffic barrier beside a white security hut. The Burj was straight ahead but access to it was strictly controlled. Swarms of tourists were snapping photographs, wishing that could get inside to experience the dream.

A burly guard in a cream uniform with a Burj Al Arab emblem leaned into the car and Clark gave his name. The man checked a list on his clipboard and nodded. He raised the barrier and the taxi drove in. Alim's people were true to their word. The Burj was expecting him.

But Clark was not expecting to see what greeted him in the atrium of the Burj. The opulence was overwhelming. The walls for as high as he could see were plated with gold, balconies and walkways from its many floors overhanging and overlooking the grand entrance. Jackson too stared in awe.

"Whoa," said Jackson not able to think of anything fitting to say.

Clark nodded. He saw a floor plan for the hotel and walked towards it, establishing that the Al Mahara restaurant was below the ground floor.

"Like before," said Jackson, "you go and do the talking. I'll keep an eye from the outside."

They went down an escalator and were met by a small framed hostess in oriental dress who checked Clark's name on a reservation schedule. He was again expected. They were led, somewhat unbelievably, to a submarine simulator and transported to the restaurant. Jackson held back and Clark was handed over to a man at a reservations desk and again his name was checked. Clark stared at the enormous fish tanks that the restaurant was set out around, fish tanks filled with rays, tiger sharks and reef sharks. Indeed no ordinary fish tanks, Clark thought, more of an undersea adventure. He marvelled at the clientele enjoying the restaurant, exorbitantly dressed westerners and what looked like local men of distinction, Sheikhs perhaps, some sharing their table with numerous women.

"Follow me sir," said the man and led Clark around the wall of aquariums towards a table set for three. The table faced the aquarium allowing the diners to enjoy their seafood platters with sharks watching from only inches away.

Facing Clark was a bald man, with a comb over. He wore a tailored grey suit and was well groomed and presented, despite the comb over. He stood to receive Clark. In front of him was a woman, her back to Clark.

"Clark Radcliffe I presume?" said the man extending his hand, "Anthony Tobias." He had a distinctive clear English accent, not unlike Jennifer Maitland's.

Clark shook the man's hand.

"This is my wife."

The woman turned towards Clark and smiled. She too extended her hand but did not rise. "Hello, pleased to meet you," she said in a familiar accent, an accent that transported Clark back home. Her face was familiar too.

"This is Delores," said Anthony needlessly adding, "Delores Tobias."

Clark nodded. She was a plain woman carrying a few too many pounds, simply dressed in a nondescript full length skirt and white blouse.

Her expression changed slightly. "Do I know you?" she asked, "Have we met before?"

"I don't know so much if we have met before," said Clark, "but we used to work in the same building, in Adelaide House. I used to be with the department of Industry and Trade Development."

She looked to Anthony who raised his hand reassuringly.

"Please sit," he said to Clark, "Would you like to order?"

Clark sat and said he had already eaten, even though he hadn't. He didn't want to be there any longer than he had to be. He accepted a glass of wine.

"Anthony told me someone wanted to speak with him about the Dubai Wire and Cable factory in Belfast," said Delores, "he didn't tell me it was someone from Belfast. Where are you working now?"

"I'm freelance," said Clark, "I've been asked by Milton White to do some investigating to clear his name."

"Ah," she said, "there's a name I haven't heard for a while. How is he?"

Clark gave her and Anthony a summary of Milton's story. Another piece of the jigsaw was falling into place. He now knew where Delores had disappeared to, and who with, and why Delores was having so many informal meetings with the Dubai team, meetings that were not in fact with the team at all but with Anthony. She had used the negotiations as cover to meet regularly with him, at restaurants and at hotels. He felt for Thomas O'Reilly.

Delores looked to Anthony. "So what can I do for you Mr Radcliffe?" he asked.

Clark decided to get straight to the point. "My findings indicate some form of attempt to cover up whatever it was that went on. Key documents were removed from the department's servers. I am trying to understand by who and why?"

He looked to Delores. She dropped her head. "Some of the evidence indicates that you Delores removed some information?"

She abruptly lifted her head and glared at him. "What? That's ridiculous. Why would I do that?"

"I have found evidence of a diary entry being removed?"

"Well, of course I would have deleted diary entries from time to time, when events were rescheduled for example."

"Would that not have been a job for your secretary?"

"Yes, I suppose you're right, but as I say from time to time I would have removed them myself."

"If they were of a personal nature, for example?" said Clark.

She looked to Anthony and then back to Clark, her eyes narrowing. "What exactly do you know?" she said.

"Did you remove a diary entry relating to a meeting with Abdul Alim at Le Meridien Hotel on the fourth of September?"

"I don't know... I suppose I might..."

"And yet my findings indicate that there were no meetings held outside of Belfast?"

She looked to Anthony again and then to the ground. "You're right. I came to Dubai on one or two occasions, but not to see Alim. I probably just put his name in as a cover. I came to see Anthony. He paid. It was all above board but I didn't want anyone to know. I was married. I was involved in an important set of negotiations. Many jobs were to be created. I didn't want to compromise my job, or the project."

She didn't mention compromising her husband.

She reached across the table and held out her hand, which Anthony cupped in his. He nodded gently to her.

"I clearly made a mistake putting one of the visits into my diary. It was something I would have done instinctively, probably after making the arrangements with Anthony on the phone. I wouldn't have wanted my secretary to organise other meetings when I was due to be away. I know I should just have recorded it as a general meeting, but as I say it was instinctive. I suppose you could say I was excited." She smiled at Anthony and he smiled back, caressing her hand in his. "It was a long time ago to remember exactly, but I suppose at some point I realised it was in my diary and I deleted it. I suppose I wouldn't have thought it would show up in files relating to the project."

"Probably some form of cross referencing arrangement. I imagine the diaries of senior staff would have been backed up and stored on a number of files and servers to allow colleagues and support staff to access them for any number of reasons," said Clark realising he was defending her.

He believed her. There was something about the way she looked at Anthony, the way he looked at her, something magical. He thought for a moment about himself and thought if he had, or could have, that something magical.

He thought for a moment of Thomas O'Reilly and the pain he had suffered.

"I spoke with your ex-husband," he said.

Delores's face stiffened, the colour draining. Anthony's grip tightened on her hand.

Anthony said, "Radcliffe, I don't think …"

"It's okay love," she said to him and turned to Clark. "How is he?"

"Now he is happy and remarried. I think he took it bad though."

She smiled. "I'm glad he is now happy. I didn't mean this to happen. It was just, you know, one of those things."

Clark nodded. One of those things he thought. Tracey came to his mind. And Siobhan.

Anthony sighed. "Are you a relationship counsellor Mr Radcliffe, or can I help you with something?"

Clark paused and looked to him. "I have reason to believe that Dubai Wire and Cable in some way manipulated the grant scheme to avoid repaying grants when they withdrew from the project."

Anthony laughed. Delores shook her head and looked at Clark.

"That's preposterous," he said, the same words Alim had used. "Why play with pennies when you have bullions of gold?"

An interesting way of putting it thought Clark. "To save face?"

"Preposterous," said Anthony again, "Listen I have no axe to grind with the Company, nor do I need to defend them. I am no longer working there remember. I resigned when Delores came to Dubai to be with me. It just seemed the right thing to do. I was not without job offers. I am currently a Board member with a chemicals corporation. Delores is on my executive staff."

He looked to her and they shared a smile. "Besides," he said, "How do you think the Company could have made it happen? As I recall it was the department in Belfast who did all the setting up, all the processing, all the verification."

Delores nodded.

"Who was the Client Executive at the department, the person who would have taken responsibility for the project after start up? I understand they reported to you Delores?" said Clark to her.

"That's not really relevant Mr Radcliffe. The project didn't get to the stage where a Client Executive had a substantive role. I did allocate it to Melanie Jones but apart from attending a couple of meet and greets she had little involvement."

"And it was you who formally closed the project?"

"Yes."

"At the Ramada Hotel?"

She glared at Clark, recollections of that night and of the following day no doubt coming back. "Yes that's right," she snapped, "at the Ramada Hotel. Now, is there anything else?"

"One last question," said Clark to both Delores and Anthony, "What did you think of Milton White?"

Delores thought for a moment and spoke first, "He was a conscientious man and a very private man. I worked closely with him but did not really know him. He was clever, some would say devious, mischievous, or manipulative. When I first took up my post working to him I was warned to watch out for him, to be careful, to watch my back, to protect myself from him. He always had the ability to smell of roses no matter what was thrown at him."

"I can concur with some of that," said Anthony, "in my

experience he was certainly a very smart man, always anticipating future problems and having contingency plans in place."

"Thank you for your time," said Clark and rose offering his hand to Anthony and to Delores, "Enjoy your meal."

They shook and Clark left the restaurant, his head again spinning as he began to add what he had just heard to what he already knew.

Jackson was waiting for him at the entrance to the restaurant. Clark nodded to him and they went straight to the front of the Burj where a fleet of executive taxis were waiting. They went back to the Seabreeze Sports Bar in Le Royal Meriden. Clark did not speak. He had much on his mind.

CHAPTER 34

Clark and Jackson had a quiet meal of grilled steak and vegetables in the Seabreeze. There was little conversation. Jackson had waited outside the Al Mahara restaurant but had seen nothing suspicious. They both noted that the intimidating presence of a shaven headed man did not seem to transcend to Dubai. That was something else for Clark to ponder. He supposed he and Jackson should talk through his thinking. That was after all one of the reasons he had confided in Jackson in the first place, and had brought him along to Dubai. But no, for the moment he preferred to keep his developing thoughts to himself.

They had to leave at six thirty the following morning and would have a full day of travel ahead of them. They had packing to do. As conversation was nonexistent they decided to head to their room to prepare for home and to catch up on some sleep.

Sleep did not come easy for Clark. Everything he had learned was running around inside him. He developed scenarios. He developed counter scenarios. He finally drifted to sleep in the early hours, Jackson's snores acting as a soothing metronome.

The breakfast Brasserie had just opened when they arrived at the lobby to organise a taxi to the airport. They grabbed a quick serving of croissants and cheese and checked out at reception. Clark paid the room account on his credit card and pocketed the receipt for Milton. The receptionist handed Clark an envelope, embossed with the crest of the Le Royal Meridien. Inside was a hand written note on Dubai International Corporations headed paper. The note thanked Clark for his time and wished him a safe journey home. The note was signed by Abdul Alim. Clark put the note in his pocket not sure what it meant. Perhaps it was a genuine message of good wishes, he thought, or perhaps its hidden context was thanks for coming, now don't come back.

The journey to the airport was uneventful. Clark was still not in the frame of mind for conversation. Jackson sensed this and purchased a James Patterson novel at the airport, something for him to bury his head in, to while away the hours on the journey home, and to leave Clark alone to his thoughts. Jackson knew Clark long enough to know he would hide within himself when he had something to work through. This was one of his great strengths thought Jackson, the ability to think through scenario after scenario to eventually arrive at a reasoned outcome. Jackson knew that was why he was so successful in the IT field. He would not give up. He would not be beaten.

By ten o'clock they were seated on the plane, similar seats to before, at the back in a window row of only two seats. Jackson sat at the window and continued working through his book. Clark closed his eyes and once more thought through all he had learned. He thought back to when it had all started, not just five years ago, but more specifically over the last week. Much had happened in the last week. He thought back to everywhere he had been, everyone he had met, all the conversations he'd had, all the information he had gathered. He thought through all the different versions of the story he had heard. He thought of the speculation and of the facts. A final picture was forming in his mind, a picture he felt answered many of the questions, but it was a picture he did not like. He could not share this picture with anyone, at least not yet. There were a couple of people he needed to speak to, a couple of things he need to check. He wished he was at home.

He glanced at Jackson and wondered how he could avoid him for the rest of the journey.

Clark slept the majority of the flight. When he awoke he feigned sleep. They arrived at London's Gatwick airport at two o'clock local time and caught the shuttle bus to London's Heathrow airport for the connection to Belfast. They had four hours to wait. Jackson read, took a walk, checked some texts and emails and made a number of calls, lengthy calls, presumably to Tracey. Clark noted there was much listening involved.

He walked around the terminal trying to keep his mind focused on what he had to do. He heard his phone ring. It was Ellie.

"Hello," she said, "Where are you?"

"At Gatwick, the flight to Belfast is at half past seven. I should be home by half past nine."

"Good. Do you want me to collect you?"

"No, Jackson and I will get a taxi."

"Okay, so I'll call round later?"

"No, it's okay. I'm shattered. I wouldn't be much company."

"Is everything all right?"

"Yes, fine. I'm just tired."

"Oh, okay then, whatever you want. I'm heading back home to my apartment this evening. I've to be at the office tomorrow morning."

"Okay, be careful."

"I'll be fine. Hazel will watch out for me."

"Okay. I'll talk to you tomorrow."

"Okay. Bye," she said.

Clark put his phone back in his pocket. He didn't want to have to speak with anyone when he got home. He had to prepare for the next day. He had to retrieve the hard drive, he had an appointment with Milton, and he people to see.

Clark and Jackson shared a taxi from Belfast City Airport. They were both exhausted, the time readjustment to their watches and body clocks not helping. They were cold too, from a dramatic change in temperature and from an absence of overcoats.

The taxi headed to Stranmillis first to leave off Jackson. Clark got out of the car with Jackson at his house. They shook hands and Clark thanked him for all he had done. He said he would be in touch the next day. He watched Jackson walk up his driveway. The door opened and there was Tracey, ready for bed in a pair of high cut loose fitting shorts and a tight vest top. She greeted Jackson and let him pass her into the house. She turned towards Clark and leant back against the door frame, cocking her leg at the knee and placing the sole of her foot on the frame. She smiled broadly and waved.

Clark got back into the taxi.

There was little he could do that night. He checked the house and went to bed. He had an early start the next day.

Seven thirty the next morning, Monday morning, and Clark was in his car heading for Strangford Lough. He pulled into his parent's driveway shortly before eight thirty. He parked beside the Land Rover Discovery and walked to the front door.

His mum was waiting for him, having heard the car arriving.

"So you're back?" she said.

"Yes Mum, how is he?"

She looked at him, her expression still cold but perhaps slightly warmer than his last visit he thought. "He's still in the hospital. He'll hopefully get home in the next couple of days."

"And how are you?"

She smiled. He had remembered to ask. "I'm tired, but holding up. It will be good to get him home and take all the strain off the running every day to the hospital."

Clark smiled too.

"Would you like a cup of tea?" she asked.

Clark looked at his watch. "No thanks."

His mother sighed.

"But, do you have any coffee?"

She laughed and led him into the kitchen.

"I'll just head to the bathroom," he said and walked the length of the corridor to his old bedroom. He opened the drawer in his old desk and lifted the hard drive, placing it in his coat pocket.

He turned around and was met with a figure standing in the doorway, arms folded and with a face unable to hide its scorn. It was a younger version of his mother.

"Hello Amy," he said.

She did not answer. She looked good Clark thought, despite the scorn. Her hair had been coloured and was well cut. Her eyebrows were shaped and she wore minimal makeup. She didn't need it. She was as pretty as she had been as a child. She was tall, just like him. She was in good shape and wore her tailored clothes well. She was a successful woman, a wealthy woman and she looked it. She had invested her share of her Uncle Charlie's inheritance in a deposit on a small property in London, a property that made her much more money when she sold it. She'd bought other properties and made more money, no doubt Spencer's advice had helped. But she was also a successful Chartered Accountant working in the City of London. He was proud of her, but it had been years since he had seen her.

"You look good," he said.

She stood upright and stared at him. After a moment she relaxed and leaned against the door frame, her arms still folded. "Why are you here Clark?"

His eyes narrowed.

"Are you here to see Mum or to collect something you left here? Mum told me you were here last week and came down to your old room. Were you hiding something?"

Clark shrugged. "Amy, I came to see Mum and just left something here for a few days…"

"So your priority in coming was to leave something and not to visit Mum?"

"Amy…"

"Forget it Clark. I'm away back to my room. Tell Mum I'll see her when you go."

She turned and walked away. She called over her shoulder, "Dad has been asking for you."

Clark looked at his watch. He screwed his face as tight as he could. She was right. He had used his parent's house as a safe place to hide the hard drive. But he had also wanted to see his mum and dad. He had thought his dad might be home. Amy had hit a nerve. He would have to make amends, but just not then. He didn't have time.

He had a meeting to go to.

And there was something on the hard drive he needed to check.

He drank his coffee staring out the window over the fields. His mother was busy preparing tray bakes. She did not speak, but she looked happy, perhaps as she had both her children together again in her house.

Clark thanked his mother and said he would be back soon. He reversed out of the driveway and sped towards Belfast's city centre for his meeting with Milton White at Café Nero in Victoria Square.

CHAPTER 35

He parked in the underground car park and made his way up the escalator to the House of Fraser.

Milton was waiting for him, coffees ready. "How did it go?" he said as Clark sat down.

"Good," said Clark.

Clark did not want to say much, if anything, to Milton but he felt obligated to keep the meeting if for no other reason as a courtesy to him for having arranged the trip.

"Did you meet with Alim?"

"I did."

"And were my suspicions confirmed?"

"Milton, I had a very interesting trip. I met with everyone I think I should have met with but I now have more information to consider and to check. I am working through it. Until I do I would rather not say anymore."

Milton nodded and rubbed his chin. "It sounds intriguing. Need I be worried?"

Clark pushed his chair back. "I really need to be going, I'll be in touch," he said holding up his mobile phone and waving it at Milton.

Clark left the coffee house and glanced over his shoulder to see Milton White sitting alone, a look of worry on his face.

He walked through the House of Fraser towards the rear doors, doors that would lead to the elevators and the car park. He saw something out of the corner of his eye and stopped. Turned with their backs to him and perusing a rail of shirts were two beautiful young women, one brunette and one blonde, both with their long hair in pony tails, both in business suits with tight skirts to their knees, both with bare shapely legs and both with red soled Christian Louboutins shoes.

Clark stepped behind a tall shelving unit displaying Ralph Lauren Polo pullovers and shirts. The two young women came towards him but stopped at the other side of the unit. They could not see him.

"I think he might like this one," he heard Siobhan say.

"I'm not sure," he heard the blonde one say in a husky voice, a voice that he recognised, a voice that he had heard many times in the last week.

Clark made his way out of the store as quickly and as discreetly as possible.

He hurried to the underground car park. His head was spinning more and more.

He had to get home and check the hard drive.

At Ethel Street he hung his coat and removed the drive from its pocket, his head pumping. He ran up the stairs to his study, powered up the computer and the drive and scanned again through the folders and files.

And then he found what he was looking for.

He stared at it. He put his head in his hands and continued to stare at it. He closed his eyes, opened them and stared at it again. He rubbed his eyes. He looked yet again. Butterflies fluttered in his stomach like never before. He breathed deeply. He didn't want to believe it. But there it was; there was no denying it, no running away.

He printed the documents on his inkjet printer.

There was more to do.

There were things people had said over the last week that were resonating with him. There were things he needed to check.

He made two phone calls.

The day disappeared. He had spoken with who he had to speak to. He had checked what he needed to check.

And then it was time, time to go and see someone. He was not looking forward to it. But he had to do it. It was time for the truth.

It was dark outside. He made his way to where he had to go. He checked his watch. He took a deep breath and knocked on the front door. The door opened slowly and there she was, looking as beautiful as ever. She was surprised but pleased to see him.

"Oh, Hi Clark," she said, "This is a nice surprise. Come in."

Clark nodded and brushed past her, saying nothing. He stood in the corner of the room beside the sofa.

"Would you like something to drink?" she said.

He shook his head and checked his watch again.

CHAPTER 36

"You still haven't told me about your trip," said Ellie.

The door knocked. Clark moved towards the knock and opened the door wide. In came DI McArdle. He nodded at Clark. Behind him came Rob. Rob was handcuffed to DC Campbell.

"Clark, what's going on?" said Ellie.

Clark did not answer. He stood with his back to the door with arms folded and stared ahead.

"Please take a seat," said McArdle.

Ellie looked at Rob. Rob looked at Ellie. Something passed between them, a look of realisation perhaps.

Ellie sat on the sofa. DC Campbell led Rob to the sofa and removed the cuffs. Rob sat beside Ellie. He stared at the ground. He did not look at Clark.

Ellie's eyes misted. She tried hard but lost the battle. The tears came. Clark's body moved forward and he instinctively put his hand in his trouser pocket for his handkerchief. Then he stopped himself. Rob continued to stare at the floor. No one spoke.

Ellie was first to break the silence. She looked at Rob and said,

"Don't say anything Rob."

Rob shook his head. "I want to tell the truth Ellie."

"Rob, I am a lawyer. Please say nothing."

"It's too late Ellie," he said continuing to stare at the floor, "I have already made a statement."

Ellie dropped her head and sobbed. "I'm so sorry Clark," she struggled to say through the tears, "I made a mistake. It was a long time ago. I …"

Rob cut her off. He was still staring at the floor. "No Ellie, It was all my fault. I shouldn't have done it. I shouldn't have involved you."

Ellie looked at Rob. "You couldn't have done it without me."

Rob could not lift his head and face anyone.

Clark remained still. He was hurting. And he was confused. He had led McArdle to Ellie's house, to her and to Rob. But he was not feeling any comfort. These were his friends. One a long standing friend with whom he had shared many nights out, had attended his wedding, had gotten to know his wife. The other was his partner, his lover. Perhaps even his girlfriend.

McArdle took over. "Right, let's hear the whole story," he said, taking a seat opposite the sofa. DC Campbell stood, leaning against the wall by the kitchen.

Clark too remained standing. He reflected on what had led him to Ellie and to Rob. It was something that Rob had said. He had said that it was a perk of being a computer security specialist that he had access to all department servers. He'd thought of what Alim, Jennifer and Anthony had said, that all the administration for the project was carried out within the department. He had checked with Ed. Ed confirmed that Rob's access gave him full input and overwriting rights. Ed confirmed that Rob was the only one with this access and that he could easily log on as another user and carry out tasks as that user. Rob's boss took little to do with checking his security audits or following up on any unauthorised access flags. Rob had exploited this complacency.

Alim, Jennifer and Anthony had stated that it was not only the finance administration that was carried out by the department but also the legal administration. This led Clark to something else. The Letters of Offer and Acceptance were legal documents. He had initially just glossed over the legal jargon on the last page of the documents, where there were the Company Seals and the signatures. He hadn't really taken any notice of the Seals, or of the signatures. But nevertheless something was niggling at him. He had checked the Letters again and that was when he'd seen it. There were three Seals on the documents, one from the department, one from Dubai Wire and Cable and one from the department's legal advisers. The department's Solicitor's Office had subcontracted its corporate assessment function to a specialist firm. The firm was Geddis, Kenny and Marshall. The Seal was signed on behalf of the firm by a sprawling signature, barely legible, but one that Clark recognised. It was signed by an Eleanor McAvoy, Ellie.

Rob began to speak, keeping his eyes on the floor. "I can't explain why," he said, "it just seemed to happen. The opportunity was there and I suppose I seen it as a challenge. Was it possible? Could I do it? Could I get away with it?"

He looked at Ellie. She looked back, a vacant look on her face.

"I met Ellie at a Government contractor conference. I was manning an exhibition stand and we got talking. She said she was currently contracting providing corporate legal services and was asking what sort of IT services might be contracted out. I guess she was there to represent all aspects of her firm, to see if there were any other opportunities for them. I was interested in her corporate legal work and we talked some about the Dubai thing. It was a big deal at the time. The whole department was excited by it. She told me she had been appointed to represent the department's legal interests. I genuinely found this interesting and asked her if she wanted to meet for lunch. It was just lunch, just a business meeting. It was nothing more. For her it was networking, establishing a new contact."

He looked for the first time to Clark, as if reassuring him that his relationship with Ellie was purely professional.

Clark continued to stare straight ahead.

Rob continued, "The conversation got onto the significance of each of our roles on the Dubai project, that I could access and theoretically control all IT actions and that she could sanction, and therefore control, the legal actions. It started as a bit of a game, a bit of talking through what we could do if we wanted. As I said, I can't explain why. It was just like a challenge. We exchanged business cards and that was that. As time went on however I kept thinking about it. I kept thinking about what I could do, what I could get away with. I had developed a plan in my head and had run over it many times. I became obsessed by it. I had to test it. It was never about the money. It was about me testing my theory, testing my system. I called Ellie and we met again. All strictly professional of course, a business lunch that she paid for, no doubt with receipts submitted."

He looked again to Clark, who still did not respond.

"She bought into it. I sold it as a system test, and not about the money. But to be honest, with hindsight, I think it was the money that attracted Ellie."

He looked at her and she turned away, tears streaming down her face.

"And that was that. I set Milton White up as the scapegoat. I had access to all the information on the servers. I was able to follow everything that was going on. I had access to all the senior staff electronic diaries. I knew he was going to the Council Of Ministers meeting on the Isle of Man and I knew he had an appointment with one of the banks. I don't know how but Ellie was able to check through her channels that he had opened an account. And I guess you now know what happened."

Rob looked up at McArdle and nodded. Clark couldn't establish if it was an acknowledgement of remorse, or pride. Maybe it was both.

McArdle knew where the money had gone. Clark had called him

earlier that day and they had met at McArdle's office. McArdle had previously frozen Milton's Isle of Man account as part of the investigation. He had a contact at the bank. With some difficulty he had that afternoon established that the money had transferred out to another account in Belfast, an account set up through Geddis, Kenny and Marshall. It was a corporate legal firm representing Milton's department and therefore aroused no suspicion from the bank at the time. The signatory on the account and money transfer documentation was Eleanor McAvoy.

Even though he knew the answer McArdle asked Rob, "Where is the money?"

Rob rubbed his hands over his face. "In an account with the Ulster Bank. Ellie set it up. She and I are joint account holders. I don't know the details. I think she set it up as some form of business account. I have never accessed it. I have never touched any of the money."

McArdle and Clark knew that as well. They had met briefly with Jackson earlier who had explained how the business account would have worked. Despite their asking he could not access the account. The Bank's financial security systems were clearly better than the department's thought Clark. McArdle was able to get access to the account however through his corporate crime channels. They learned that there had been a number of withdrawals over the years, large but not significant amounts. All withdraws had been made by Ellie. Clark had thought of her ultra modern apartment, the one they were all sitting and standing in, the black convertible car, the clothes with top of the range labels. He assumed that she earned a good income, even though she had reverted from corporate legal work to conveyance work, but clearly she was not earning enough.

"As I said," said Rob, "it was never about the money, but I suppose at the back of my mind I knew it was there if I needed it, maybe to fund an early retirement, or whatever."

Rob exhaled a heavy sigh. "I knew Milton had an appointment in

Fiona's diary last week, two weeks ago or whenever it was. I keep an eye on all the senior staff's electronic diaries, just one of the routine things I do, for security, just to make sure everything is ok, no bugs or whatever."

Not a very convincing reason thought Clark, assuming Rob liked to keep an eye on what was going on at the upper echelons of the department just because he could.

"I made sure I was in the corridor around the time of the meeting just to check it was him and then afterwards I made sure I was behind Fiona in the canteen queue at lunchtime. I brought it up casually asking if it was Milton White I had seen earlier outside her office. She told me he had come back and was asking questions about what had happened with the Dubai project. I of course got a bit nervous. I had as good as forgotten about the whole thing. Yes, from time to time my path and Ellie's would cross when we were out."

He looked at Clark. "But that wasn't really very often. It was usually just the boys out for the night. And we didn't really talk about our wives and girlfriends when we were out anyway. So it wasn't really something that haunted me.

"But as I said, I was nervous after I spoke with Fiona. She told me she had sent Milton to you Clark. I wondered why. I knew it was you who had found the bank codes before and I wondered what you could do for Milton now. I know your expertise, finding data, making sense of code.

"So I went back to the servers and found in my security flags that Dubai Wire and Cable files had been copied to an external device, a portable hard drive. This was five years ago. I had missed it at the time. I then suspected Milton had something he wanted you to examine."

Clark looked at Rob and spoke for the first time. "Why did you delete the documents five years ago?" he said.

"There were two reasons. Firstly I wanted to check if I could get away with it, get away with accessing documents under Milton's user code. It was just part of steering the blame towards him. The second reason was that I was at one of the final meetings, just as an observer at the back of the room. My role was to listen and consider if there might be any IT security implications in what was being agreed.

"My name was included in the minutes as having been in attendance. But no one would have noticed I was there. I wasn't required to contribute anything. As I said, I was invisible at the back of the room. But I wanted to get rid of anything with my name on it that associated me with the Dubai project. I deleted a number of the final documents just to be sure."

"And why did you delete the inspection records?" said Clark.

"I had to. I was asked to carry out a system security check on the inspection process. I couldn't get out of it. My name would have appeared against the inspection records as having conducted the check. I couldn't pin this check on anyone else as I was the only one who had the authority and access to carry it out."

"Would there not have been hard copies of the documents on files somewhere? Did you get rid of them too?"

"No, I didn't, but remember we had just moved into an era of electronic file management. Hard copies were discouraged. Existing files were put into storage and the likelihood of someone cross referencing an electronic file with a paper file was pretty slim. It was a chance I took. They have probably all been disposed of by now anyhow."

"So you knew Milton had given me something with copies of the Dubai files and you sent someone to try and retrieve it?" said Clark.

"Not me," said Rob and he pointed at Ellie with his thumb.

Ellie spoke. "I'm sorry Clark," she said again, "you were never supposed to get hurt. It was Glenn, my brother Glenn. I had asked him to try and frighten you away from Milton after Rob had told me that woman in the department had sent him to you. The first night you met him outside your house he was just there to scope around, find out where you lived, that sort of thing. But you came home early and startled him. He followed you the next day and saw Milton give you the drive.

"He broke in to try and get it. I know I could have given him my key but he wanted it to look like an authentic and random break in, to divert any suspicion. And then he followed you to the factory, to scare you off, and again at your house but it was never meant to get physical. After your two neighbours came in Glen said he'd had enough. I'm so sorry Clark."

"Why did you not look for the drive yourself when you were in my house?"

She looked away. "I tried," she said, "but I couldn't find it. And besides, you were always in the house with me."

"But why Ellie? We have been together for the last four years. Have you been scoping me for four years, keeping an eye on me? Is that what this has been?"

She broke into tears again. "No Clark, what you and I have is genuine. We met remember all those years ago at that seminar. You sat beside me. We talked. We met again. Public Sector contracting is a small family Clark as you know. There was nothing unusual about you and I meeting like we did. I didn't know you had any connection to the Milton White thing when we met. I didn't know for some time. I didn't know for a long time that you knew Rob, or that Rob knew you. Rob and I rarely spoke in any case.

"By the time I did know we had a relationship, a strong relationship. I fell in love with you Clark. I still…"

"What about Declan Sommerville?" Clark asked Rob, cutting Ellie off, leaving her to her tears.

"Clark," said Rob, "you know it was a terrible accident. There was nothing anyone could have done." He looked at Clark, "I know this has troubled you and I hope you can find some comfort, some closure. That night I was in the office. My system flagged that Declan was accessing the Dubai files. I went to see him. He wasn't at his desk. I went out to the landing at the stairs and there he was, sneaking a quick cigarette. He just dropped in front of me. I went home, didn't know what to else to do. The next day it was found that he'd had a massive heart attack. There was nothing anyone could have done. He was dead before he hit the ground. It was his time. He would have died no matter where he was."

"So that's how you rationalised it then Rob? You were there. You could have done something."

Rob looked away.

Clark at last knew the truth. He had finally heard what happened that night, although he didn't know what if anything Declan had found. He didn't suppose it mattered any more. He had spoken with Declan's wife he was satisfied that there was nothing anyone could have done.

He walked from the door to the main window and stared along Chichester Street towards the City Hall. His head was still spinning. He leaned his hands on the window frame to steady himself. Inside his stomach fluttered. He looked to the ground below the apartment. There were two marked police cars together with Campbell's unmarked car. There were four uniformed police officers waiting, waiting for Rob and for Ellie. Reality sank in. What had he done? Could he not have confronted Ellie and Rob and maybe sorted it out without involving the police? No, they had betrayed him. He had thought they were his friends. He had done the right thing. He had suffered for years, but his suffering was nothing compared to Milton White. Milton had been framed. He had been accused. He had lost his job and his reputation. His lifestyle had suffered, and his health had suffered. And all because of my friends, thought Clark, all because of Rob and of Ellie. Yes, he had definitely done the right thing.

He heard McArdle speak into his radio. A moment later there was a knock at the door and two uniformed policemen entered the room. One escorted Ellie to the door, and the other escorted Rob.

Ellie turned to Clark as she was being led away. "I'm sorry Clark. I love you."

Clark ignored her and looked at Rob. Rob lifted his head to look at Clark.

"Clark," he said, "Angela knows nothing about this."

Clark nodded.

McArdle held out his hand to Clark. They shook. No words were exchanged. DC Campbell nodded.

They left Clark alone in the apartment.

CHAPTER 37

Clark awoke early the next morning. He had walked home the previous night in a daze. He had gone straight to bed and tossed and turned for hours. Sleep eventually came.

He had been ignoring his phone. He looked to see he had missed a number of calls from Jackson. He would call him later.

He made breakfast and put on some music, some Leonard Cohen. Mood music, it seemed appropriate. He picked up the Gibson and picked along with the melody. His mind was all over the place. He couldn't settle. He did some barbell and dumbbell reps in his study.

The phone rang again and he looked at the screen. It was a number he had got to know over the last week. It was the number Milton White's personal assistant had used to contact him.

Clark answered the phone. It was Milton White himself.

"Good Morning, Clark," he said, "and thank you for all you have done. McArdle has just left. I am no longer suspected. He has assured me he will do all he can to put things right."

Clark couldn't think what to say. He was pleased for Milton of course, but at what cost? He had found Milton's retribution amongst his own friends. Milton might have relief and satisfaction. But Clark did not. His own life had been exposed, and corroded. He was hurting. He was angry.

"I'm also sorry," said Milton, "I believe the answer was not in your favour."

Still Clark could not speak.

"There is someone I would like you to meet. If it is all right with you we would like to meet you at your house. Can I say we will see you in thirty minutes?"

"Okay," said Clark and hung up.

Thirty minutes later there was a knock at his door. He hadn't moved from the club chair. He rose and opened the door. There was Milton and behind him was a tall broad shouldered young man with closely cropped hair. Clark stood back to let them in. They both nodded as they went into his house. Behind the young man stood a young woman, with long blonde flowing hair and flawless complexion. She smiled a beautiful smile and said "Hello," in a soft husky voice. Clark nodded and she too went into his lounge.

The young man and the young woman sat on the sofa. Milton sat on the club chair whilst Clark remained standing.

"This is my son and daughter," said Milton, "I wanted you to meet them. You to them however are not a stranger. Gwyneth has been talking to you and I believe also has been keeping a track on you?"

He looked at his daughter and she looked away.

"I can assure you that was not in the plan. Jonathan has been my chauffeur and has been in my shadow to make sure I was okay physically. I didn't want to over exert myself, what with my weak condition.

"At least I can now get on with what is left of my life. So thank you again. My family would like to thank you."

He nodded towards the sofa.

Jonathan stood and shook Clark's hand. Gwyneth stood too and raised herself to her toes, kissing Clark on the cheek. He smiled appreciating the gesture from both of Milton's children.

"My wife is still in Sligo," he said, "We need to decide whether to come back to Belfast or to stay there. Gwyneth and Jonathan are both living in Belfast. Gwyneth is an Accountant with Petersons Global and Jonathan is a Structural Engineer with Fergusons. They have both managed to maintain their careers despite what happened with me, thank goodness. They have been living in the family home, hopefully keeping it intact." He raised his eyebrows to them and they both laughed.

Clark raised a smile also. He looked at Gwyneth.

"I have a confession," she said, her voice distinctive and familiar, "I had asked Siobhan to talk to you, to call you."

Clark gave her a cold stare. He did not like the thought he had been used.

"But hear me out," said Gwyneth, "let me tell it from the start. I work with Siobhan at Petersons. We were out with some other colleagues a couple of Friday nights ago in the Apartment Bar and you came in. I recognised you from a picture my dad had. Siobhan said she recognised you from years ago when she worked with you. At that stage I didn't know if you were going to meet with my dad the following morning at the Palm House, so I asked her to bump into you and strike up a conversation, to find out what you were doing the next morning. A bit of a farfetched story I know, but we were drinking. It was like a girly dare."

Clark nodded.

"Anyway, after that I asked her to call you a couple of times before you were due to see my dad, to make sure you were going to turn up, to check up on what you were finding. But here's the thing Clark. She fell for you. She genuinely fell for you. That second night she met you in the Apartment she was treating it as a date. She was really annoyed with herself that she had upset you. She wanted to make it up to you. Even yesterday when you were meeting my dad in

Victoria Square we were in House of Fraser and she was looking to buy you a present. She knew you liked clothes and was going to buy you a pink shirt. I told her I didn't think it was you."

Clark smiled again. She was right. He liked clothes but he wasn't sure pink was his colour.

Milton rose from the chair. "Thank you again," he said and shook Clark's hand, "If there is ever anything I can do for you just let me know. Oh, and please let me cover your expenses from Dubai."

"That's okay," said Clark and showed them to the door. He waved them off and went back inside.

He spent the rest of the morning tidying the house, doing anything just to kill time. He was about to call Jackson and arrange to meet up with him later that night when the phone rang again.

'Now what?' he thought in seeing Fabian Townsend's name on the screen, the managing partner of Chesterton and Williamson.

"Please hold for Fabian Townsend," said Charlotte, his secretary.

"Clark, I just wanted to say we got sorted out with that other thing. Good notes, thank you. It didn't take much to pull together a final report. I called to say I have just been invited to submit a tender to provide Digital Investigation Services to the police. There could be a lot of work coming out of it, a lot of regular work. Your name was specifically mentioned in the conversation.

"I would like you arrange a familiarisation meeting with the potential client. The contact name is a Detective Inspector McArdle. I will send his details by email. Thank you, talk soon." He hung up.

Clark smiled again.

He sat back in his chair. He thought through all that had gone on in the last week. He thought through everything that was going on in his life. He thought of his job, his friends, his family and his relationships with women. These were all the systems of his life, and he had allowed every one of them to fail in some way. He had compromised a client in work and had suffered the wrath of the source of much of his freelance work. It looked however like he might just have survived that one thanks to McArdle. He had friends but how did he treat them? He had accused Jackson, his oldest friend, of betraying him. He had betrayed Jackson by allowing feelings to develop with his girlfriend. He had not allowed meaningful friendships to develop with Rob and Ed. With Rob it was probably justified but Ed had proved to be a good solid friend when he needed one. It had been Ed who had taken him to see Declan's wife. It had been Ed who had helped him at the end in piecing together the facts against Rob. He had allowed a relationship to develop with Ellie for four years without really getting to know her. On reflection he knew little about her. He had never met her family. He knew she had a brother but could barely even recall his name. He had never taken the time to even look at her family photos. He had never let Ellie get to know him. They didn't discuss things they should have discussed. Maybe if they did he would have learned things long before he did. And then there was his family. He missed his family. He wanted to talk with his dad; he wanted to confide in his mum. He wanted to laugh with Amy.

He decided then he would make every effort to put the systems of his life right.

He would give his work the effort and respect it deserved but would not let it take priority.

He would spend time with his dad. He would apologise to his mum. He would have it out with Amy. He would clear the air. He would apologise to her too. He would grovel if he had to. He would make it good with Amy.

He would make more of an effort to open himself to Ed, his wife Caitlin and his wonderful kids Conor and Francois.

He would cement his friendship with Jackson. He would give him his blessing with Tracey. He would fight whatever feelings he had for her. He would avoid her if that's what it took.

And there was one more thing he needed to do.

He lifted his phone and called Siobhan.

ABOUT THE AUTHOR

Allan McCreedy lives in rural County Down, N Ireland with his family. A graduate of Ulster and York universities Allan has worked across a number of government departments. Systems Failing is his first full length novel. Double Figures, a second novel featuring Clark Radcliffe is coming soon.

Printed in Great Britain
by Amazon